NOW GREAT LYNX

By

Elli DeLing

ACKNOWLEDGEMENTS

My husband Wesley Andrews created the cover and has consistently encouraged, discussed and edited this book. Other members of the Little Traverse Bay Bands of Odawa Indians have also reviewed and made suggestions for revisions, in particular Frank Ettawageshik, Yvonne Walker-Keshik, Eric Hemenway, Beverly and Neewin Wemigwase, Alice Yellowbank, Carla McFall, and Simon Otto. John Ernst and Priscilla Whiteford also made several technical suggestions.

The Ann Arbor Writers Group and the Breakout Writers have been of great assistance in recommendations for editing and revising this effort. I have learned a great deal from them about the craft and art of writing over the past two years. The encouragement of AAWG members: Skipper Hammond, Kim Fairley, Patricia Tompkins, Karen Wolff, Rachel Maitra, Karen Simpson, Bethany Neal, Dave Wanty, Shelley Schanfield, Ray Juracek, Kay Posselt, Janet Cannon, Ellen Halter, and Donnelly Hadden - has meant a great deal, and I have attempted to make as many of their suggested revisions as possible.

The title of this book 'Now Great Lynx' was used as a chapter title by Thomas Overholt (see the bibliography).

Note: Don't look for Cathead Island on any map. It exists only in this book.

TABLE OF CONTENTS

LIST OF CHARACTERS:
Spirits:

Shibizhee (Great Lynx, Underwater Panther) – John Mishipsea
Nanabozho
Thunderbirds
White spirit reptiles, snakes, fish
Ganoozow-makwa (Long-tailed Bear)
Spirit bears
Mishi-Ginebig (Great Serpent)
Spirit serpents
Water spirits
Memegwesiak (mermen-merwomen)

Humans (Two-leggeds):

Nem-kee Ishkoday – tribal elder, spiritual leader (Chip's
                                            great-uncle)
Louie St. Sable – tribal police chief (Chip's father)
Chi-Payan (Chip) St. Sable – tribal educator (Louie's son)
Sam Keshiawas – deputy tribal police officer
Lorna Mazur – deputy tribal police officer
Jack Derrick – local mainland sheriff
Basil Chiwaygan – tribal economic developer
Jerry Higgins – injured quarry worker (Barb's husband)
Barb Higgins – postal worker (Jerry's wife)
Neewin (tribal kid, brother to Beanie & Mayn-gun)
Beanie (tribal kid)
Mayn-gun (tribal kid)

Elizabeth (Tizbet) Mueller – teacher (daughter to Angeline & Henry)

Angeline Mueller – (Tizbet's mother, Annie & Lorette's sister)

Henry Mueller – (Tizbet's father)

George Olmstead – visiting scientist, friend to Muellers

Annie Martine – retired schoolteacher (Tizbet's aunt)

Lorette Kipway – tribal chair (Tizbet's aunt)

Toby – laid off quarry worker

Nancy Cloud – head of Jingtamok committee

Dan Ebbot – local coroner

Lee Kinwah – cousin of Louie's at Thunder Bay, Ont.

Bobby – tribal fisherman

Jason Keshiawas – son of Sam Keshiawas

Yvonne Keshiawas – daughter-in-law of Sam Keshiawas

ANISHINABEMOWIN – Anishinabe language (words in this book)

Note: Spelling is used for non-Anishinabe reader's pronunciation. Correct spelling can be found on the Internet. One source is Ojibwe.lib.umn.edu – Ojibwe Dictionary.

Anishinabe = the people (Native Americans of Northeast
                                    N. America)
Kitchi-gami = big lake
Nem-kee Ish-ko-day = Thunder Fire
Migwetch = Thanks
Baa-maa = (see you) later
Ah-nee = Hello
Boo-zhoo = Hello (bon jour)
Jingtamok = pow wow
Chi-Pyan = Big Paul
Dakon-way-winnini = the man who grabs you (policeman)
Makatay-maingun = Black Wolf
Mayn-gun = Wolf
Muhkuhkee-que = Frog Woman
Muh-kuh-kee = Frog
Ahau = Yes
Nee-win = four
Ganoozow-Makwa = Long Tailed Bear
Memegwesiak = mermen and merwomen
Mishi-ginebig = Great Serpent
bidossigay = coming light

CHAPTER 1

CATHEAD ISLAND, LIMESTONE POINT ANISHINABE
RESERVATION,

EARLY SPRING

Shibizhee - the Great Lynx - heard a strange sound. He looked around in the dim light of the phosphorescent mosses on the limestone walls of the underground cavern. Rock above his head crumbled and small fragments rained down. His small spirit companions brushed past him to shelter themselves under a low rock ledge. Large chunks of stone tumbled from above and splashed into the small shallow stream running through the floor of the cave. He roared loudly, but the sound was nearly drowned out by the crashing of larger and larger pieces of rock. Clouds of dust filled his nostrils. He sneezed and ran a paw across his whiskers.

A massive piece of the top of the cave just missed him and he spread his huge feline body as flat as possible against the wall. Where the roof had been an enormous hole had opened. He looked up and was blinded by a broad shaft of intense sunlight. Pain shot through his head. He could see nothing. He dug his claws into the debris-strewn floor of the cave and slid his long tail back and forth. He roared again, a massive lion's roar, and the sound echoed through the cavern.

Something heavy crashed into the cave, accompanied by a sharp smell. He recognized the odor. Oil. He reached out with one paw and touched a hard flat surface. He backed away.

Shibizhee drew on the strength of his powers and forced his yellow-green eyes to adjust to the sunlight spilling down into the cavern. The pain in his head lifted a bit. As the dust cleared, he looked around and saw his small white reptile companions still hovering under the rock shelf, plastering themselves against each other.

Sunlight reflecting from the copper scales that covered his body cast iridescent rainbow discs of color on the walls. Distracted for a moment, he raised one paw to catch an image, but as he grabbed at it, his movement turned it away. He tipped his great horned head and frowned at the curious spots of color, and realizing what they were, he jerked his massive shoulders in disgust at his stupidity.

The large object that had crashed to the floor of the cave was bright yellow with round black things attached. A two-legged creature lay next to it, making sounds, bleeding from his head and stomach. Shibizhee had not seen a human since his imprisonment, but he knew the above-ground species. When he was still free in the world above, the Anishinabe humans of the Great Lakes who called him 'Underwater Panther' used to put gifts of tobacco to him in the water. Since he was the supreme spirit of water and those under the water, he had accepted the gifts as his due and occasionally did kindnesses to help them. Of course, a human could also be a tasty meal.

A groaning sound came from the man and Shibizhee began walking toward him. He could smell fear on the wide-eyed man that lay there staring at him. Shibizhee stopped and turned away, again inspecting the opening above. The man was not important. What was happening... what was now happening...? He looked around at the place where he had been trapped for millennia.

At one side of the cave, crumbled rock had created a sloping pile of gravel. His small companions rushed to it, slithering and scrambling to the world above. He watched them go, pale lizards, snakes and frogs that had lost their color during the years in the cave. They would be blinded for some time in the world above. He hoped they would be safe in the new environment.

He caught his breath as he realized he could now escape the hated cavern where Nanabozho had trapped him so long ago. Their battles over the ages had seemed endless. Nanabozho, earth spirit and trickster, had won that time, but now Shibizhee could once again take his rightful place - Supreme Being of the Underworld. He could shape-change into anything. His powers would be enormous.

Shibizhee followed the small ones up the sloping rock. He dug his sharp claws into the rim of the opening and leaped free of the cavern. As he breathed in clean air, his tongue came out to join his nose, flehming in an ecstasy of smells. The spikes on his back lay flat and his long forked copper tail curled with pleasure.

Through a mesh barrier he saw the great lake, blue water sparkling and moving. He went over the barrier in a fluid leap and ran, great heart pounding like a rapid drum as his paws dug into mosses under sacred cedars. Stiff-legged, he slid down the embankment. The sand of the beach under his feet felt soft. He strode through the waves into water that gradually covered his sides and back. Shibizhee bent his great horned head and went under the surface, strong webbed paws pulling on the deep liquid of his beloved great lake. The loud ecstatic purring in his throat reverberated through the waters of Kitchi-gaming.

===============================

Basil Chiwaygan heard a rumbling sound coming from the quarry across the road from his house. He felt a tremor under his feet for a few seconds, and then it stopped. He put down his fork, pushed himself away from the table and went to look out the front room window.

"What the hell?" A large cloud of dust was rising over the quarry. He heard sounds of rocks falling. There was a loud crash, and then nothing. Silence.

He opened his front door, letting in the cool spring air, and went out in his stocking feet to the small front porch. The cloud over the quarry was blowing away on a stiff breeze from Lake Michigan. He went back inside, grabbed his cell phone from the kitchen table, and called Louie St. Sable, the Tribal Chief of Police.

"Hey, Louie, I think we've got some kinda thing going on over at the quarry." As Limestone Point Tribal Developer, he had worked hard to get the limestone quarry up and running, providing jobs for tribal members. He always kept an eye on things across the road.

"I really don't know, but I'll check it out. Bunch of dust, crashing sounds, maybe something fell." He reached around with one foot under a footstool for his shoes and pulled them toward him one at a time with his big toe.

"O.K. Call you back." He put on his shoes, pulled a jacket out of the front closet, turned off the coffee maker, grabbed his keys, and headed out the back door to the garage.

There was a high cyclone fence around the quarry and he wasn't about to climb it. Driving around to the entrance would be quicker.

The gate to the quarry was open. Although it was after working hours, some of the quarry workers put in overtime, so there might be someone on site. Basil drove past the big pole barns that housed the quarry equipment and office, but didn't see anyone. There was one car in the employee parking lot - Jerry Higgins' old rusted black Chevy. Basil parked next to the car and got out.

A large pit had opened up, probably a couple of hundred yards across. Rocks were still tumbling in around the edges. "Holy crap!" He walked gingerly across an open area toward it.

"Hey, Jerry!" Silence.

He looked around. Through the fence, he caught a glimpse of something shiny that reflected sunlight, moving toward the lake. Then it was gone. "Hey, Jerry!" He thought he heard a voice, but wasn't sure.

Testing each step, he got closer to the pit. "Jerry, you down there?" A big backhoe was sitting next to the pit and since it hadn't fallen in he climbed up and stood on the bucket.

From the higher point he could see down into a huge opening in the earth, gravel and rocks still slipping down the sides, raising clouds of gray dust. One of the big yellow dump trucks was in the pit, lying on its side.

"Hey, man - you in there?" Basil stood on tiptoe, hanging onto the backhoe, leaned over and looked down. Jerry was laying on his side, propped up on one elbow, his leg at an impossible angle.

"Yah! Get me outa here!" Jerry was covered with gray dirt. The hole was at least fifty feet deep. There was no way Basil could get him out by himself.

"Hold on, I'll get some help."

He called Louie again and told him what had happened. As he was talking, he looked through the fence toward his house and saw something white moving through the field of high brown dead weeds.

"Louie! We've got a cave-in here, enormous. Jerry Higgins musta been workin'. He and a truck are both down in the hole. Looks like he got hurt. We'll need some help gettin' him out."

CHAPTER 2

CATHEAD ISLAND - ANISHINABE RESERVATION

LATE SPRING

Something was not quite right. Silence. No sounds of birds and insects. The elderly Anishinabe man stopped walking and looked into the woods next to the road. A cedar fringed pond lay between the road and Lake Michigan. It was a sacred place where a spirit being had been seen generations ago.

That silence. Perhaps he should check it out. He put his khaki shoulder bag on the ground in the culvert next to the road. Moving silently, not stepping on dry twigs, he went carefully through a stand of cedars and stood at the edge of the algae crusted water.

He reached out one wrinkled hand to steady himself against a tree and heard a blue jay announce his presence. A thirteen-striped chipmunk sat completely still on the branch of a cedar, one paw raised, listening.

Past the cedars, the big lake and pale beach beyond glistened in sunlight, but the shaded woods turned the surface of the pond to black glass. Distant plashing rhythmic waves of Kitchi-gami were the only sound. Nem-kee Ish-ko-day St. Sable, the 86 year old traditional leader named 'Thunder Fire' felt a chill go up the back of his neck. He swallowed and breathed in the musky odor of the place.

He heard it before it appeared, and hid looking through a broken place in a tall weathered stump.

A huge cat-shaped head lifted from the depths of the pond. It was covered with coppery iridescent scales that reflected light, with curved white horns upon which huge patches of algae slid back into the water as a large creature pulled itself heavily onto the mossy bank.

Nem-kee recognized it at once... Shibizhee... the underwater panther.... a spirit being to which the offerings were made by people going out on the big lake.

Clawed feet crushed ferns and leaves as it walked out onto land, making deep prints in the earth. The enormous cat was at least forty feet long, covered with the shining copper scales to the forked end of its long tail. Curved spikes protruded from its spine. Pale yellow-green eyes reflected the dim light. Its mouth opened, revealing a reddish colored tongue and sharp feline teeth. The curved horns behind the short copper covered ears shone white in sunlight.

Nem-kee felt cold and his hand trembled as he grasped the dead wood. His grandfather told him about Shibizhee on winter nights. He only half-believed, but he still dropped a bit of tobacco in the water when he went fishing. No one had seen the spirit for centuries. Unless, of course, as a shape-changer, it was in another form.

Perhaps this was a dream. But he felt the smooth wood under his hand, heard the sounds of the waves, and saw the copper-scaled panther as its long tail whipped back and forth nipping off the tops of several flowers and scattered their white petals. No, his dream senses were never this sharp.

Nem-kee Ishkoday held his breath, not daring to move or make a sound. His felt his heart beating and wondered if the creature could hear it. Would it attack him? His sense of fear at being attacked was equal to his curiosity and wonder.

Shibizhee stood on the mossy edge of the water on all fours, taller than the smaller cedars, more than twice a man's height. Bending his neck, he looked down and found a patch of mushrooms growing on a mossy log near his front feet. With one claw, he grasped the nearest fungus, tore it from the log, and stuffed the white substance into his mouth. He half closed his eyes and then opened them, exposing bright orbs with long black oval feline pupils at the centers.

Walking forward, Shibizhee pushed himself off his front

feet, reared up and back – supporting weight on his back legs and tail. The spiked protrusions on his spine compressed and became a single ridge as he came erect. His front feet clawed at air for a moment for balance. Standing on his hind feet, his head turned, surveying the higher shrubs and trees where life was suspended.

One clawed front paw suddenly reached out and grasped the chipmunk that had maintained its stillness. The small animal was quickly crushed as the talons closed on its striped fur, blood running down as life left its body. Shoving the crushed tidbit into his jaws, he barely chewed before the snack followed the fungus into his throat.

He turned his head toward the place where Nem-kee was hiding and looked directly at him, aware. Nem-kee's heart pounded more quickly. He held his breath.

Shibizhee's eyes met Nem-kee's. Then he nodded in acknowledgment. It seemed a gesture of respect. Finally, Nem-kee breathed in, a long slow intake of air. He nodded his head in response. What did it mean? A flow of warmth ran through him; his heart and breath steadied. Had Shibizhee somehow calmed him with assurance?

He understood what happened next from the traditions he was taught, but watched open-mouthed at the transformation.

Motionless, still standing, the panther's outline blurred against the background of cedars. The white horns tipped far back and disappeared into the spiny ridge on his back. One foot raised, Shibizhee stretched, and then his feet thickened, claws shortening, broadening. His body became blurred darkness, his head lifted, his nose rounding.

Then his head came down, and there were no white horns, only a dark burred bear-shaped head with small dark eyes against a coat of black fur. His body thickened; the long tail disappeared entirely. Only a small tuft remained at the base of the dark rounded back. He dropped to all four legs - Mukwa - the black bear, a familiar presence in these woods.

15

Nem-kee had actually seen a shape-changing. He caught his breath, wanting to turn and run, but afraid to move.

Shibizhee-now-bear lifted his head and made a growl of triumph. He walked slowly around the rotted wood of the fallen tree where the fungus had been, and went into the forest. In a moment he was gone beyond the trees.

A few birds flew in to perch on branches. Nem-kee stayed where he was, not trusting movement. He didn't know how long he stood that way, but a familiar stab of pain in his back made him change his position. He finally let go of the tree.

Then he saw movement in the forest. A round white ball of light glowed through the trees. It disappeared and reappeared in another place, rested momentarily in the branches of an oak, and moved on.

The light avoided the sacred cedars and the birches with their small thunderbird markings of spirits that were the enemies of Shibizhee. Had he transformed again? Was he now the ball of light told about in traditional stories?

The blue jay called a warning and birds that had returned to trees around the pond lifted and flew off with a rushing sound of wings pushing air beneath them.

The ball of white light came through the trees, and Nem-kee ducked down, hoping it was not headed toward him. It sped toward the pond, hovering over the glassy surface for a moment, then dove swiftly into the murky water. There was hardly a ripple as the light disappeared.

Was Shibizhee gone? Nem-kee wondered why he had been allowed to see it. Was he chosen to see the wondrous spirit? He didn't consider himself special, although his knowledge of the old traditions was honored and were taught to those who cared to listen.

Nem-kee stood looking at the pond for a moment and turned slowly to walk back to the road into sunlight. He picked up his bag, slung its strap over his shoulder, and climbed out of the culvert up to the road.

Perhaps his package would be at the post office. Considering what he had ordered, he wondered the night he dreamed about it had been a premonition of what he had just seen. He had always acted on the instructions given him by his own spirit protectors in dreams. He reached into his shirt and clasped a small medicine bag that hung around his neck.

Taking out a small soft deerskin bag of tobacco from his pocket, he poured a bit of the pungent crushed leaves into his palm. What spirit would be strong enough to confront Shibizhee if it became necessary? Nanabozho, certainly. But he was sleeping up at Thunder Bay. No one had seen him for generations. Would he answer a call for assistance? It wouldn't hurt to try.

Nem-kee lifted his offering skyward and spoke the words taught him. He dropped the tobacco on the ground. Would the Earth Spirit respond?

Nem-Kee shuddered slightly, his brow knotted with thoughts of protection, of somehow trying to protect the people from the ancient spirit beast. Or was he supposed to protect the spirit being?

===============================

Coming into the village, Nem-kee walked toward a white frame building with an American flag flying from the pole in front - the post office and the Higgins' home. The post office itself was an add-on in front that Nem-kee had helped build. He had sometimes worked as a carpenter when he was young, and then when he got older, he sold wood carvings to the tourist shops.

Yes, think about the post office.

Think about his carvings. Think about anything but the spirit he had seen shape-changing.

He couldn't do much carving now, and most of his old carvings had been sold. Some were left, and his grandson

17

helped him arrange for one carving to be made into hologram pendants in Chicago, to sell at the Jingtamok over the weekend. He hoped that they would be all he expected. He went into the post office, stepped up to the counter and pushed the buzzer.

Barb Higgins bustled through the door at the back that led to her kitchen wearing an apron over her post office uniform, wiping her hands on a towel.

"Oh, Nem-kee! You come for that package? She bent down to reach for the box that had his order inside. "It came kinda late. Almost didn't make it to the Jingtamok." Her hair was up in plastic curlers under a brown hairnet that had seen better days.

"Thanks for calling to let me know it was in. How's Jerry?" He took the package. He remembered Barb as a girl, but now she was over fifty years old. She had many wrinkles in her face, evidence of a lifetime of hard work and a pack-a-day smoking habit.

She looked away and he could tell that things were not so good. "Oh, some better. Not much." She wasn't one to complain. Her shoulders lifted and then sank under the blue-gray uniform shirt. Her husband Jerry probably wouldn't make it to winter and they both knew it. He was hurt bad in the limestone quarry cave-in a few weeks back, and his body was just giving up. Some people said it was cirrhosis because of his drinking, combined with the accident.

"I thought about retirin'," she said. "But I wouldn't have nothin' to do. Could just take care of Jerry. But I can do this and look in on him, too. He just lies there watchin' the TV all day."

"Hang in there, Barb." He put the package under his arm, and started to open the door, and then half turned. "You got any other mail for me to pick up?"

"Already took it out on my route, but figured you'd want to pick up the package yourself." She grinned at him, and they both smiled at how she knew his habits.

18

"Migwetch." He used the Anishinabe slang for thanks. "Baa-maa, Barb" (see you later), closed the door behind him, put the box in his bag and adjusted the strap on his shoulder.

He hoped that the pendants would surprise and might even protect people at the Jingtamok from the spirit being. Remembering the Shibizhee, his jaw clenched. Would pendants made from a small thunderbird carving be enough to stand up to the Shibizhee?

Nem-kee headed for his usual spot on a bench facing the town of Shipsea's main street. He sat down and leaned back, bag by his side, and watched tourists from under the shade of his baseball cap. Some of the men wore shorts and had hairy white legs. They usually followed their wives, carrying packages. Amused, he smiled broadly, dark eyes twinkling.

The tourists were as familiar as the gulls overhead, loud and assumptive about their right to dominate the little town of Shipsea with their demands. Since the 1800's tourists had come to Cathead Island. They were tolerated by the tribal people along with the non-tribal 'summer people' who leased land from the tribe for their cottages.

He looked around at the small harbor town, the boats bobbing on the water between two long white piers. The side street to his left arched to the top of the hill and the cemetery where his wife and two sons were buried. Down the street to his left was the road to the limestone quarry, fenced off after the cave-in earlier in the year. Ahead was the road to the causeway that connected the island to the mainland.

He got up and went to the vending machine in front of the general store, got himself an orange soda, and returned to his seat on the bench. He held the cold metal can in deeply tanned wrinkled fingers, sipping slowly. What day was this? Oh, yes, Monday. The Jingtamok would begin on Saturday. They used to call it a Pow-Wow, but the tribal language department people said it should be called by the right name in the language.

He had already spoken for his trader stand to sell the

pendants. Thinking about that made him consider whether the Shibizhee would cause problems. A lot of people would be on the island over the weekend. He should tell someone. There could be big trouble.

CHAPTER 3

"Hey, Chi-Pyan!" The boy ran across the road, waving as he approached. "What'cha doin' in town? It's a nice day for fishin'."

"Sure is! Hope it's nice for the Jingtamok." He smiled at his small cousin. "Are you going fishing?"

"I might. Beanie says we're goin'. Baa-maa!" The boy ran off, long black hair flying, to join his brother, a taller boy wearing a red shirt and a pair of jeans. As Chip looked at his little cousins, he remembered days when he was that small, going fishing on Lake Michigan in Cathead Bay. Days spent with Tizbet Mueller in the summers of their childhood and teen years were memories he cherished the most.

Chip and his small cousins had the same straight nose and feathery eyebrows over large dark eyes. Their mouths were similar, the lower lip fuller than the upper one. Instead of being bound in tight braids like Chip's, their hair was long and black, flowing loosely down their backs like most of the Indian kids on the island. Their skin was the pale tan color that the kids always had in the spring before they were out in summer sun.

Chi-Pyan (Big Paul) St. Sable was tall, with the broad shoulders and narrow hips that were his inheritance. Called 'Chip' by nearly everyone, he was a handsome, impressive man who moved gracefully. He listened well and only spoke when he had something to say.

For the past few months, Chip had lived with his father on the reservation in one of the tri-level houses built back in the 1970's. After graduating from the University of Michigan with his master's in education in January, Chip had returned home to help the work toward the building of an island school. With the new casino on the mainland bringing in money, the dream of the tribe having their own school was close to reality at last. He hoped it would stem the tide of dropouts from the public school system on the mainland.

Of course, money owed to the investors in the casino would have to be paid back before the tribe would realize any great amount from the casino. It would months before the school was built, but Chip had been promised the job of principal, and he was paid by the tribe to work working with the architects and design the curriculum.

Chip's dad, Louie St. Sable, was known as 'Dakon-way-winnini or 'The Man Who Grabs You' - police chief on the island reservation. Of course, there was a full complement of security people at the casino, but that was on the mainland. He had a couple of part-time deputies that he could call in, and deputy Lorna Mazur manned the police station desk.

Chip was grateful for the improved financial security that he and his father enjoyed now that the tribe was more affluent. There were tribal jobs, but no one as yet got any profit sharing until the casino debt was paid.

He went to his car, opened the back door and put the bags of groceries on the seat. As he started to get in, he saw his great-uncle sitting on a bench across the street and waved to him. Nem-kee had probably walked into town for his mail. Instead of his usual smile, the old man looked solemn, a deep crease in his forehead between his eyes. He called out and motioned for Chip to come over.

================================

When Nem-kee saw his great-nephew go to his car, he got an idea. He could talk about it with Chip's dad Louie. As head of the tribal police, Louie should be warned. He called out a hello: "Ah-nee!" in the Anishinabe language. Chip waved back and walked across the street toward him.

He was glad Chip was back home. A lot of folks moved away to go to the cities for work. Chip was one of the few people who went away to get an education and then came back to work for the tribe. But to many of the elders, school reminded them of their times in the hated Indian boarding schools and were places to avoid. To the ones who didn't go to college, they might think he considered himself better than them. It would take time for Chip to regain the trust of some folks after being gone.

"Ah-nee! What's up?"

"I need to talk to your dad. Something kinda important." Nem-kee stood up.

"How about a ride out to our place? I think he's home."

"Sure. Migwetch." He picked up his bag and put the empty pop can inside. No point in wasting the 10 cents refund for the can. They headed across the street to Chip's car.

Nem-kee got in on the 'shotgun side' and Chip opened the door on the driver's side just as another car drove past. A young woman honked her horn and waved at them, Tizbet Mueller, probably back for the Jingtamok. Nem-kee thought for a moment, was she one of his great-grandkids? Then he remembered. Her mother Angeline was a daughter of Mary and Ben Raincloud, a different family. Angie had married a university professor and they had a cottage on the island. Tizbet was their only child.

Chip waved at her and stood for a moment watching her drive down the street. Nem-kee remembered when Chip and Tizbet were young, and how they were always together. He wondered if they still were friends, but held back from asking about something personal.

They passed by the pond and Chip saw Nem-kee's jaw tighten. Something was bothering the old man.

Chip drove slowly on the gravel road to his father's house. He waited for Nem-kee to talk, but the old man remained silent, looking straight ahead, clutching the bag on his lap.

His dad was standing in the yard watering tulips and narcissus that had sprung up in the spring sunshine. Louie was

23

also a tall man, with the beginning of a belly that strained his tan t-shirt. His short hair was graying on the sides, and he had a small gray moustache. He lifted his chin in the typical Anishinabe gesture of recognition or assent. His eyebrows lifted in surprise at seeing Nem-kee.

"Hey! What's up?" Louie said.

"Gotta talk," said Nem-kee as he got out of the car. Louie motioned for them to sit on the porch, and Chip got a bag of groceries and the mail out of the car.

The two older men ignored Chip and went to sit on the old wooden porch chairs. They didn't speak until Chip went into the house. He could hear their voices, but couldn't make out what they were saying. He put away the few groceries and began fixing dinner.

He wondered what Nem-kee was concerned about, but in Anishinabe tradition, it would be rude to question anyone about their personal business. Nem-kee and his father would tell him what it was about when they were good and ready.

CHAPTER 4

Shibizhee walked into the lake on the sand of a small island across from the Cathead Island Indian reservation. His copper scales gleamed in the sunlight with liquid iridescence, his eyes molten yellow-green as the inner lid came over them to protect them from the water. Swimming gracefully, massive shoulders and thighs stroking, his long tail acted as a rudder and the spiny protrusions on his back helped direct his movements. Between each of his claws there were thin webs of flesh, and he spread his feet wide to enable faster movement.

He dove nearly to the bottom of the cold lake and then came up for air, breathing deeply through broad nostrils before diving again. His white horns gleamed like ivory as he tossed his head, throwing off ribbons of droplets that glistened as they fell. It was good to be alive and free from the humiliating prison and the deadly sameness of his days in the cavern. This was his element, in the deep waters of Kitchi-gaming.

He tasted the water, drinking deeply at first and then more slowly, holding the lake water on his tongue. It had a strange foul taste, nothing he could place.

Finally, the realization came to him. The dark oil that came up sometimes from the earth, rotted remains of vegetation and the ancient reptiles he had not been able to help when the earth turned to fire so long ago. They were large beings, some larger than Shibizhee himself, and they died so quickly.

As the most prominent spirit among many, charged with responsibilities over the underworld beings - fish and reptiles - each with their own spirit - he had felt their loss with great sorrow. The years wore on, and the great ones bodies became part of the underworld itself.

He tasted the sadness of their loss and shook his head in disgust, blowing through his nostrils, growling slightly. Then he dove beneath the water and turned back to his new home on Whitefish Island.

===========================

Louie watched through his living room window as Chip backed out of the driveway to take Nem-kee home. His uncle looked small sitting in the front seat of the car. He was old now, but his mind was still sharp, and Louie believed his story. As a child, he heard stories about Shibizhee, and the pond was always considered a place where he was sighted. Who knew how many generations had lived and died since the last time someone saw the spirit creature there? There was no point in telling anyone about it, but Louie knew a warning when he heard it.

His phone vibrated in his pocket. "St. Sable here."

It was his cousin Lee Kinwah at Thunder Bay on the Ontario side of Lake Superior. "Louie. Darndest thing happened here. Earthquake."

"Kind of unusual. A bad one?" Louie asked.

"Nobody hurt, no damages. But you know those hills they call 'The Sleeping Giant'?"

"Yah. Where Nanabozho is supposed to be sleeping." It was only one of several places where the old earth spirit was 'sleeping.'

"Well, there was a rumbling last night, hey, woke me up. I went back to sleep, thought it was thunder. When I woke up, the damn hills were gone, flatter than a pancake."

"No shit!"

"Now everyone in the tribe here is freaked out, saying that Nanabozho woke up and went missing."

Louie just stood there in the middle of his living room, phone pressed to his ear. He caught his breath. Should he tell Lee about what Nem-kee had seen? He cleared his throat.

"Um. Uh. Lee." He cleared his throat again. "We've had something kind of unusual happen here, too. It might be connected."

"Earthquake?" asked Lee.

"No. Nem-kee just left. He told me about seeing something this morning…."

======================================

"Honey, would you mind going to the store for me?" Tizbet's mother asked. "I need more yeast for the frybread dough."

"Not at all." Tizbet stood up quickly from the book she was reading and stretched, her chair nearly tipping over behind her. She grabbed it before it fell, grinning at her usual clumsiness.

"I could use that dry yeast, two jars if you can get it, and if not, about two dozen packets. The Jingtamok Food Committee is sure taking a lot of time this year." Angeline reached for her purse that sat on the kitchen counter.

"No. My contribution." Tizbet waved it away. She grabbed her own bag and car keys from the table. "You want to come along?"

"Oh, no! I'm so busy right now. There's a lot to do. Thanks for helping out."

Elizabeth Mueller, known as Tizbet, had completed another year of teaching in the city, away from her family and the northern forests she loved. Returning here this summer was a real treat after fighting traffic in the northwestern Chicago suburbs. She grew up in Ann Arbor, but spent most of her summers at her parent's cottage on the island. She and her mother Angeline were members of the Cathead Island tribe, but her father was a white man, Henry Mueller, a retired professor of botany who spent all of his time now at their island home.

Tizbet had her own space, the two-bedroom cabin that had been the summer cottage of her youth. A tribal member, her mother had inherited the land. Eventually, her parents built their retirement home on the property, and gave her the old log cottage.

Tizbet was tall and thin. Her smooth olive skin, shoulder-length straight dark hair and dark brown eyes were striking. She wore little makeup, and ran a brush though her hair without much thought, more to get it out of her eyes than for style. Her features were a mixture of her parents, the Germanic genes of her father apparent in her firm jaw and chin, and from her mother, a generous mouth that smiled easily, straight fine brows, thin nose, and dark, deep-set, almond-shaped eyes. Her mother, like many of the Indians on the reservation, had some French ancestry, and this combined with the rest of her heritage to give her an almost Eurasian appearance.

She avoided questions about her Indian ancestry. Occasionally in college she had helped out at Indian student functions as a volunteer. The poverty in which many of the Indians had grown up compared to the affluence of her own life made her feel apart from them.

As she drove, images of her teenage years came back in a rush as she remembered the times with Chip St. Sable. Perhaps she would see him at the Jingtamok. Unconsciously, her foot went down harder on the accelerator. She knew that Chip was here, working for the tribe.

Driving into the little town of Shipsea she saw old Nem-Kee sitting on a park bench near the hardware store, wearing his usual baseball cap, sipping a can of pop. He waved at her and she waved back, smiling at the familiar figure. He was so gentle and soft-spoken, like many of the older Indian people on the island.

The jars of yeast were not to be found, and she nearly exhausted the supply of yeast packets with her purchase. Tizbet came out of the store and headed for the post office.

"Got any mail for the Muellers?"

"Sure, it's all ready for you." The petite woman behind the counter smiled. "You home from Chicago for the summer this time? It's been quite a while since I've seen you."

"Right. How did you know where I was?"

"Well, it wasn't the moccasin grapevine this time, just the U.S. Postal Service - return address on your letters to your folks." Barb Higgins' eyes twinkled, and as she smiled, Tizbet noticed that more of Barb's back teeth were missing.

"How's your family?" Tizbet took the packet of letters held together with a rubber band. She remembered the Higgins children who were about her own age.

"Oh, they're fine. Moved away, of course. The girls are married now, living in Detroit, doing fine. The boy is down in Lansing, got a good job there. But my husband, Jerry, he isn't so well. He got hurt in the quarry cave-in this spring; been in bed most of the time since."

"I'm sorry to hear that." Tizbet saw the pain behind the other woman's eyes, and realized that there was more than she was saying.

Going back to her car, she heard the gulls setting up a ruckus out on the causeway as two small boys walked along the road carrying fishing poles. They reminded her of the times as a child when she and Chip had gone fishing. So many memories of those days.

What if Chip had a girlfriend now, here on the reservation? That thought was disturbing. Well, she would just have to wait and see. She would have to see Chip again this year, spend time with him. Maybe she could get him out of her system once and for all.

Then she saw Chip walking toward his car. He turned and went toward Nem-kee as she drove past, and they both waved at her. The same old feeling about Chip ran through her and she made herself take a deep breath.

CHAPTER 5

Swimming underwater, Shibizhee saw a school of fish he didn't recognize. He had seen others of the new fish species that had invaded Kitchi-gaming - the great lake - during his absence, and was concerned about how to fulfill his responsibility to them. Like the reptiles on the mainland, there were fewer of them. He tried to communicate with the new species, but they didn't recognize him, and rushed away, their leaders taking them quickly to avoid harm.

He brushed against objects half buried in the sand of the lake bottom and stopped swimming to look around. There were similar objects in and around the places of the humans. He had taken different forms in order to investigate the new upper world and had seen such things. So much had changed since his imprisonment. The dwellings of the humans were no longer rounded lodges; they lived in buildings with straight edges and had things in them that he had learned about in the weeks since his release. The language they spoke was not the same as that of the humans before his imprisonment, although some of the old words were retained. With his powers, he could understand any language whether it was animal or human, and could 'hear' the thoughts of those who primarily communicated with gestures. Sometimes what he heard was disturbing.

Taking the form of a small lizard, he had been able to fasten himself on the places humans called 'windows.' He saw the humans performing tasks that were strange to him, cooking food that came out of containers kept in 'cupboards' and 'refrigerators.' He investigated in the form of a small flying insect and learned a great deal inside the buildings, which it was a bit confusing due to the multiplicity of the lenses of the insect eyes. Any form he took seemed to have some disadvantages.

Seeing humans using machines to perform things that would have been difficult if not impossible before he was trapped, he devoted many days learning about the objects and their uses. Computers and televisions fascinated him.

He moved again through the water, but when he tried to drink, it tasted strange, as though it had some substance in it. He half-gagged and spit out the water. He knew now what had happened to the lake and the water. The humans had nearly destroyed everything he valued.

He reached the shore of the small island and walked out onto land, his copper scales shining in sunlight. Shibizhee shook himself, drops of water flying out onto the sand. He lay down on the grass that bordered the beach, reached out with one sharp-nailed paw and crushed a bunch of wormwood. Bending his nose to the feathery leaves, he breathed deeply of the healing odor, clearing his head of the lake smells.

So much was different, and he thought of the time before his entrapment in the underground cave by the half-human spirit Nanabozho. Shibizhee had been part of the great circle of life, a strong spirit among others. For thousands of years, he had responsibility for the creatures of the underworld - the fish and reptiles - and they were strong and abundant. He had lived under the big lake or in limestone caves along the shore, eating only the weak or the old ones of his children to keep their species strong, not destroying those who needed to live their lives fully. There were always problems, of course, with some of the small underworld spirits that were constantly fighting for power, and with other greater spirits like himself with the unending egos. Nothing was perfect, and maintaining balance was always a challenge.

Shibizhee lifted his head and stretched out in the warmth of the sun. He thought of Nanabozho who created the earth forms - the life that lived above ground - and who taught the humans many things. Many stories were told about Nanabozho that Shibizhee had listened to when humans talked in the boats on the lake. There were long periods of time when he got along well with Nanabozho, but they also had altercations.

33

The above-earth powerful sky spirits had their own realm, with a multitude of air and sky beings. Just as some of the underworld and earth spirits created problems, sometimes young thunderbirds caused storms and other enthusiastic disturbances that showed their strength, but were generally peaceful, with only occasional serious problems like tornadoes.

Humans that occupied the area had shown the spirits respect with gifts of food and tobacco. They performed ceremonies, a part of the great circle of life themselves, working to maintain balance in a world always full of problems. Of course, like the humans and other species, sometimes great and small spirits fought to maintain power over one another. Even among the smallest living beings, there were battles and difficulties. Balance was an ideal never completely achieved.

Shibizhee looked up at the clear sky that was darkening as the sun disappeared behind the mainland trees. His scales reflected the setting sun, a rose pink coat of color. He stood and slowly walked the beach. His thoughts whirled, making rest impossible.

Seeing a small fire across the lake along the shore of Cathead Island, he thought of how some of the humans were still keeping their traditions. They used the shells of turtles for rattles in their ceremonies, and had named the land Turtle Island. Some of their clans that were descendants of fish and reptiles kept their old beliefs. He always felt closer to those clans than the others from earth and sky beings. The people sometimes told about him, the great Shibizhee, and believed that if they could find one of his copper scales or obtain a piece of one of his ivory horns, it would heal their illnesses.

Since his release from the underground cave, there was a time when a boat capsized and a two-legged human fell into the lake and drowned. Thinking it was an offering, he had accepted it, enjoying the sweetness of the flesh. His anger at human desecration had overpowered him and he had thought it was a gift to appease him. In the old times, if humans fell in the lake and it was possible, he would keep them from drowning and return them to their villages. Some of the humans told stories of how he had found lost children along the shore and taken them to their homes, carrying them on his back. If they were already dead, however...

Then he remembered the final clashes between himself and Nanabozho. In rage, Shibizhee had killed Nanabozho's brother Makatay-maingun - Black Wolf. Nanabozho vowed revenge and invaded Shibizhee's home, the underworld.

He tossed his head back and forth, hissing his old hatred of Nanabozho. His clawed feet grasped the sandy earth, remembering how Nanabozho had retaliated by killing Shibizhee's beloved mother, Muhkuhkee-que - Frog Woman, flaying her skin, removing it to wear as a disguise so that he could escape to the upper earth.

Yes, he had been angered, and he had taken some of the boats and people during that chaotic era. He had eaten the people, and they had been very good to eat. The people gifted him with white dogs with red-painted feet, hoping to appease him. But he hated the dogs; they had hair that caught in his throat. The people could eat those dogs. Not him. He spat his distaste into the sand, pacing faster, crushing a patch of beach grass in his anger, caught in the memory.

In that last ancient great battle, Nanabozho called the Grandfathers. Because they loved Nanabozho more than Shibizhee, they sent the big older winged Thunderbirds that shot bolts of lightning to punish Shibizhee for his actions. Huge lances of fire came down from the sky. He was injured again and again. First on his front legs, on his back, on his legs, and on his head. He felt as though he were burning all over, with great waves of pain that felt like a million needles, penetrating even the copper scales on his skin. The sharp and biting thrusts of lightning came through the beautiful iridescent copper scales to his softer flesh beneath.

He had tried shape-changing, perhaps to turn into a rock that would be impervious to the lightning. But he had not been quick enough. Avoiding the thunderbolts took all his energy.

He had turned, diving far down into a tunnel underwater that led to his lair, deep under the limestone. Emerging into the cave, he felt safe seeing all his beautiful underground white creatures. The familiar cool rocks cradled his aching body.

Then something unimaginable happened. He heard the rumbling and crashing, the crumbling of the entrances to the cave. Nanabozho had sealed him in by tumbling tons of rock over the entrance. He had sought to escape through another entrance, but that was also blocked by thousands of tons of rock. Entrapment. He was trapped for millennia in that cave.

At that thought Shibizhee stopped pacing and walked back up the beach. The sun had disappeared and his scales were dark now, no longer reflecting light. He was only a shadow against the rocks and trees of his island.

Freedom to move about gave him unbelievable pleasure, but he remembered the cave that was his prison for so long. There was water in the cave, and the small pale creatures that were trapped with him provided food and entertainment when he toyed with them. They would do as he bid them, and he enjoyed watching them run and hide when he was in need of meat or was too aggressive. He had forgotten why he was there at times, only living day to day, surviving. There were many lost years when he only slept.

Then, several weeks before this day there were sounds of human machines that rumbled above the cavern, crushing layers of rock into thousands of pieces. He escaped the cave.

The small spirit beings that had been in the cave - lizards, snakes and frogs - had scattered, making their separate ways out and up the limestone rocks to hide in the forest. He could have called some of them to him, but he gave them their freedom. He could hear their small thoughts and small voices.

For days afterward, taking the form of a small frog, he had heard the humans talking about the cave-in at the place they called 'the quarry.' There was also talk of Shibizhee coming out of the pit in the cave-in, the man who lived through the cave-in told of seeing a large animal covered with copper colored scales. Other humans laughed at the story and said they did not believe what the man had told, not believing that Shibizhee existed.

Some of them told stories about Nanabozho, and sometimes even stories about himself. Some believed that he was evil. The black robes had told the Anishinabe that he was their evil spirit being, the Devil. Some of the people who went to their missions and churches believed those myths. They showed no respect, but some people still put tobacco in the lake, as a gift or because they feared him.

Now, in anger, he threw his iridescent white horned head back and growled, a large cat growl that bordered on a roar. The spikes on his back stood out in sharp relief against light misting of fog at the edge of the water. He lay down on the beach, his forked tail switching back and forth.

At the small pond near the lake, he had seen one of the humans, an old Anishinabe. The person had looked at him and watched his shape-changing, recognizing the Shibizhee, knowing his power. A smell of fear came off the old man, but he did not run away.

He thought of the taste of sweet human flesh, how it nourished him. Eating the old one would have given him some immediate satisfaction, but there were many humans and the old man looked tough and stringy.

He had not seen any evidence of Nanabozho. There appeared to be no one to challenge him. Yet there had been a sense of something in the old one.

Rising up on his back legs, his body shuddered and he stretched his limbs, tossing his great head back and forth. He needed food, and would go into the cave on this island now.

The shape change into a human was not as easy as the others, and took more energy to accomplish. He drew strength and forced himself into the familiar human entity but it took long minutes. Finally, he felt the sand beneath his feet that were now in soft moccasins. Holding his arms before him, he saw the muscle and sinew that made him strong, and looking down at his legs. Flexing them, he felt their hardness. The breech cloth that went between his legs and hung down front and back from a deerskin belt was comfortable, and he ran his fingers across its softness. He now was a tall man, strong and handsome. He called himself John Mishipsea.

Turning away from the beach, he walked to the cave. He had used it in human and other forms in the past, and the small rocky island was still deserted, a suitable place to live away from the people on the mainland and Cathead Island. He could not fit through the cave opening in his true form, but in human shape, it was possible.

He moved a thick juniper aside and entered, one hand sliding along a ledge. A flashlight he had appropriated from a building on the mainland was where he had left it. Using its beam, he walked down a small tunnel into the wide open space of the main cave.

He had made a bed in the old way of juniper branches covered with hides. A large flat rock was table height and he had placed a cut piece of log next to it for seating.

Mishipsea opened the computer and turned it on. He accessed the internet and prepared himself to gather information about the changed world. His face was reflected on the screen of the monitor. With light tan smooth skin, dark hair and green eyes, his human features were not of any race but a combination of all. He wore his hair in a long pony tail much like many of the Anishinabe, with a strand of white hair on either side. Deep lines furrowed his cheeks from each side of his nose to his mouth. With thin lips and a serious expression, he seemed almost scholarly in appearance. His hands on the computer were fast and precise.

His shift into a ball of white light was quick. He hovered over the computer, entered it, and sped through the masses of digital data. It was something he had done several times before, but there was always more to absorb. Gaining familiarity with this new world had become an obsession.

Coming out of the device as a white light form, he moved away from it and shifted again into human form more quickly, this time with renewed strength.

He had found most of the information he wanted about land and water changes caused by the humans, and had learned how to store that information in the computer. Taking human form on the mainland, he had posed as an elder unfamiliar with computers and was shown how the device worked. Going through the instruction manual as a ball of light was faster than reading it in human form. Purchasing the computer meant acquiring money, which had been another challenge.

It had taken nearly an entire day to find a human that he could change into one of his small turtle spirit beings in order to take the man's identification and money. Since the man was a tourist alone on vacation, and came from a place far from the island, there was no local knowledge of his disappearance. The man's wallet and identification were next to the laptop, and Shibizhee smiled, remembering his first attempts to use the cards to obtain cash, and learning the system to make credit purchases. An alert message appeared on the laptop screen. The battery was getting low. He had no way to obtain electricity in the cave. He was getting dependent on the device to obtain information, and resented his inability to have more control over it. The devices were useful, but their maintenance was irritating.

Having lights in the cave was also desirable. In his cat-like form, he had no difficulty seeing in the dark, but in human form it was difficult.

He could not immediately create electricity. Not being one of the sky spirits who controlled that force along with lightning, he must bring that power to the cave in human and other forms. Back on the mainland, he found what he needed at the hardware store. As John Mishipsea he bought a solar powered generator, cords with plug-ins, and a string of LED lights. Some of the new inventions of the humans could make his plan easier to accomplish but he wished for a simpler time.

It was dark before Mishipsea finally stood and stretched, rolled his shoulders and bent to place his hands on the stone floor of the cave. Remembering to plug in the hated equipment, he turned off the lights and lay down. Keeping to his human form, he turned on his side and slept.

CHAPTER 6

Barb and Jerry Higgins sat at the kitchen table, Jerry with his back to the stove, Barb facing him at her usual place, angled so that she could see anyone coming into the post office. Jerry sat quietly, holding his coffee with both hands as if savoring its warmth. This was one of the few days he had been able to get out of bed. They had enjoyed few times like this since the quarry cave-in.

He had severe internal injuries. Above his waist, he was in fair condition, but several respiratory infections had weakened his body's ability to heal itself. The major damage had been to his liver, spleen, and other vital organs.

The most frightening times were those when he vomited blood, requiring a quick trip to the hospital, transfusions, and a slow recovery. They had been to the doctor the day before, and the blood tests were disheartening. His liver function was still very minimal, and he was showing signs of jaundice, the whites of his eyes growing more yellow by the day. His history of heavy drinking hadn't helped things any. Combined with the injuries was a progressing case of cirrhosis. The doctor had given them little hope, and didn't recommend surgery. He didn't believe Jerry would live through an operation.

They sat silently at the table, their hands inches away from each other, but not touching. She had held him in the night when he had finally broken down. In forty years, she could count the number of times she had seen him cry on the fingers of one hand. Today they had to get on with the business of living, however short a time they had to be together.

"I wish there was something we could do. I feel so helpless!" Barb's voice was angry, rare in someone with her usual calm disposition.

Jerry was tired, but hated to go back to bed or to the couch in the living room.

41

He lifted the cup and sipped a bit of the hot coffee. His hand trembled and the liquid nearly spilled. He put the cup down too fast and it hit the saucer. Fatigue showed in his face and the weakness of his arms.

"Maybe I need to get one of them copper scales off of that panther thing I saw at the quarry. The Indians call him 'Shibizhee.' They say if you can get a scale, it will heal you up real quick, fix anything." He grinned, knowing she didn't believe he had seen anything that day he got hurt.

"Yah, right," she said. "If that don't work, I've got a bridge to sell you."

He smiled, but remembered seeing the thing even if no one believed him. It was only for a few seconds, but he remembered its horned head and eyes, and how the sun had reflected off the copper scales covering its body.

"How would you catch him?" Barb was glad that he was talking with her; they had too many silences in the house these days.

"A net? No, he's got sharp teeth and claws, could bite right through that. I guess I'd have to use something as bait."

"So what kind of bait do you give underwater panthers? Maybe underwater lady panthers?" She saw a customer coming toward the post office and got up. "Whoops! I'm getting company."

"I'll just stay here for a while. Don't worry about me, honey."

He watched her as she went down the steps into the post office, pushed himself out of the chair, and walked to the sink. He held onto the table and then the edge of the cupboard, and broke out in a cold sweat. He opened the door under the sink, bending over in agony, reaching behind soap containers for a bottle. It was nearly full, a fifth of whiskey.

Mixing booze with pain killers was madness, but it really didn't matter anymore. It was the only way he could get through the days. His liver wasn't going to last much longer, anyway.

He tipped up the bottle and drank deeply, wiping his mouth with the back of his hand.

He carried the bottle into the bedroom and put it on the night stand. There was no point in hiding it from Barb, she knew he had continued drinking but she refused to buy it for him. It would last a day or so, and then he'd have to get his buddies to bring him another. He felt the warmth in his gut, and the hurt subsided some. He knew it would return with fury later, but for the time being he would try to forget it.

He put on a jacket. Needed to get outside and now he could manage it. Be able to do what he had planned. Maybe it would make a difference.

Barb wouldn't understand. She only half believed in that sort of thing. She had always been the practical one. Even when the kids were little, it was Jerry who read stories to them, and Barb who taught them how to do things.

So now, when he didn't know whether he would still wake up from one day to the other, she was still going to the doctors, dragging him over to the hospital for more tests. They always heard the same thing. But this... this was different. The doctors didn't know about this. It could work, he'd heard about it ever since he was a little boy. The Indians knew about things like that. But he needed a small white dog with red feet for his sacrifice. That was part of his plan.

He went in the kitchen and looked back under the sink. He could hear Barb talking to someone out in the post office. He got the round container of latex paint, the one with a shiny red cap. He had used it to spray paint the bird feeder earlier in the year. He shook the can, assuring himself that it still had some paint in it and slipped it into his jacket pocket.

As he stood, a sharp pain hit him in the stomach and he held onto the countertop with both hands for a moment, his head down, catching his breath. If he just rode out the pain, it would go away. It was like riding a wave, or a horse. He would grasp the pain, ride it out, and then it would fade.

When it began to subside, he turned cautiously, so as not to bring it on again. Holding onto furniture and appliances, walking stiffly, he went out the back door.

The road to the lake was too far; he knew he couldn't make it unless he used the car. The keys were on the rack by the door. He lifted them carefully and went outside, closing the door silently behind him. He opened the car door, took the can out of his pocket, and put it behind the front seat.

It was only a few steps to the neighbor's yard. He knew Fay Gordon was gone to visit her daughter over on the mainland. Her little dog was tied up in the back yard, a tiny white mongrel with a fluffy tail and a small face. He went up to the dog and it wagged its tail, glad for company.

"Hi, there! Want to take a ride?" He untied the rope that fastened the dog to a tree and walked it over to his car.

The dog wriggled excitedly, loving the attention and pleased that it was going for a ride in a car. He put the dog on the seat beside him, and it immediately sat up on its haunches, putting its front paws on the door, looking out the window. Jerry reconsidered, reached over to and pulled it onto his lap, patting its head. "I think you'll be more comfortable in the trunk." Someone might see him with the Gordon's dog and wonder about it.

He wrapped the rope around his hand and still holding the dog, got out and went around to unlock the trunk. He put the dog in the trunk and it looked up at him inquisitively before he slammed down the trunk lid.

He backed out of the drive quickly, before Barb could hear the car leaving, and headed for the lake shore road. He drove too fast for his condition, and the car wove from one side of the road to the other a couple of times as his vision blurred and then cleared.

Jerry parked on the side of the road and got the paint can, looking both ways before taking the little dog out of the trunk.

He wrapped the rope around the dog tightly, and then around its legs, immobilizing it. The animal whimpered.

Holding the little dog away from him, and checking the wind for direction, he flipped the cap off the can with his thumb and sprayed each of the dog's four little feet with red paint. As the stinging paint hit the dog's tender flesh, it made a high-pitched sound of pain. He tossed the paint can into the bushes beside the road.

Then he patted the dog's head, cradling it next to him, and it calmed down, but its entire small body was trembling in fear. The paint on the small feet smeared his jacket.

Jerry walked down the path to the lake. Small waves came in and then receded in gentle rhythm. The day was warm, with only a slight breeze coming in across the water. He held the dog out in front of him.

If he could get close enough, if he could get that old underwater panther to come to him, he could grab one of those copper scales. The whiskey and pills were catching up with him. He stumbled and nearly fell but grabbed a tall scrawny juniper just in time.

Fay wouldn't be too pleased about her dog, but she'd probably think it got loose and somebody ran over it. That happened a lot on the island; the dogs just went off to die if they got hit by a car.

He felt the pain again, and brought the dog to his chest and his belly, pushing against the pain. Well, soon it would be over. One way or the other.

He called out over the shallow waves. "Hey, panther! Hey Great Lynx! Hey, I need you, so come here. There's a dog here you can eat, real tasty dog here!" The little dog looked up at him, twisting its head back to look at his face.

Jerry stood with the dog at the edge of the lake as long as he could, and finally went over to a log and sat down, still holding the little dog against him. Against the pain.

================================

Jerry Higgins was in a stupor, holding the dog against his burning gut as the whiskey and pills kicked in. He saw Shibizhee emerge from the lake through a haze. The huge copper-scaled cat looked at him with large yellow-green eyes, the white horns on its head dripping water. It walked cat-like, claws digging into the wet sand at the edge of the lake.

Jerry half stood, still holding the dog. It trembled uncontrollably, making small whining noises in its throat. He held out the dog with a drunken grin. He saw the head of the creature with its white horns, and beneath the haze in his mind he realized this was what he had been seeking, the cure for his pain and the doctor's death sentence.

"Here, I brung ya somethin'. Maybe you could give me one a them scales to fix me up." His voice slurred, and the last words he spoke were lost as Shibizhee reached out with one paw and took the little dog from his hands.

The dog quieted as Shibizhee set it down carefully in the sand. It was bound tightly with rope, and Shibizhee used one claw to loosen the binding. He wrapped the rope that was fastened to its collar around a small bush.

Jerry collapsed onto the ground, sitting with his legs straight out in front of him. He looked up at Shibizhee and smiled, pointing at the dog. "That's for you."

Shibizhee moved his head back and forth, negating the gift. He had no desire to eat the dog. The hair would get caught in his throat, and there was no need to kill it. He understood the offer from the obviously ill man.

He ran one paw down his side and dug out a single copper scale, leaving a small bare spot of flesh. A small spurt of blood came out of the spot and he pressed it, stopping the flow.

Jerry saw the Shibizhee's sharp nailed paw holding the copper scale as it came toward him and shrank back. The scale was the size of a small saucer, like a large smooth fish shell, but

46

as thick as his thumb. It felt warm and smooth as Shibizhee slid it down Jerry's neck, across his chest and down his belly. He left the scale next to Jerry's hand. Then the enormous spirit panther turned and walked back into the lake.

Picking up the piece of copper, Jerry held it to his stomach. It gave off some heat that seemed to penetrate, flowing through the pain and lifting it from him. He took a deep breath, and healing warmth permeated his lungs and gut. A second breath lifted more of the pain and he breathed it out. He lay back, heavy with relief. Sleep wrapped him in a blanket and the piece of copper fell out of his hand onto the sand.

===============================

Louie St. Sable was driving into Shipsea when the beeper on his belt signaled a call from Lorna at the office.

"Hey. What's up?" He released the button on the radio and waited for a reply.

"Barb Higgins says she can't find Jerry. He took the car. She sounded pretty worried."

"Okay. I'll check it out." He had a bad feeling about this; Jerry hadn't even been out of the house in the last month. It was rumored that his buddies were sneaking booze to him to help kill the pain. The doctor had prescribed pills, and was only a matter of time before the combination caused either a problem or a final solution to his suffering.

Louie knew that Barb wasn't the type to bother anyone with her concerns. He pressed down harder on the accelerator.

She was standing in front of the post office, arms folded around her waist holding in her anxiety. Tears made paths down her cheeks and her nose and eyes were pink.

"I don't know where he's gone to, Louie." Her voice was throaty, and broke slightly.

He put a hand on her shoulder. "Hang in there, now. When did you notice he was gone?"

47

"Just a little while ago. I was pretty busy there for a while, and he had gone in the bedroom to lie down. I went in to check on him, and he was gone. He took the car. I kept thinking maybe he had just gone to the store or something. But you know he hasn't been out at all lately."

"Let's go inside, I want to look around." Louie followed Barb. She locked the door and pulled the shade indicating that the post office was closed. She walked ahead of him into her living room.

"Had he been drinking?" Louie knew that was a strong possibility. "Mixing it with the prescription drugs?"

She didn't answer, shrugging her shoulders, keeping her back to him as they went through the kitchen. She collapsed on the living room couch and put her head in her hands. Through the doorway to the bedroom he saw the unmade bed and the whiskey bottle on the night stand.

"Did he leave with anyone?"

Barb shook her head. "No. I couldn't exactly go out looking for him with no car, and if he was as drunk as I think, he wasn't in any shape to be driving."

"So he took the car. Anything else?"

"Fay Gordon from next door called. She can't find their dog. I think he took it with him."

"Gordon's dog?"

"The little white one."

"Was he friendly with the dog?"

"Well, yes and no. Not super friendly." She looked away from Louie, and walked past him into the kitchen.

"There's something more, Barb. What is it?" He followed her and leaned back against the kitchen cupboard.

"This is stupid. But we were talking about how he thought he saw that underwater panther thing at the cave in. He said it ran right past him. It's supposed to have those copper scales and we were joking about how if you get one, it will heal anything." Barb looked at Louie now, and he stifled a desire to

48

groan. "We were joking about how to catch him and get one of those scales, use something as bait."

"Like a white dog." Louie's voice was low. He remembered the old story about gifting the creature and asked "With its feet painted red?"

"Oh, crap!" She stood up. "We got some paint to fix up the bird feeder..."

Barb went to the sink, opened the cabinet door, and felt around behind bottles and cans. "There was a can of red latex spray paint in here. It's gone."

Louie didn't respond right away. He shook his head, biting his lower lip. It was just crazy enough to be true. "Where do you think he'd go to find the panther thing?"

She hesitated, looking out the window toward the empty yard next door. "Probably down by the lake. When we were kids, they said there was a monster there."

"I think they said that because they didn't want you to go swimming by yourselves." Louie wanted to put some sense into this. "He's probably down there right now, sleeping off his drunk with that dog right next to him."

"With its feet painted red!" Barb grinned. "Boy, are the Gordons going to be mad."

Driving with Barb riding shotgun in the police car, they were both quiet. Louie hoped they would find Jerry, but he had some doubt. There were dozens of places that a sick man could go on the island. Or over on the mainland.

Then he saw the car parked ahead on the side of the road.

"He's there." Her voice was low. She reached for the car door handle.

"I'll go and check it out. You just wait here, okay?" He pulled up behind the Higgins' car and stopped. "Just wait here."

He ran down the path, waves breaking on the beach the only sound. Branches caught on his uniform but he didn't notice it. That damned Jerry! Worrying Barb like this.

Coming out of the cedars that edged the beach, he stopped. Jerry lay next to a large log, snoring loudly. The Gordon's dog was lying next to him, fastened by a rope to a small bush. Its paws were red with paint.

He looked down and saw the claw marks in the moss and mud. They were reptilian in shape, deep, from a heavy creature. The claws had sunk into the ground much deeper than a man's footprint, or even that of most bears. A thick shiny fish-scale shaped piece of copper was lying next to Jerry in the sand.

Louie reached in his pocket for his cell phone with its camera. Taking photographs of the tracks would prove they were there. There would be a lot of questions. With one foot, he wiped across the claw marks.

He picked up the copper and slid it in his pocket with his phone. Leaning over, he grabbed Jerry's shoulder and shook him.

"Time to go home, buddy."

Jerry opened one eye and then the other. He looked up at Louie and grinned. "Fixed me up, he did. Bi' guy."

"Uh-huh." Louie helped Jerry to his feet. "Barb's waiting for you. She'll drive you home."

After being untied, the little dog trotted ahead of them, red feet prancing up the sandy path dragging the rope. Barb got out of the police car and ran back to them.

"Oh, my goodness. Just look at that dog's feet!"

"It'll wash off," said Louie.

"I'll do that right now." Barb grabbed the car keys out of the ignition so that Jerry wouldn't get them and put them in her pocket. She took the rope and led the dog down the path to the lake.

Louie fastened Jerry's seat belt and shut the car door. "You gonna be OK?"

Jerry nodded. "Better'n OK now." His eyes focused for a minute. "Where's my copper?" He started patting the pockets of his cotton shirt.

Louie hesitated before taking the copper scale out of his pocket and handing it to him.

"Yup, don' hurt nowhere. An' he didn' even wan' th' dog. How 'bout that?"

Barb came back to the car with a wet dog trailing behind, shaking the water out of its coat. Its feet were a pale pink now, but the paint was gone. Louie didn't envy her having to explain that to her neighbors.

"I'm gonna have to keep a better eye on Jerry." Her mouth was set in a grim line and the circles under her eyes looked even darker. "Thanks a lot for everything."

Louie waited until the Higgins' car made a U-turn and headed back to town before he followed them. It would be interesting to see if Jerry's health improved over the next few days. Somehow, he thought it would.

CHAPTER 7

John Mishipsea pushed a grocery cart in the large store on the mainland. He wore the new light blue t-shirt and tan pants he had purchased at Wal-Mart. He had discovered that by changing into a small ball of light and entering an ATM, he was able to compress the cash and then bring it back to its normal size. Having observed other humans using money they took from small leather wallets, he had purchased a similar one and some clothing.

He wanted to blend in with the two-leggeds so that he could learn more about them and this new world. Functioning as a human was a constant irritation. It showed on his face, jaw tensed and brows pulled together as he tried to decide on which package of meat to buy.

A man ahead of him had stopped to talk to another man coming from the opposite direction. Mishipsea was at first angered by the two carts blocking his way, but listened to their conversation.

"Holy shit, do you see the prices on meat?" said the man in a gray t-shirt and jeans. "Just feeding the family...."

"Yeah, we haven't had a steak in months now."

"We can't afford much of anything since the quarry closed."

"Yeah, unemployment barely covers it, the wife is really pissed."

"Mine, too. And the kids keep asking for stuff."

"Can't afford crap anymore."

"If those assholes had paid more attention, that cave-in wouldn't have happened."

"We thought about getting out of here...."

"So did we, but with her mom depending on us, and no other jobs out there, no way to move someplace else for work, either."

52

"Us, too. Same old same old."

"Have you tried fishing lately? I was out all day Saturday and only got a couple of those carp. All little bones. The wife is pickling them."

"Haven't tried that, but my brother shot a deer and gave us some of that."

One of the men turned and saw Mishipsea standing behind him. He moved his cart out of the way. "Sorry."

Mishipsea nodded and went around them without picking up a package of beef. He could come back for the meat. The conversation was unsettling.

He hadn't thought about the effect of the cave-in on others except the man who had been injured and offered the white dog hoping to be healed. Evidently, there was another kind of injury. He knew that men working at the quarry had been paid money for the time they worked, but he wasn't that well informed about how the exchange of money for labor actually functioned. The cave-in had given him freedom, but it seemed to have also caused problems for some of the humans.

He studied the colorful pictures on the hundreds of boxes of cereal and wondered about their contents. The need for so many things to choose from was a mystery to him. One entire side of a long aisle had candles, and yet the humans had electricity for light. There were many things that confused him and seemed to make no sense.

Coming to the boxes of sweet cakes, he took a box of Twinkies and put it in his cart. He was developing an appreciation for some of the human food. The jerky he had eaten was all right as it didn't spoil, but he liked his meat fresh. He headed back to the meat section and picked up a wrapped package of steak. Although he ate meat raw in his true form, as a human the meat digested better cooked over the small fire in the cave.

He walked down the street to the marina and onto the dock, his new shoes making a slight squeaking sound on the painted boards. The small boat he had purchased was tied up next to a catamaran with furled sails. Putting the bags in one of the side lockers next to another package of clothing and a warm blanket, he sat down and started the engine.

An overcast sky blocked the warmth of a high sun. There was no wind. The lake had only slight ripples except for the foaming wash behind the boat. He thought of how simple it was to remain in his true form, and how he had become dependent on the human inventions. It was nearly impossible as a two-legged to find anything to eat around his cave, and he had exhausted the few berries that grew there. In his true form, eating fish from the lake was possible, but they had a bad taste.

Pulling the boat up onto the shore and taking his parcels into the cave, he thought of the times he had seen people taking bags from their cars into their homes. In human form, he was not so different from them. Having taken the money to buy food and clothes, he could get what he wanted. But he had seen the contents of the carts of many people in the stores who were obviously limited to what they could afford.

The quarry itself had caused serious destruction, yet these men whose ancestors had been farmers and hunters had depended on it to provide food for their families. Perhaps if the regulations he had read about had been followed, there would have been employment without pollution. He felt another surge of anger at the man who had created the problem.

Mishipsea sat down at the computer and lifted the cover. The screen was lit up. He remembered turning it off before he left for the store. He touched the mouse and a face appeared on the screen – a familiar face, one he hadn't seen in thousands of years. Nanabozho. The same Anishinabe features, black hair and dark eyes, dark tanned skin. The same self-satisfied smile. The same deerskin shirt trimmed with brightly dyed porcupine quillwork. No!! It had to be some kind of joke.

The voice was the same, and as his ancient enemy looked into his eyes from the computer screen, he heard the old laugh. "You are surprised?"

Mishipsea let out a cat-like hiss of anger and slammed the top of the computer down. He pressed the button on the side to turn it off. He stood up and then sat down again, curious. He lifted the cover again. The computer was supposed to be turned off, but the face was still there.

"No!" He felt himself changing. Anger rose like bile in his chest, bitter in his mouth. He closed the computer and strode out of the cave. By the time he reached the water, he was himself again, copper scales glinting in sunlight. He thrust himself deep, letting the chill of the lake cool his fear.

CHAPTER 8

Basil Chiwaygan walked through the tribal casino, his eyes darting right and left, checking on the number of people playing slots and table games, a good showing for early morning, a lot of gray heads in the place - retirees with money. Once the investors were paid off, the tribe would be raking in the do-re-mi. He smiled broadly and waved at his niece dealing at one of the blackjack tables. He hoped she was getting good tips, but working the morning shift; it wouldn't be as much as if she worked nights, but she had kids and worked while they were in school.

The conference room was prepared for his meeting with the new group of investors for the limestone quarry. A white tablecloth covered service table set up with coffee and trays of pastries. He checked the long table and chairs and walked around straightening the pads of paper and pens with the tribal logo at each place and the tray of bottled water in the middle.

He made a quick trip to the bathroom and inspected himself in a mirror. His new suit had been tailored in New York and fit perfectly. The shirt and tie were expensive, and his shoes cost more than most people spent on groceries in a month. It was important to make a good impression. Besides, the little gifts tossed his way and which he helped himself to over the past couple of years covered a few personal expenses. He deserved it, working all hours of the day and night. The people in the tribe simply didn't appreciate all that he did for them. His salary certainly wouldn't cover squat with today's prices.

He returned to the conference room and saw his guests coming down the carpeted hallway. He walked toward them smiling broadly, the new caps on his teeth gleaming.

"Welcome!" He shook hands with the four men, grasping each with his other hand in what was considered sincere warmth. "How was your trip?" The men had flown in a private jet from Chicago and were picked up at the airport in a limo he had rented for the occasion. Basil had not yet been able to get the tribal council to spring for a tribal limo, and the casino shuttle busses wouldn't have been appropriate.

He grunted a sound of disgust, just thinking about the tribal council. A bunch of candy-assed do-gooders and tree-huggers. They were tight with money that could go to impress the big-time investors with a little bling. Instead, they stuck to the old traditions, thinking that money for the Jingtamok was more important than paying for things that would really count. The last batch of speculators he brought in were turned off when they found out that tribal members got a yearly bonus based on casino profits. When they saw the tribal budget and how much was spent on the elders for health care, housing, a new senior center and trips, they simply laughed and walked out.

This time it would be different. The group of men in the room had only seen the tribal business financials, not the yearly tribal governmental fiscal report.

Once the men had their coffee and pastries and were seated, Basil closed the door and took his place at the head of the table. He folded his hands in front of him, stilling their tendency to tremble a bit. Knowing that drinking exacerbated his diabetes was one thing, stopping his penchant for Jack Daniels on the rocks was something else.

For the next two hours they developed plans for restarting the quarry. His figures were approved for buying equipment and covering startup wages and supplies. It would take millions to clean up the cave-in and buy new equipment. Once the quarry was operational, it wouldn't be long before they started showing a profit again. A cement plant on the mainland would be their biggest customer and orders were already in. He already had talked with the council and received approval for the percentages of interest that could be paid on the investment. However, several of his visitors expressed concerns.

"Wasn't there some problem about ground water pollution? I heard something about that," said a portly man with a ruddy face and jowls. "We sure as hell don't need any damn feds sticking their nose in." The man looked around at the others. Two of the men nodded agreement.

"Not to worry," said Basil. "I've got them right where we want them." He smiled and leaned back a little in his chair, relaxed and confident. He rubbed his right forefinger and thumb together. Payoffs were a part of doing business as far as he was concerned. He knew just the right people to encourage.

The man who had questioned him cleared his throat. "We don't want to be involved directly...." He straightened his tie with one pudgy hand. "You'll take care of it?"

"Absolutely." Basil knew he had these investors right where he wanted them. They saw him as the point man and trusted him to get things done. "What about safety regs? I heard that some guy got hurt in a cave-in." A younger man with a skeptical look on his face had been writing on the pad in front of him. He sat with pen poised, eyebrows raised. "Are you making any changes? We don't need a lawsuit."

"That's all been taken care of," said Basil. "You can come in once we get going and check it out yourself." He knew that they hadn't the foggiest idea of what to look for regarding safety issues. The insurance policy was set up to cover liability and he had been assured that the new operation would be safer. The state regulators couldn't come on the rez and poke their noses into tribal business, and it usually took years before any of the feds showed up.

"We don't want any of that union crap, Chiwaygan. Set up a pay scale and stick with it. This isn't a charity, y'know." A tall gray-haired man seated at Basil's left spoke in a deep voice, looked around the table and got his expected approval. "You don't have to go along with that here on the rez, do you?"

"Not so far, we don't." The tribe was the biggest employer in the area. As Economic Developer, Basil had fought any unionizing of tribal government employees, casino employees, or employees at the other tribal businesses. People complained about low wages, but he was more concerned with profits. Besides, the council had insisted on giving everybody health care insurance. Even with the Indian Health Service providing for some of the needs of tribal members, there were so many white people working for the tribe that health insurance was felt by council members to be fair. Basil wasn't that concerned with being fair but he had been voted down when he complained.

After the meeting was over and he had assurance the investment funds were being deposited in a tribal account, he escorted the men to the formal dining room where they were treated to the casino chef's best efforts and driven back to the airport.

Going to his car an hour later, he drew the envelope of cash that had been given him from the inner pocket of his suit jacket. Sitting in the driver's seat, he counted the bills. More than enough to convince the right people to turn a blind eye when he cut corners and a sizeable amount for himself. He put the car in gear and headed for home.

===========================

Tizbet was nearly at the entrance to her parents' driveway, mail and grocery bag from the store on the car seat next to her. A truck passed and she waved at the laughing Indian kids, their radio blaring music. Another car approached from the opposite direction. She recognized the driver, Basil Chiwaygan, the tribal Economic Developer. She tapped her horn, stopping the car as he pulled up alongside her.

He looked tired, dark wrinkled circles under his eyes. He was precisely groomed, as usual, with short hair and a white shirt and tie. Worry and aging lines on his face combined with reddish blotches on and around his nose. His complexion had always been bad as a youth, and his cheeks had deep pock marks.

"Hi, how are you?" she asked.

"Fair to partly cloudy. Haven't seen you for a while, where you been?"

"Teaching down by Chicago. Elementary," she replied

"That sounds like a challenge!" He grinned, perfect white teeth a testimony to excellent dental work.

"Sure is!"

"You'd better stick around; we're going to need teachers right here on the Rez."

"Well, maybe." She hadn't thought about teaching here on the reservation, yet she hadn't signed a contract for the next school year.

"See Chip about it. He's going to be the new principal. Needs someone to help him get the school started."

"I'll do that, thanks!"

"Glad to see you back. Gotta get home, there's a game on TV!" He drove away without saying goodbye, and Tizbet remembered that it was considered bad luck, that you would never see each other again. That was why 'Baa maa pii' (see you later) was the usual expression used.

Before Basil and his wife Susie moved to Green Bay where he went to business college, they were always at the evening forty-niner parties where drummers and singers played forty-nine social songs. He had returned from college to help open the quarry in order to provide jobs for tribal members, but after the cave-in, the quarry had to be closed. He started hanging out with men on unemployment at the casino bar. Tizbet's mother told her Basil had a drinking problem and she had seen Susie with bruises just before she left with the kids. Louie clammed up about it when her mom had asked if Basil was abusive.

Tizbet had plenty of concerns about Basil. It was rumored he'd pulled strings to avoid some of the environmental and safety regulations in getting the quarry operational. She checked it out by accessing tribal records on her computer back in Illinois. She found documents of interactions between the tribal Economic Developer and state and federal regulatory persons in Lansing and Washington, D.C. Her concerns were justified. Basil had convinced others there was no need to follow regulations in regard to runoffs from the quarry. She couldn't find anything about any enforcement of safety regulations, however.

One of her cousins worked in the accounting department and got the information Tizbet requested. When she checked Basil's tribal expenditures, it was obvious he had used the casino and tribal hotel to arrange for expensive meals, transportation and luxuries for government regulators. She understood something about how they had been convinced to go along with relaxing the rules that were supposed to regulate the quarry and wondered if there was more to it.

Water used in the crusher at the quarry had gone down a small creek into a larger stream, and then into Lake Michigan. The ground water around the quarry had dried up and clogged with calcium chloride. There had been no testing for toxic chemicals or environmental reviews.

Tizbet's disappointment with Basil went through her like a bad fog.

As she neared her parents' house, her thoughts and feelings were strong enough to flow to one of Shibizhee's nearby spirit beings.

===========================

Muh-kuh-kee - the large spirit frog in the tall grasses - looked first to the direction that Tizbet had taken, and then down the road where Basil's car was just disappearing over the next hill. It put one webbed foot out onto the road, then another, and quickly hopped to the green moist swamp at the other side.

At least three times larger than green frogs native to northern Michigan, his skin was the white of non-color, nearly translucent, an absence of color. His eyes were black, not the expected pink of an albino, and his mouth was large, red inside, a slash of violent color in the colorless flesh. Small sharp teeth rimmed his mouth, sharp as needles, teeth never seen in a frog.

Like the other spirit beings that had escaped the underground cave with Shibizhee, he had powers to understand the languages and thoughts of others, animal and human. Tizbet's concerns about Basil's role in the quarry's effect on the local environment were absorbed. This was something that concerned Shibizhee, and spread into the wider network of smaller spirits.

He puffed out his throat, gathered air and produced a deep guttural croak that echoed through the swamp. His voice was echoed by his brother in the hollow of a swale that led down to Lake Michigan. It was answered by another sound, a rumbling from the direction of a small island across the water.

===============================

In his human form on the beach of Whitefish Island, Shibizhee released a scream of anger. That one of the two-leggeds could have created such destruction was incredible. Only powerful spirit beings should create changes, and then because it was necessary. It was his responsibility to protect the small ones. The results of such a thing were obvious. He had seen stunted and disfigured frogs, turtles and snakes. The fish he once knew were reduced in numbers or gone entirely, with new species that Shibizhee had developed in other earth area now in abundance in Lake Michigan. Even the research he was doing on the computer verified what he saw in the water and on the land. Humans knew what was happening, but people like the man Chiwaygan supported those whose sole interests were based on greed.

He dropped to all fours and howled his anguish, feeling himself changing. Arching his back, he felt the familiar weight of the copper scales, horns and claws. He felt his tail extending, the forked barbs at the end as it tore through beach grass.

He had learned where Basil lived. The underground river beneath Cathead Island ran directly under the man's house. Shibizhee walked into the water and dove beneath it.

CHAPTER 9

"No luck with the jar of yeast, had to get the packages," Tizbet said, putting the grocery bag on the kitchen counter. Her mother got up from her chair in front of the television and came into the kitchen.

"That's O.K. See anyone in town?"

"I picked up the mail, saw Barb. And Nem-kee in his usual spot. He was talking to Chip. Lots of tourists. Just saw Basil on the road. He doesn't look so good."

Her father came out of his study smiling, and headed for the coffee maker, cup in hand. Her mother began pulling pans out of the oven.

"Did I tell you that George Olmstead is coming up here?" Henry filled his cup and sat down at the kitchen table. George was one of his professional friends who visited her parents every summer.

"When?" Tizbet took silverware out of a drawer and began setting the table.

"I'm not too sure, today or tomorrow, I think." As a retired botanist, Henry occasionally kept his hand in professionally, and his paper on the varieties of wild violets in the county had been published this year. The visit by the well-known biologist, George Olmstead, was something Henry looked forward to, as he had been cut off from face-to-face professional conversations with his fellow scientists for several months

"Ever since that cave-in, I've been getting calls about the white reptiles and the snakes that were seen by those fishermen. I told George about it. Albinos, maybe, but they could have been trapped in an underground cave and lost their pigmentation." He sipped his coffee. "He has contacts with ichthyologists and herpetologists, if more expertise is needed."

"Yah, the icks-and-erps fish and reptile guys will be interested," said Tizbet. "Well, maybe George can help you look into it. I haven't seen any of the little creepy-crawlies, have you?" She looked up at him and smiled. Angeline put their lunch on the table and both she and Tizbet sat down.

"No, I haven't seen any, either. But the people over by the quarry have been reporting sightings for weeks now. I suppose there were some underground caves that had water in them, a way for insects to get in and out so they could eat. The cave-in must have disturbed their habitat." Henry picked up a spoon and began filling his plate. "I can't find any research about the types that have been seen. At least no white lizards or frogs in this part of the country have ever been reported."

"One of the older women at the Food Committee meeting said she saw a big white lizard in her garden," said Angeline. "It really scared her."

"Usually there are only a small number of a population that lack pigmentation; albinos aren't usually found in large numbers." He scowled, thinking. "Some of the kids said they saw several white lizards coming through the grass out by the quarry one day."

Tizbet passed a bowl of peas to her mother and made no comment. It sounded as though the kids were making up stories. She had enough experience with children and their scary stories to be somewhat skeptical.

"The story I heard about those fishermen was that they threw them back in the creek. No chance to prove their story." Her father scowled. "It would have been smarter to keep at least one for evidence."

Angeline cleared her throat and laid down her fork. "I know they'd all been drinking, and Louie laughed at them, but when he saw that guy's ankles that got bit; he took it a little more seriously. But I know those men, and they were probably aggravating the situation." She picked up her fork and resumed eating.

Tizbet could see that her parents were taking the stories seriously and refrained from criticizing them for telling what sounded impossible.

After they finished lunch, Tizbet went out the back door and walked the mossy stone path to her cabin. She unpacked her suitcase and did some cleaning in her small kitchen and bathroom. She thought about Chip, and the possibility of getting a job here on the Rez. Maybe she could see him and talk about it. His dad's number was in the phone book.

Chip answered on the second ring. They agreed to meet at the restaurant in Shipsea. Tizbet ran a brush through her hair and applied some lipstick. She grinned at herself in the bathroom mirror. Chip had seen her grow up, spent countless hours with her when they were awkward teenagers, and was only now seeing her as a woman. Or would he? Would she always seem to be his old adventurous friend?

==============================

Tizbet's aunts were on their way to the Tribal Center after stopping to see their sister Angeline Mueller about food for the Jingtamok. Annie Martine drove too fast, as usual, but Lorette didn't say anything about it. Of course, Lorette's right foot was pressing hard on the floor of the car on the rider's side.

"Are you staying in the office this week, or heading out again?" Annie asked. As Tribal Chair, Lorette Kipway was often away on business trips. She had spent the morning working at home without the constant interruptions at her office in the Tribal Center.

"Staying in," said Lorette. "With the Jingtamok coming up this weekend, can't afford to be gone."

Annie drove up to the new low brick building and stopped in front of the entrance. Lorette got out and reached in the back seat for her briefcase. She had been on the job for eight years, and the worn leather briefcase was her constant companion.

"I'll be over at the Jingtamok grounds later on if you need me," said Annie.

"I'll probably catch a ride home." Lorette was conservative about expenses, and rode to work with someone else if she didn't need her car that day. She was the same about tribal expenditures, and this continued to win votes for re-election.

Essential for any Indian leader, Lorette didn't set herself above other folks. She greeted the receptionist and a couple of secretaries as she walked down the hall to her office: "Boo-zhoo!" The greeting came naturally. She didn't know if it was Anishinabe or a variation of "Bonjour," but really didn't care. The receptionist called back "Ah-nee," another form of greeting.

Dressed in a tan pants suit with a white blouse open at the neck, low heeled shoes, and her graying hair pulled back in a tight bun, she didn't wear a lot of jewelry like some of the other women working at the Tribal Center. She thought some of them wanted to look more Indian, with long beaded earrings and necklaces. Most were mixed blood tribal members, and only a few elders were full blood Anishinabe. Lorette herself was part French.

She put her briefcase on the desk in her office and went to the window. A fly was caught between the window and the screen. She opened the window to free it and it dove for the doorway.

A cup of tea would be good. Lorette smiled as she walked past the windows of the tribally run preschool program on her way to the Senior Center. The kids were singing in the language - Anishnabemowin - the song about the raccoon that her own grandmother had sung to her.

Most of the children looked Anishinabe, but there were a few blondes and those with light brown hair. Lorette did wonder what the non-Indian island parents thought about their children learning to speak Anishinabemowin, but no one had ever raised a question about it, so she didn't.

The elders were grouped around the big round table with their craft projects when Lorette entered the room. In the afternoons, they liked to play cards and gambled with toothpicks instead of money.

"Hey, Lorette!" Her great-aunt called to her, and she went over to give the older woman a hug. Lizzie was so tiny and frail now, perched like a small bird in the upholstered rocker. Her hands were still agile and a new pink and purple afghan was taking shape.

"Still at it?" She smoothed her aunt's hair back from her brow.

"Should be done with this one by the end of the week." Her hands moved in and out with the crochet hook, eating up the thick pink yarn.

Lorette made herself a cup of tea. "Everyone ready for the Jingtamok?"

"Oh, we're ready all right!" Old Emma Pipawme grinned and held up a pair of dolls to sell at the Jingtamok senior booth. She had dressed the dolls in replicas of traditional Anishinabe clothing with tiny beaded jewelry, tiny hands holding small beaded bags.

Back in her office, Lorette leafed through the stack of mail. The phone rang. "Ah-nee. Lorette here."

It was Louie St. Sable. "Got interesting news." He told her about Jerry Higgins.

"Just a crazy idea. Jerry took Fay Gordon's dog and painted its feet red. I saw some footprints over there that looked.... different ... Took a picture of them. I'll show you. I'm going to talk with Nem-kee and check out some things. It might tie in with something he told me earlier."

===============================

Annie drove into her driveway, and pulled up to the little wooden house nestled under huge oaks and pines. The yard was a mass of spring wildflowers, and a bluejay raucously announced her return.

Annie was a tall, large-boned woman that carried her considerable weight well. Her white hair was braided and wound around her head, pinned down securely. Her round brown face was wreathed with the kind of wrinkles left from a lifetime of smiles, with snap black eyes and two large dimples in her cheeks that accented her full mouth. She had retired from teaching biology at the high school over on the mainland and now spent most of her time on the island.

She went into the house thinking that she should get in touch with Angeline about the Food Committee supplies for meals at the Jingtamok. With all the dancers and traders coming from far off, by Saturday there would be a good six or seven hundred people at the Jingtamok grounds, and the tribe provided some meals for the visitors. There were supposed to be huge pots of corn soup, and she had ordered buffalo meat. It should be in at the store, so she would have to go and get that and take it to the freezer in the pavilion.

Angeline would be supervising the making of fry bread. Everyone always thought they had to have corn soup and frybread. Annie grinned to herself as she thought about how frybread was probably just some old French recipe for gallet. At least she made hers from scratch, not like the girls nowadays. Some of them just bought frozen bread dough and let it rise, pinched off a hunk and dropped it in hot fat. Now, that wasn't real frybread. Not like her mom used to make, or her grandma.

She went to a big pot steaming on the back of the stove and lifted the lid to check its contents before picking up the long-handled spoon to stir the murky mass of mullein plants and water. She was making cough medicine today, the way her grandmother had taught her. She wasn't a member of a medicine lodge, and realized that they had much better traditional ways of healing, but she could make a simple herbal tea.

She stirred the mixture, scooped out a cup of mullein tea, ran it through a fine mesh strainer and carried it outside to her rocker on the porch. Across her wildflower yard, there was a flash of movement as a doe turned and ran into the woods. The wig-wag of the white hair under the tail was the last thing seen. Annie smiled. The doe always came to check her out, and then melted into the forest. Curious. Just like Annie herself.

She surveyed the yard, cupping the tea in her hands, blowing across the steaming liquid to cool it down. There were lots of violets this year, and some jack-in-the-pulpits coming up in the yard. Birches that rimmed the yard at the edge of the woods had small leaves, and she noticed that the leeks already had started to die out, their leaves turning yellow and brown.

She sipped the tea, her rocker squeaking a slow rhythm.

In the warmth of the sun her head nodded and then bent as she fell asleep and the empty cup slid from her hand to her wide lap. The doe tiptoed out from the woods to resume eating new grasses at the edge of Annie's yard.

The dream was horrible. So real, all the images flooding her brain. A bathroom with tiled walls, a ripping and tearing sound as though something large was being broken. A man being pulled and crushed. Something had him by the leg. He was screaming.

She awoke with a start, crying out with a small sound. The cup slid from her lap onto the porch floor. She looked around the yard and then down at the place where her cup had fallen. Leaning over, she picked up the cup and carried it to the kitchen.

She had always had dreams like this, and they were usually premonitions of actual events. Too many were about death, and she hated them.

She speed-dialed Lorette's number at the Tribal Center. "Lorette, please. Well, get her!"

"....Hi, hey, I just got a flash of something.... right......
don't know who, but it was a man, in a bathroom, tiled walls.
Something had him by the leg, a crashing sound, screaming.
That's all."

Lorette asked: "Do you know who it was?"

"I don't know. I think someone here on the Rez. Didn't
want to scare you, just wanted you to be prepared."

===============================

Lorette hung up her phone. Annie's voice had sounded
tense and higher than usual. Coming so soon after the call from
Louie.... the old stories.....

Chills ran up her spine and the backs of her arms. This
wasn't the first time Annie had warned her about something.
Over the years she had learned to pay attention to Annie's dream
warnings. It would be only a matter of time...

CHAPTER 10

On his way back from a meeting on the mainland, Basil Chiwaygan passed the quarry. The gates were closed; a chain and lock had already started to rust. He drove to the end of the road, into his driveway, and parked under the big pine that he had planted twenty years before. He walked up the steps heavily, grasping the metal railing. It was hard to go into the empty house.

After Susie left with the kids he spent most evenings at the casino bar in an alcoholic haze. The men there knew he had done his best and didn't blame him for the cave-in. He didn't know where his family was, and his mother-in-law wouldn't tell him.

He looked in the freezer and found a frozen Salisbury steak dinner with a promising picture on the top of the box that exaggerated the contents. After zapping it in the microwave, he carried it to the living room and turned on the television. It would be a half hour before the game started. He could be at the office, but after dealing with casino investors for two nights and a morning, he had to take time off when he could.

The call on his cell from Lorette came just as he finished eating and watching the pre-game talking heads. He turned down the sound on the TV. He probably should have gone in to work, and he didn't want her to know that he was home.

"Hi. Don't want to bother you. I need some good news." She sounded tired.

"That's O.K. I'm just finishing up some things over here on the mainland. Might take a while. What's up?"

She didn't answer right away. He waited. There were more silences in Anishinabe conversations, folks not feeling they had to fill them with sounds. Then she asked: "How was your meeting?"

72

"Oh, I think they're interested in re-opening the quarry. At least they're interested in how to put their money into something so they have an excuse to come up here, out of the city and onto the golf course."

"Basil, the casino is still just breaking even, and there isn't any way the tribe can do it. We have to pay off the casino investors. Can they put up enough money to get the quarry re-opened?"

"Not sure. Can't keep them on topic. They keep talking about people they know, places they are going to, and I couldn't keep up with all the rounds of drinks. Probably I'll be in deep trouble if I hang around with them very long." He had been trying to cut down on his drinking and she knew it.

"I know it irritates you to have to deal with millionaires when we've got so many out of work here," she said. "I really appreciate your efforts."

"It would be easier if we didn't have to follow all those EPA regs."

Lorette's voice changed somewhat, with more force behind it. "Don't you ever do that again, Basil. Look at the environmental damage that was done. I wish you had talked with Council before taking it on yourself....."

He couldn't answer. The runoff from the quarry had nearly ruined the island's wildlife and caused a high degree of toxins in the lake. His jaw tightened. He had tried to speed things along, that's all. He hadn't thought it would matter.

She changed the subject, telling him about Jerry Higgins.

"That's really crazy."

"He has only a few months to live," said Lorette. "He must have been desperate."

"It's too bad he couldn't have got a job at the casino," said Basil. Some of the quarry workers had been able to get employment, but with Jerry in serious condition it wasn't an option.

"Yeah. Well, I've got to go. Thanks again."

73

Basil thought about another man who had been affected by the cave-in but did get a job at the casino. Toby. He lived in a trailer over on Lakeshore Road, in a strip of places that always looked like somebody had started to have a dump and decided on residential instead. Toby had a bunch of kids, a plump wife, and a backyard full of ancient, rusting cars. His kids had hung a hangman's noose from a tree in the front yard some years back and it was still there, a kind of mute reminder to strangers.

Smiling, Basil remembered the last time he had been out to Toby's place. The family's attack chickens ran free around the place, with a tendency to peck at people's ankles, so Basil had talked to Toby through the car window about a job in maintenance at the casino. With tribal preference in hiring, it had been easier to find him a job than a non-tribal person.

Taking his tray to the kitchen, Basil figured he might as well take a shower and headed for the bathroom. There was a rumbling sound, and he thought it was strange that a truck would be coming down the road with the quarry closed. He could feel the vibration through the floor of the house. It had been months since large trucks had gone down the road. He stood in the hallway at the bathroom door, thinking about going to look out the living room window, but then shrugged it off. Tourists were always driving around, gawking at the Indians.

He took off his jacket and tie and hung them on the bedroom door knob. He really needed to relax; he could feel the tension on the back of his neck. Stretching, he rotated his shoulders and moved his head back and forth a few times, trying to work out the kinks. It was no wonder he was up tight, with all the stress.

He tried taking deep breaths as he unbuttoned his shirt and tossed it on the floor. Letting the rest of his clothes fall, he walked naked into the bathroom. The floor seemed to shake a bit as he put his weight on it. Cursing himself for feeling afraid, he realized that he wasn't used to being alone in the house. He just hadn't noticed the floor shaking with the family around and probably just scaring himself over nothing.

Standing at the sink using his electric shaver, he felt the vibration again under his bare feet, this time somewhat stronger. His face in the mirror reflected a growing feeling of apprehension. He'd check it out after his shower.

He got out the towel and shampoo and put them on the back of the toilet. Opening the glass shower door and turning on the water, he heard a gurgling sound deep in the pipes under the bathtub. The gurgling stopped. He turned off the water and listened. Had that happened when the water was turned on before? The house was so quiet now, maybe he hadn't noticed.

He turned on the water again, pulled up the knob for the shower, stepped into the bathtub, and pulled the glass door shut. The hot water felt good on his skin, and he let it run down taking away some of the tension and tiredness.

Eyes shut, reaching for the soap; he heard something thump on the bottom of the tub. His heart leaped. He caught his breath and then shook off his fear. The damned soap had probably fallen. He opened his eyes and looked down through the steamy haze.

Where the drain had been was a large hole broken in the bottom of the tub. He reached out one hand and braced himself against the wall. The bathtub was coming apart! He felt his heart pounding in his chest. Overwhelming fear rushed through him at what he saw coming out of the widening hole.

A large scaly claw at the end of a leg covered with coppery scales was feeling about what was left of the bottom of the tub. It waved blindly, brushed across the skin of his ankle, and then grasped his leg in a tight grip. The pain was sharp and immediate. He tried to pull back but it held his leg in a steel grip.

The tub was now cracking and breaking in large pieces. Horrified, trying to lean against the side of the enclosure for balance, he fumbled with the sliding glass door, trying to escape.

He heard a sound like someone howling and realized that it was his own voice. The shower was still spraying, steam escaping into the bathroom. He grabbed at tile walls, trying to pull away from the pressure on his leg, and managed to step out with one foot just before the entire tub broke.

An enormous copper-scaled creature burst upward into the bathroom and he screamed again. His arms reached out to find something to grab, something to help him pull away.

Filled with terror, his last keening sound suddenly stopped.

===============================

Shibizhee carried the man's skin in his teeth as he swam under the water to Whitefish Island. He dropped it in the sand and lay down beside it. His anger was gone with the destruction of the person responsible for the desecration of his small kindred beings. Would his action change anything? Or had he accomplished nothing but vengeance?

He stood and stretched, he gradually taking the form of John Mishipsea. He brushed sand from the front of his shirt and pants. The skin lay like a long piece of tripe, folded in on itself, tousled hair on one end, and nails of the feet at the other. He spread it out to dry, placing rocks along the sides so that a wind wouldn't blow it away.

He pushed aside the juniper at the entrance to the cave and turned on the light so that he could see to open a bottle of water from the mainland. The water in the lake was too foul to drink.

Seated at the computer, he turned it on and tried to concentrate. Since Nanabozho had appeared on the screen that one time, he was always apprehensive when he turned the thing on, but his old nemesis had not appeared since.

Mishipsea had saved some of the websites for university libraries with information about pollution by herbicides and pesticides, and brought up a site for a college in Wisconsin. On a whim, he clicked on the department of Native Studies. One of the course descriptions was about Great Lakes Native Legends. There was nothing written about him, Shibizhee. On the side of the page there was a reference to the university museum and he went into that. The portion about museum exhibits showed a picture of a twisted fiber bag with his image woven into it. The image was silhouette, blocky and crude. The bags looked old, and reading the caption he saw that they were made by Anishinabe women in the 1800's. He remembered seeing bags like that before he was imprisoned.

More pictures of artifacts on display in the museum showed the pottery and tools of early people who lived in the Great Lakes area. A picture of a large display case with life-sized Anishinabe people dressed in old style clothing caught his attention. He enlarged the picture and saw the detail in beadwork applied to the leather. One of the figures wore a man's long shirt with designs of turtles made with small seed beads in bright colors. The caption under the photo said it was a donation from a man who belonged to the turtle clan and had inherited it from his grandfather.

Mishipsea turned off the computer, whirled and became a blur. He compressed into a tiny ball of light, whirled out of the cave, lifted high in the air, and headed west at incredible speed. The museum was in Madison at the university. He compressed himself into an even smaller orb and entered over one of the closed museum's massive entrance doors.

The gallery where the life-sized dioramas were located was dark and the glass protecting them was thick. He penetrated the glass as the ball of light and then took his human form in order to examine the various figures. Half of the side of a bark covered lodge took up the back wall. Several Anishinabe figures were seated around a small replica of a fire pit, and others were standing. He spotted the figure of a man wearing a long shirt, leggings and loin cloth. The process of removing the

77

shirt and other regalia from the mannequin was much like removing the skin from a victim, except that he felt none of the rage. He touched the display figure, minimized it and removed the shirt and regalia. Then he touched the figure again and it regained its original size.

He laid the mannequin on the floor of the display and put on the shirt and regalia. A bright light flashed into the display case, blinding him for a second. Mishipsea had heard nothing. A museum guard holding a heavy flashlight was silhouetted against the dim light of the outside hallway.

Mishipsea froze in place, taking on the pose of the figure he had just undressed. The guard moved closer, flashing the light around the display case. Mishipsea's leg muscles started to twitch, and he kept his eyes half open, hoping that if he blinked the guard wouldn't see it. He just wanted to get out of the place. No point in having to hurt the guard.

Then the guard turned his flashlight up to light his own face. Mishipsea caught his breath and swore. Nanabozho! Damned clown. Tricked again.

Mishipsea whirled and became a blur, compressed into a tiny ball of light and whipped through the thick glass. He shot directly at Nanabozho, spun around the man spirit rapidly and then out the galley to the outside. The sound of his enemy's laughter followed him across the great lake.

CHAPTER 11

"Give it here, man!" Beanie ran after his brother in the woods between the lake and Basil Chiwaygan's home. His younger brother Neewin sprinted through the trees ahead of him, around bushes and moss-covered large rocks, laughing and holding a long fox tail at arm's length. "It's mine! Dad gave it to me!"

"No he didn't! He promised the next one was mine!" Beanie had about had it with his brother, always taking everything for himself.

There was a sudden loud crashing sound and a flock of birds rose above the trees. A low rumble like thunder resounded, followed by more crashing noises.

Neewin stopped running and Beanie caught up with him.

"What was that?" asked Neewin.

Beanie shrugged and pointed in the direction of the sound. "Something big must'a fell."

"Maybe an airplane crashed," suggested Neewin.

"I didn't hear no airplane."

Beanie led the way through the woods toward the sound. The fox tail was tucked into Neewin's back pocket, their argument forgotten. Coming into the clearing, they saw clouds of dust rising into the sunlit air.

"Where's the house?" asked Neewin.

"It's gone, dummie."

"Must be it caved in."

They stood close together, breathing heavily although running hadn't winded them. "We'd better be careful." Beanie felt a cold finger of fear go up his spine and raise the hair on the back of his neck. "Stay back. I'll go check." He shoved his brother in the chest with his forefinger to make sure he stayed put.

Beanie walked slowly forward. The ground under his feet might give way. He wouldn't go too close. Just enough to see. He ran back to his brother.

"The house fell in the hole," he reported. "We'd better call Mom."

===

Lorette picked up the stack of opened mail and began sorting it into piles on her desk. She let her desk phone ring three times as she finished dealing out opened letters. "Lorette here."

"Beanie said what? Oh, my God!" She hung up and immediately called Louie. "You'd better get over to Basil's place. It sounds like another cave-in. I don't think Basil was there, I just talked to him, and he was over on the mainland."

She tried calling Basil back, but there was no answer.

===============================

Louie and Sam Keshiawas parked along the road next to the beginning of a driveway across from the quarry. Beyond the short patch of asphalt was an enormous pit, a haze of dust still rising, motes catching the sunlight. Crows sat in the trees at the back of the clearing behind the pit, commenting loudly. Louie shut off the engine and got out, testing the ground with every step. This spot was only a few hundred yards from the cave-in at the quarry. Did it mean that there would be more? Another underground cavern?

"Holy Wah! Another one!" Sam echoed Louie's thoughts.

"Thank goodness Basil wasn't home."

"You're sure about that?" asked Sam.

"Lorette had just talked to him; he said he was over on the mainland, just got out of a meeting." Louie hoped she was right. He had no reason to think otherwise, but Basil had been known to take off and not show up at work. Hopefully, this was not one of those times. Since they were young, Basil had also been known to stretch the truth or just not bother letting people know what was up with him.

"Lorette asked me to check on the place before giving him a call." Louie tried calling Basil but there was nothing but voicemail. He left a message and shoved the phone back in his pocket.

"I don't think it's safe to go down there right now," said Sam. "It's still caving in around the edges."

"Yeah." Louie stepped gingerly as he got closer. The roof of Basil's house was on an angle, just showing up over the edge of the pit. "I'll see what we can muster to get down there and check it out. But I sure as hell don't want to try it now. We'd better do something to keep people away from it. Someone could get hurt."

"We've got police tape in the car."

"Good idea, Sam. There are enough standing trees and bushes; at least it might discourage anyone until we can put up stronger barriers." Louie headed back to the car, Sam behind him.

While Sam got the tape, Louie called the local county sheriff Jack Derrick, and then the Coast Guard station. He leaned against the side of the tribal police car as he talked.

"They can't get a helicopter over till morning, got an emergency out on Drummond. Their Search and Rescue team is tied up with that, so we're on our own. Jack will come and help out." Derrick was an old school friend of Louie and Sam's. The reservation wasn't his jurisdiction, but he had training that would be helpful.

"What about Chip?" asked Sam.

"I can't deputize him. Remember? No two immediate family members in the same tribal department." Louie grimaced. Damn regulations, and Lorette was a stickler on that stuff.

"Well, he could just be an interested bystander like the rest of us when we help out."

"He used to call it slave labor when he was a teenager,"

said Louie. They both smiled at the memory of Chip helping out at the police station, mostly cleaning floors and filing reports.

"I'll give Basil another call. He's got to be someplace." Louie tried his cell phone again with no result. "Has he got a girlfriend over there?"

"I heard there was someone that works at the casino or the hotel. Never saw her."

Louie hoped Basil was tucked in safe somewhere on the mainland, not in what remained of his house. As they worked to get the police tape all the way around the pit. Standing on higher ground looking down into the chaos below, he saw a flash of something metal reflecting sunlight. Window glass? It seemed brighter than glass. Metal? A car bumper? He got as close as he dared to the pit and saw dark topsoil and rocks spilling downward. The big pine tree that had been in front of the house lay partly across the roof, it's huge roots exposed, brown sandy soil sifting down. There was no way anyone was going down there over the edge today. Not until it stopped caving in.

"I'll try him again. Probably should let Susie know," said Louie.

"She moved all her and the kids' personal stuff out when she left."

"This will get out pretty quick, better she hears it from me." Louie reached for his cell phone again. He had Susie's number. Too many things happening all at once. Lorette was on her way and would want to see this for herself.

"Hey, Susie. I got bad news about your house." Louie nodded, listening. Then he nodded again."Yup.... No...... I don't think he was here......."

When Susie finally ran down, he flipped the phone shut. "She says Basil always likes to watch that Canadian hockey team on TV and they're playin' today."

"He's a big hockey fan."

"He told Lorette he was doing stuff over on the mainland."

"Crap. He might be down there."

"If he is...." Louie looked around for some way to get over the edge of the pit, but saw the earth slumping all around the rim. Maybe a crane... No, that would be too heavy. The 'copter would have to be used to get people down in there.

Another huge chunk of the rim of the pit cascaded downward, taking several of Susie's rose bushes with it. He remembered when the family dog had died and Basil buried it under one of the rose bushes. Now the dog's bones were probably in the pit. Louie hoped that Basil wasn't down there, too.

==

Tizbet ran easily along the soft dirt on the side of the road. Her feet tingled in the old comfortable running shoes. Umbrellas of mayapples were nestled under the trees along her parents' driveway. Yarrow was just starting up; feathery leaves a promise of the tall plants to come.

It would be good not to have to go back to the city, but teaching jobs were scarce in this area; she had tried before. It was a matter of waiting for someone to retire or die. Most of the local teachers seemed to be in pretty good shape. There wasn't much chance of a job with the local public schools.

She could live here, fix up the cabin, and make it ready for winter. Expenses would be considerably less. Of course, the job wouldn't pay as much as she was earning now, and she wondered about benefits. If she could get a job at all. Her parents would probably spend part of the winter in Arizona living in a trailer at a retirement park. She had never spent a winter on the island. Snow removal would probably be a major activity. She could stay in the winterized house.

Her father had not exactly been rude to Chip over the years, but he had made it clear that she could do better. Sending her to Europe for the summer that last year of high school was an obvious attempt to get her away from Chip. She wondered what he would think if Chip was her boss, and perhaps more.

She was still considering possibilities as she went into her parents' house. Her father and George Olmstead were having coffee.

"Tizbet! Good to see you!" Olmstead stood up and put out his hand. She shook it firmly, following the old-fashioned protocol her father and his friends seemed to require.

Her mother bustled about serving fresh rolls and homemade strawberry jam. George Olmstead complimented her. Angeline smiled noncommittally, embarrassed at the attention.

Tizbet listened to her father and George Olmstead plan their excursion. She was glad to see her dad so involved and excited. He had been holed up with his research for months, and she had detected a tinge of depression since her return to the island.

"There are supposed to be all types of land and water based white creatures according to the locals," said Henry. "Of course, the stories could be exaggerated. But no one seems to be questioning the phenomena."

"There was a cave-in at the quarry? Is that correct?" asked Olmstead.

"Oh yes. There definitely was a cave-in. A large cavern opened up, and supposedly there were white creatures that escaped. They all seem to be either amphibians or reptiles that would be able to climb or crawl out of the cavern. No reports on any white fish," said Henry.

"And you say they have black eyes? That is pretty strange. Most albinism exhibits eyes that are pale or pink."

"I find that hard to believe, too. Some of the stories have come from fishermen who were drinking rather heavily. It

84

happened back in the spring, when the Indians around here go spear fishing."

"Probably a good idea to check it out, anyway. Gives me an excuse to have an adventure with my old buddy." Olmstead laughed and finished his coffee. "So where are we going?"

"I figure that the best place to start out would be the underwater caves along the shore. There's a limestone outcropping there that is inaccessible on foot. We'll have to take my boat."

Tizbet sat quietly listening to their plan and exchanged amused glances with her mother. The aging white haired men were like little boys in their enthusiasm. It was refreshing to see her dad so involved that he was sitting on the edge of his chair, hands waving around as he talked.

The men got up from the table and began putting on light jackets and caps. "We'll be back around five or so, Angie," said Tizbet's dad. "Take you out to dinner if you want."

Her mother smiled. "Sounds good, but I could have something ready here."

"No, don't bother. And you can wear that pretty blue dress you've been saving for a special occasion."

Tizbet remembered going with her mom to buy the dress when they were in Ann Arbor. Her mom bought it to go to a friend's funeral. It was the only time she had worn it. It seemed like her mother had avoided wearing the dress since, as though it might be tainted somehow. She saw a slight grimace on her mom's face that was quickly hidden as she smiled at the men going out the door.

========================

Henry's small boat bobbed in the water as he sat waiting for George to emerge from his initial dive. The water suddenly broke, and his friend's head appeared wearing goggles and mouthpiece, his face ruddy from the icy cold Lake Michigan waters. He had a muscular body and wore a black diving suit, fins, and a small air tank. He pulled the mouthpiece out to talk to Henry, adjusting a spear gun that hung from a nylon strap across his chest. Short barbed spears and a net specimen bag were tucked into his black pocketed vest.

"I think I can see some underwater caves off to the west there. Do you want to follow me along the banks?"

"Sure, just give me a minute to start up." Henry pushed the ignition switch and guided the boat behind George's strong strokes. When they were a few feet from the rocky shoreline embankment George dove under the water. After a minute he emerged and floated on the surface as Henry pulled up alongside him.

"This is the place. In fact, I saw some light-colored fish or eels. A couple of dozen of them, just going into one of the caves. There were also a few of these, but I only got one of them, some kind of water snake." George held up the black net specimen bag with a lump of white flesh inside and let it drop to his side. "The motor must have scared them. I think I'll go in and give them a look-see."

Henry turned off the engine. "Be careful in those caves, George. This limestone rock may be fragile."

"Right." George replaced the mouthpiece again, and turning downwards, flipped upside down in the water, his swim fins making a churning splash.

Henry shut off the motor. He was glad that George was wearing the diving suit. The waters of Lake Michigan were cold in early summer, and a person could only stay in the water a very few minutes at this time of year without protection. The lake was relatively safe, especially on the south side of Cathead Island, in the bay between the island and mainland.

Henry looked through half-closed eyes at the glare of sun on the water. The lake was a deep blue-green and clouds scudded across the sky. It promised to be a clear weekend and he hoped so, for the sake of his wife's people. So many were returning for the Jingtamok.

===========================

Shibizhee heard the calls of the small spirit beings in his mind, feeling their fear and the agony of the one that had been impaled by tearing metal. He swam rapidly to the place where a man in black diving gear was just going into one of the underwater caves along the shore. A shadow on the sandy lake bottom made Shibizhee look up to see a boat riding silently on the surface.

Seeing the net bag with the body of a small water snake, he read the mind of the diver. The man wanted that diminutive body to examine, not for food. The killing had been senseless, with no reasonable purpose that made sense to Shibizhee. He was enveloped in anger.

He watched as the man reloaded the gun with a barbed spear. The diver didn't see him, one hand on the gray rock at the entrance to the cave. Reaching out with one claw, Shibizhee twisted the gun from the man's grasp. It was attached by a strap that went across the man's chest, and his entire body followed the gun. He was spun around to face Shibizhee and his eyes widened in fright beneath the plastic window of his face mask. With one slash of sharp nails, the man's mouthpiece was whipped from him and bubbles of air escaped upward toward the surface.

The diver pulled away and lifted toward the surface, arms above his head. Shibizhee pushed his feet against the sand and reached up. His claws and teeth just missed the black rubber suit.

CHAPTER 12

Henry heard a loud splash about fifty feet away from the boat and sat upright. Olmstead was swimming rapidly toward him. He started up the engine and turned the boat toward his friend.

"Just a minute," he called, and rapidly covered the space between them.

Olmstead treaded water next to the boat and looked up at George. His eyes were bulging, and his mouth made a soundless O, diving goggles and mouthpiece gone. He reached out and grabbed the side of the boat and tried pulling himself up. Henry reached out to help him, but Olmstead's fingers slipped on the wet surface and he went down under the water.

Henry took off his shirt, kicked off his shoes and let himself over the edge of the boat, feeling terror close his throat. The water was like a knife edge on his unprotected body. He was not a strong swimmer or diver, but in his fear he pushed himself down beneath the chill water, eyes opened, searching. The limestone rock stood out in sharp relief, gray underwater and pale tan above with lines of iron-stained yellow, pock marked with small caves.

The water was clear and he could see George gradually sinking down to the rocks and sand on the bottom of the lake. Holding his breath, he reached out, threw one arm under the other man's chin and pulled him to the surface.

After a lifetime of academic pursuits, Henry was in no shape to rescue someone from the chill waters of Lake Michigan, but somehow he did it. He shoved George over the side of the boat and pulled himself up, his chest heaved with exertion. He shuddered with cold and fear. He grabbed George under the arms and pulled him into the boat.

Olmstead lay on the bottom of the boat, and Henry turned his head to the side, straddled him and pushed on his back. Lake water gushed from George's mouth and he coughed, expelling more water.

"Holy shit, George! What happened?" Henry sat back in his wet clothes, shivering as the cool air hit him, body crying out for heat.

"Did you see it?" asked George.

"What?"

"Some kind of animal thing. It grabbed at me."

"I didn't see anything."

"It was huge. Shiny. Big white horns, really angry."

Henry didn't know what to say. George Olmsted must have had some kind of hallucination, maybe a stroke or some kind of medical problem. He sounded irrational. There were no animals like that in Lake Michigan.

"We'd better get back to shore. Neither of us is in really good shape right now." Henry wished he had brought a blanket or warmer clothes. He sat behind the wheel and revved up the motor. Heading for shore, he felt like he wanted to push the boat to its limit, but knew how much the old thing would take. He reached in his pocket for his cell phone, but came up empty. It was back at the house.

They were passing the petroglyphs on the rocky wall along the shore. The ancient raised rock carvings were colored with muted pigments. He had seen them many times but never really examined them.

The first petroglyph was of a boat, with two stick figures in it. Next to the boat was the image of the Great Lynx. What was it that the people around here called it? Shibizhee. The figure was that of a cat, but with a long forked tail and horns. He tried to remember - what was it? He had heard something about the petroglyphs. Then he remembered. They were found at places where the people made gifts to the Shibizhee. Some of the tribal people dropped tobacco in the water when they went out on the lake. Maybe he should have done that, but he hadn't smoked a cigarette in twenty years. No tobacco.

A gust of wind hit him, turning his back to ice and raising goose bumps on his arms. He shuddered as the chill reached the back of neck and ears. His wet hair was plastered to his head.

He felt a sharp pain in his chest and coughed several times. The dive in cold water had taken its toll. The pain subsided some as he turned the boat into the marina. Behind him in the boat, George coughed and gagged, and Henry heard him spitting out the remainder of the lake water.

"I lost the specimen, and the spear gun. That thing knocked it right out of my hand," said George. "I lost it."

Henry didn't say what he thought George had lost.

===============================

Henry and George drove into the driveway at the Mueller's home, wet clothes clinging. They had left the boat at the dock. Henry still felt pressure in his chest, and couldn't seem to stop shivering. He stumbled as he got out of the vehicle, grabbing the door to maintain his balance. His left shoulder and arm started to hurt, and there was another pain in his chest.

"Angeline? Honey?" He went in through the screen door and saw her standing in the kitchen. He reached out and pulled her to him.

"What's wrong?" She held him close. "Henry! You're chilled clear through!"

George came in behind him, dripping water on the kitchen floor. "Damndest thing I ever saw," he muttered. He headed for the guest bedroom and dry clothes.

Angeline looked up at Henry sharply. "Did you guys cramp after eating? If you did, I'll never forgive myself for not reminding you to wait. Henry... you're all wet!" She was babbling, putting up a wall of sound.

"George had some kind of accident. I don't know. I just jumped in to help him back into the boat." They went into the

90

living room and Henry stood there looking confused, his entire body felt like ice with cold and shock.

"Here, sit down." She grabbed a blanket from the couch and wrapped him up in it. He sat down on the footstool and she sat on the couch next to him.

"Oh, no, Henry! "You went in that cold water?" She rubbed his chilled hands and tried to warm them. Henry nodded, his mouth tightening over clenched teeth and then took a deep breath.

"What happened?" She sat rigid on the couch.

"I don't know. He saw something like white fish and snakes down there. Then he said something grabbed his equipment and ripped it off him." His voice faded and he put his face in his hands.

"I'll go and get you something to warm you up. Stay right there, don't move. Keep that blanket around you." Angeline ran to the kitchen, and filled a cup with coffee and took it back to Henry, who was still sitting huddled on the footstool.

"Here, drink this."

He sipped the hot liquid. Then the pain hit him in the chest, a pressure like a huge hand pressing down. He felt a numbness in his left arm, running up to his neck and face, and the coffee cup in his hand dropped to the floor, the brown liquid spreading out onto the carpet. The last thing he saw was Angeline's face as he felt himself falling.

===============================

Angeline went to the door as soon as she saw the police car pull in next to the ambulance. She waited on the back porch as the Chip and Louie walked up to the house

"Boozhoo, Angie. Where is he?" Chip saw Henry lying on a gurney in the living room, wrapped in a blanket. Paramedics had him hooked up to a heart monitor and an IV was already dripping into his arm. He was pale and his hands were gripping the edge of the blanket. An oxygen tube snaked to his nostrils.

"We're leaving for the hospital." said Angeline. "Tizbet is out jogging, she doesn't know about this yet."

Chip went to the door. "I'll see if I can find her."

As he stepped outside, he saw Tizbet. She was wearing a red sweat shirt and pants, dark pony tail swinging, running up the driveway. She had heard the ambulance siren and ran back to the house in a panic.

"It's your dad," Chip called. "His friend was diving in the lake and had some kind of accident, so your dad went in after him. Got chilled. Might be his heart. They're taking him to the hospital. Somebody should drive your mom."

"I'll get my keys." Tizbet ran to her cottage as Chip went in the house.

Tizbet handed her keys to Chip. Neither she nor her mother was in any shape to drive, but they would need a car at the hospital on the mainland. Angeline stood by the door to the kitchen, tears running down her face, her hands twisting together around a wad of tissue. George Olmstead was in the living room sitting in a rocking chair in dry clothes, just staring straight ahead.

Louie stood next to the gurney, a heavy sense of responsibility carving his features into bronzed concern. Chip had never shared his father's job and had seldom seen this expression. He memorized the lines in his father's face and the graying short hair, a picture etched in his brain, something he knew he would remember long after this day.

Henry turned his face toward Louie. "We were in George's boat; it's down at the dock. He was scuba diving along the rocks there looking for those white fish and eels.....by the petroglyphs. He went under and then came up talking nonsense. Lost his equipment and the specimen he speared. He got back to the boat and I jumped in to try to save him, but he couldn't pull himself up, so I got back in the boat and pulled him up."

"You just go get yourself taken care of," said Louie. "That's what is important right now."

Henry nodded, his hands clutching the blanket. "Thanks."

Louie turned to Angeline. "I've got to go take care of another situation."

Chip was standing next to the couch where Tizbet sat hunched over, hands on her knees. "I'll go to the hospital with them."

Louie shot a quick look of relief at his son. "Check in with me."

"Will do."

CHAPTER 13

Tizbet relaxed a bit. Her father was conscious and seemed alert. She knew that she was a mess, and her bare feet dirty on the bottom. She was still holding the shoes she had taken off so that she could enjoy the feeling of the moss and grasses. She crossed her feet and tried to tuck them back as close to the couch as possible

Tizbet got up and went into the kitchen, balancing herself at the sink as she put on her shoes. Her mother followed.

"Dad looks terrible." Tizbet spoke in a low voice close to her mother's ear.

Her mother held her close for a second and looked into her daughter's eyes. They kept their voices low so that the men in the living room couldn't hear their conversation.

Angeline said "He's chilled and exhausted. I think something is really wrong. He passed out for a minute, and I called the paramedics. They seem to think it's his heart. This may have been coming on for some time. You know your dad, he wouldn't complain."

The paramedics were ready to load her father into the ambulance, and Tizbet held the door for them as they went through with the gurney, the IV pole just missing the top of the doorway.

"We'll be right behind you." Tizbet called to her father. Chip came out, following Angeline who had put on a sweater and carried her purse.

Louie's police car drove away in the opposite direction toward the quarry and Chiwaygan's, red and blue lights flashing. George Olmstead had managed to get to his car and sat waiting for the others so that he could follow them to the hospital.

Chip followed the ambulance, hands gripping the steering wheel. He glanced over at Tizbet beside him and looked in the rear view mirror to check on Angeline in the back seat. They focused on the sounds of the siren and lights of the ambulance ahead of them. Nobody spoke. George had said he would follow them.

Tizbet felt as though she were caught in some kind of vortex, whirling down and down. Annie had called her mother about Jerry. Now George almost drowned. Chip suddenly there, after all these years. Then her father, perhaps having a heart attack. She mentally stopped herself and got a grip on reality. Too many things happening too fast.

They drove into the Emergency Parking area at the hospital. Chip had barely stopped the car before Tizbet got out and ran into the building just ahead of him and her mother.

The attendant pointed them to the Emergency Room area, and met Louie in the waiting room. Henry had been taken into an examining room immediately. The hospital ER resident was with him.

"It will be a while." Louie took Angeline to the desk to sign admission and insurance forms and finally a nurse came out to take her back to see her husband.

Louie came back to Chip and Tizbet. He pulled his cell phone from his pocket. "I've gotta make some calls," and went out to the lobby.

Chip and Tizbet stood facing each other. They didn't speak at first, and then Tizbet reached out and touched him on the arm. She felt herself trembling and the tears finally came.

He put a hand on her shoulder and pulled her to him. She clung to him in her confusion and the remembered warmth was still there. He felt strong and safe. Neither of them spoke for a long moment, and then she stepped back, looking into his eyes. That one look said everything. She turned, carefully, and her voice was harsh with the emotion of the moment and her fear for her father. "I'm really worried about him."

"He's a tough old mutt." Chip reached out, gently holding her upper arms, smiling down at her. Her hair was a mess, she had no makeup on. Her faded red running clothes were worn and frayed. She had stopped in the woods to

95

examine the roots of a plant and her fingernails were black with dirt.

"You're beautiful, do you know that?"

She looked down at herself ruefully and grinned. "Not!"

"I really don't care." He pulled her back to him for one more long hug before letting go.

They sat down on the couch, each half turned toward the other. "Seems like we've both been away too long."

"Yes," agreed Tizbet. "It's been so long. I always hated my father for sending me away from you and the island."

There was a short silence, and then Chip spoke. "Your dad thought he was doing the right thing for you back then, Tizbet. He just wanted the best for you. Don't hold it against him."

Tizbet leaned back against the couch, feeling Chip's arm at the back of her neck. "I've missed this place and the people - more than I realized. It just seemed great to be back and see everyone again." A shadow went across her face. "Everything was going pretty good, but now... It might just be a mild one. He looks pretty good."

"I'll wait here as long as you need me," Chip said.

She hadn't been in to see her father yet, and it might be some time.

=============================

Angeline sat by Henry's bed. Tizbet stood next to her looking down at her father in the high hospital bed. A tube trailed down from the IV bag hung on metal rack fastened to the bed into his hand under a bandage. Round white patches on his chest had cords that led up to a blinking monitor with glowing green continually moving wavy lines.

"So I'm alive, Babe. Didn't even come close." He grinned up at her. "So don't get your hopes up."

"Hopes!" She snorted and punched him playfully on the arm. "I'm not surprised. Diving into the lake at your age... you aren't exactly a tadpole, you know."

Henry grunted and pulled the sheet up to his chin. "

Angeline smiled and reached over to smooth the hair back from her husband's face. She was relieved that it hadn't been a serious heart attack, but the doctor said that Henry had come very close. He was going to have to stay in the hospital for observation.

George Olmstead stood in the door to the hallway. He was pale and his hair was standing on end. He went to Henry's bed and stood there, arms clasped behind his back. "Sorry I put you to so much trouble."

"Just glad you're ok," said Henry. "This was probably coming on for a while."

A nurse came to the door and told them that their visiting time was up, and that her patient needed rest.

"Okay, Dad. We're getting kicked out. We'll be back!" Tizbet leaned over and kissed her dad on his forehead. He smiled up at her and nodded.

CHAPTER 14

George Olmstead went to the hospital visitor's parking lot and got in his car. He sat with his hands gripping the steering wheel. He knew what he had seen in the lake, but talking about it with everyone concerned about Henry didn't seem right. So he kept his mouth shut. Would anyone even believe him? He'd heard Henry tell his daughter that George had been talking nonsense, so obviously, Henry didn't believe him.

"What I need is a good stiff drink," he said aloud to himself. He turned on the ignition and headed for the nearest bar. He hadn't eaten anything since morning, and now it was early evening, but he didn't feel hungry. The street lights were already on and there were only a few cars parked in front of the stores.

He saw neon lights in one of the storefronts advertising Bud Lite and Coors and pulled into the parking lot. There were quite a few trucks and vans, but his was the only one that looked as though it had been washed recently.

The heavy wooden door opened out, and he went in trying to adjust his eyes to the semi-dark interior. A long bar took up all of the space on his left, booths along the wall to his right, and a few tables in between. A pool table at the back had a hanging lamp over it, and two men were playing pool. A long hallway behind them went to the back door with rest rooms along the side. It looked like there might be a kitchen at the back behind the bar. Just another local northern Michigan oasis, a wet spot in the desert of a million trees and lakes.

A big dark-haired bartender looked up as George walked in without pausing as he wiped a glass. There were several people at the tables, and a few at the bar.

George went to the bar and sat on a stool in front of the bartender. "I'll have a double shot of Laphroiag."

"Do what?" asked the bartender.

"Laphroiag. Whiskey."

"Never heard of it." The bartender had an amused expression on his face and George wanted to punch him. The image of the copper-scaled huge cat flashed in his mind and he felt his elbows pull in sharply and his back straighten in a spasm of memory. It didn't matter what the hell he drank, he just needed to take the edge off.

"Single malt. Whiskey. Double shot."

The bartender turned and got a bottle off the mirrored shelves behind him. "Will this do?" It was a cheaper brand, but George nodded.

The whiskey wasn't as smooth as he was used to, but it went down just fine. He pushed his glass toward the man behind the counter. "Another."

"Where are you from, friend?"

"Ann Arbor."

"Enh, Downstate. What brings you here?"

"Visiting a friend. He just had a heart attack." George felt the whiskey warming his stomach and started to relax.

He thought about saying something about seeing the big copper-scaled cat, but decided against it. The guy would probably think he was nuts.

He felt someone sit on the stool next to him and looked over at a big Anishinabe fellow wearing a tan jacket over bib Carharts. He had on high boots, and a black baseball cap. A long black pony tail hung down his back.

"Boo-zhoo," the man said. "That's hello in Indian talk."

"O.K. Whatever you say," said George. "You ain't from around here, hey?" The man half turned and grinned. A liberal waft of beer breath hit George in the face. "Just visitin'?"

"Yes." George fiddled with his empty glass. "You live here?"

"All my life."

"Good place," said George. He pushed the glass toward the bartender again for a refill.

"I like it. Me and my brothers just got in from setting nets. We fish for a living." He tipped back his beer bottle, wiped his mouth with the back of his hand and set the bottle on the bar.

"Oh." George had never met any Indian fishermen before and wasn't sure what to say.

"How come you decided to come here?" the man asked. "Gonna do some fishin'?"

"Not exactly. A friend invited me to help him check out the white reptiles and fish that people have been seeing."

With the next drink, George's tongue loosened considerably, and he found himself sitting with the fisherman and his brothers in a round booth at the back of the bar. They smelled like a combination of beer and fish, and dwarfed him with their size and the bulk of their thick work clothes. After he found another glass of whiskey in front of him, he bought a round of drinks, and then another. They were very jolly fellows, and seemed to enjoy talking with him.

"D' you guys ev'a shee any white fish er reptilzhs?" he asked, his tongue slurring.

"Oh, yah. We seen them."

"Lotsa them things."

"D' you shee a bi' cat?" George tried to sit up straighter but seemed to be sliding sideways. He noticed that the men didn't answer, and a couple of them got up from the table.

"Did you?" The man who sat next to him pushed his shoulder against George as he asked the question. "You see something like a big cat?"

"Yes. Under d' water....I did see it. Bi' cat... all shiny like." George sat up as straight as he could. "Took away m' gear. I had one a th' white snakes. Took it away fr' me."

The men across from him exchanged quick glances and both of them lifted their beer cans at the same time, tipped them back quickly, stood up, and put the cans on the table. One of them said: "Well, we gotta go. Interesting story." The man next to George slid out of the booth and stood for a minute looking down at him. He didn't say anything, but turned and followed the others out of the bar. The door swung shut behind them.

The bartender came over to the table and put a slip of paper in front of him. "Looks like you're picking up their tab." George fumbled with his billfold and removed his credit card. The writing on the paper was blurry, and he just handed it over with his card. "I'll have another."

Writing his name took some doing, but he managed it. He didn't notice when the lights in the bar started dimming and other people left the building. He didn't hear the bartender empty the cash register. He didn't see a tall man with long dark hair worn in a ponytail, or the two white streaks of hair on either side. The man came out from the back after the bartender left. He didn't hear that man lock the door from both the outside and inside, and walk away laughing.

A small gray mouse ran around under the tables, nibbling crumbs. The neon sign next to the clock over the bar flickered. George lay on the padded seat behind the big round table at the back of the bar, his mouth hanging open, drool sliding onto the leather.

===================================

A police siren sounded outside and registered somewhere in George Olmstead's brain. He felt something wet under his cheek. The side of his face was stuck to a smooth surface. He sat up and bumped his head on the edge of a table. The only light came from a streetlight outside and a neon sign over the bar. He was sitting behind a table. His skull felt heavy and his brain wanted to escape the pain inside.

He tried standing, but the room was spinning too quickly to the right and he sat back down. Must be that old inner ear problem again. Maybe if he had a drink, he would feel better.

He slid to the edge of the booth, braced one hand on the table and stood up. The room spun a bit to the right again, but calmed enough that he could make his way stumbling between tables to the bar.

Where was everyone? The place had been full of people, and they were all gone.

"Hey." Maybe the bartender was in the back room. "Hey!"

The only sound was the fading wail of the police siren. Everyone had gone home. Why was he here?

A sudden flood of memory slid into his head and he saw again the enormous shining cat that reached out with one paw and ripped his gear from his body. What the hell was it? Yes. The big cat thing. He saw it, godammit. It wasn't his freaking imagination. His stomach tightened as he remembered about Henry. But Henry didn't believe him. Nobody did. He needed a drink.

Well, if the bartender was refusing to answer him, he'd just help himself. He hung onto the bar and walked unsteadily around to the back, tripping on a heavy rubber mat and falling face first onto it. Crap.

He pulled himself up by hanging onto a shelf behind the bar and bumped his shoulder on one of the tap beer spigots. Righting himself, he saw a half full bottle of whiskey. Cradling it against him, he unscrewed the cap, tipped it back and took a good mouthful, feeling welcome warmth in his gut as it traveled down.

Probably ought to get out of the place. Go back to the motel. His laptop was there. He could do some research on those white snakes and lizards. Probably some explanation about their albinism. Locals said there was a cave-in. Maybe they were trapped underground.

He reached in his pocket for his billfold, pulled a bill and laid it on the bar. That would cover his drink. Might as well take the bottle with him.

Going to the door took some time. The tables kept getting in his way. He shoved a chair aside and it tipped over. It also was a while after grabbling with the doorknob before he figured out that it wasn't stuck. It was locked. From the outside. Shit.

He took another drink of the whiskey, and went back behind the bar. Maybe someone could unlock the door and let him out. His cell phone. Patting his pockets, he realized that he didn't have it on him. Probably left it in the car.

There was a phone next to the liquor bottles with a phone number taped to the shelf next to it. From the light of the neon sign, he could just make out the numbers on the phone and started punching. Slowly. Checking each number.

After quite a few rings, a voice answered. "Yah? Whadda ya want?"

"When doesh d' bar open?"

"Eight o'clock." Must be the bartender. There was a sharp crack in his ear, and then a dial tone.

George enjoyed a liberal amount of Black Label and tried again. Maybe the bartender didn't understand him the first time. "Y' shur yer comin' t' open d' bar?

"Yes, at eight, dammit!" Crack. Dial tone.

George had another drink. What did the bartender say? Was it something about being late? Or did he say 'eight'? The bottle seemed to be empty. He felt it slip out of his hand and heard it roll on the floor.

He held up the phone to the neon sign again, and very carefully punched in the numbers. This time, he didn't get a chance to say anything. The voice on the other end shouted: "I'll be down to open up and let you in at eight!"

"I don' wanna be let in.... I wanna be let out!"

The policewoman was understanding and made sure he got to his motel room. She even opened the door for him and took off his shoes after he sat down on the bed.

He didn't dream about the big cat until just before he woke himself up screaming.

CHAPTER 15

The moon was low in the sky as Tizbet and Chip left the hospital together. Angeline had refused to leave, and a bed was being made up for her in Henry's room.

Dinner in the hospital cafeteria had been unexciting, but adequate. Angeline had picked at her food, anxious to get back to Henry. The doctors still insisted that he had experienced only a slight heart attack, but she wanted to be sure he was all right. Chip and Tizbet drove back to the island. He followed the lakeshore road to a public beach parking lot, pulled into a space and turned off the car lights.

"I hope you don't mind, just want to spend some more time with you," he said.

"Sure. Good idea." She smiled in the darkness of the car, the only light coming from a street light behind them.

"Your dad's a tough old duck." Chip grinned down at Tizbet, and she looked up at him and smiled. He put one arm around her shoulders, pulling her close. "He's lucky. That water is incredibly cold, and even when you're in top shape and used to it, it can put you under."

"I guess he was scared for George. Probably too scared to think about himself"

Neither of them spoke for a minute. Chip suggested they take a walk. He kept his arm around her shoulder.

Tourists and summer people usually deserted the beach on the island in the evenings. It was the best time for young people to build driftwood fires and drink beer. Couples wandered off to be alone. Sometimes the tribal boys took a drum down to the beach and they sang forty-niner social songs. Supposedly forty-nine songs, but it was hard to keep track. Chip and Tizbet had been to many forty-niner's as teenagers. Those were good times.

If she stayed, it could be like that again, Tizbet thought. They both had changed, and yet there was something the same. His arm felt good around her shoulders, and they walked together comfortably.

"I need to know everything about you. Where you've been. What you've done. When was the last time we saw each other?" she asked. "Three years ago? Four?"

"Well, let's see. Graduated from high school here, went into the army. Military Police, served in D.C."

"I remember that part. Let's see, we saw each other when you were working on your master's, didn't we?"

"That was the time we met at that awful Greek restaurant, wasn't it?"

"Oh, gads, yes! The waiter burned the souvlaki!"

"I knew about you." he said. "Your dad talked to Nem-Kee, and Nem-Kee talked to Annie, and Annie talked to my mom." He chuckled. The tribal moccasin grapevine was notorious.

His arm dropped from her shoulder to catch her hand. She matched her steps to his as they walked.

"My mom wrote some, but she didn't seem to know exactly what you were doing. And of course, you wrote sometimes, too. But not often enough."

"You weren't exactly the best letter writer yourself!" They laughed.

"So what's the degree in?" she asked.

"Education."

"Just what the tribe needs."

Without talking, Tizbet felt the same linkage with Chip she always felt. It was this way each time, even when they had met away from the island.

Then he drew her to him, holding her close, as he had in the waiting room at the hospital. Only now they were under trees. They kissed then, and it was like the times on the beach, in the caves.

"This is incredible." He spoke with his lips on her hair, still holding her close, and she felt her ear against his chest, hearing his heartbeat. "Somehow, here on the island, it's as though we were never apart."

It was quite a while before they left the shelter of the trees and went onto the beach. They walked in synchrony, then stopped again and she reached her arms up and around his neck, feeling the braids against her arms as she drew him to her. He held her face in his hands, and then tilted her chin up with one hand and kissed her again. She drew him close with both arms, wanting more of him.

The moonlight was silver on the dark water that moved in slow deep waves toward the shore. Its broad band of light went from the mainland across to the island, as though one could walk on the shimmering path. Far down the beach there were a few flickering driftwood fires.

She looked up at the night sky. The myriad of stars were hidden in the city where she lived; only the brightest could be seen. Here, it seemed that the sky was full of stars, and she threw out her arms as though she could reach out and hug them. "I love it here. So many stars."

"The ancestors said the stars were the campfires of the ones that went before, campfires of the old ones." His voice was soft and deep. "See there? That's my great-great-grandfather!" He pointed at one bright star.

"I like that, but there goes my astronomy class." She saw his head jerk back a bit at her attempt to make a joke. Maybe he took the old stories seriously.

She looked back at the beach before her. A movement caught her eye and she saw a round white light near the trees that seemed to rise and float, and then move quickly to the right. It darted into the trees and was half hidden and then came toward the beach again. "Hey, did you see that?"

"What?"

She pointed and he watched with her as the light lifted again, rising to a point just above the trees, darted quickly to the left, dove down, and then went into the trees again.

Chip talked softly, almost in a whisper. "I've heard about people seeing a ball of light that moves like that. The folks around here say that when you see a ball of light, someone will die."

"I'm really not into that sort of thing," she said. "There's probably some explanation for it. Maybe just some kids fooling around."

"I don't see any kids," said Chip.

The bright sphere came toward them in a rush. It grew in size until it was as large as a person and stopped to hang in mid-air a few feet in front of them. They both moved back and ducked down.

"Holy wah!" Chip reached out and grabbed Tizbet's arm, pulling her away from the threatening orb. "What the hell......"

Tizbet was frozen with fear for a moment. They ran back up the beach, trying to distance themselves. The bright sphere followed them, but stayed a few feet away.

Suddenly it grew smaller, to the size of a baseball and flew out over the water. Chip and Tizbet stopped running and watched as the ball of light dove under the gentle waves, floating for a few seconds just beneath the water and then disappearing completely.

"I don't think that was kids fooling around," Chip said.

"It scared me silly," she said. Her heart was still pounding and she gulped in a deep breath.

"Maybe it was some kind of spirit."

"That's just superstition!" She turned and started marching toward the car. He caught up with her but didn't take her hand.

"Maybe. I'm going to see if anyone else has seen this. There's got to be a reason..."

"Well, it sure isn't some kind of spirit crap. I don't go along with that."

He didn't respond. She could feel that her rejection of his words had put up a wall between them. Probably he felt that the old beliefs were important to him and he still clung to them. She had always prided herself on being objective and practical. It didn't seem that all his education had made any difference when it came down to things like this.

Perhaps they were not as similar as she had thought. The mood of a few minutes before was broken. He handed her the car keys and she drove him back to the police station to pick up his car.

CHAPTER 16

Nem-kee went into the woods to get a mess of cowslips. They were good cooked like spinach, with vinegar or mayo. He cut off a bunch, flowers and all, leaving the roots to regenerate. He reached in his pocket for a small handful of loose tobacco, pulled it out with three fingers, bent over and placed it in the dark soil, murmuring "Migwetch" to thank the plant. Although some folks would say the tobacco protected the roots from insects the old way was best, gifting the plant for providing food.

As he walked up the path to his door, he saw that the Tribal Council must have sent someone over to pick up the old refrigerator he had set up in the side yard. They sure were fussy nowadays about anything extra lying around the yard. Now, if he wanted a place to store things away from raccoons, he'd have to go to the dump to find something. This time it would go out of sight back behind his cabin.

The tribal housing department had offered him an apartment in Senior Housing, but he held out to keep his own place. Men were a rare commodity in the senior community, and he could take only so much of ladies bringing over casseroles. He hung his cap on a hook behind the door.

The phone rang, his old friend Annie Martine. "Can I come over? You got time?"

"Always time for you. I'll put the tea on." The way she drove, it wouldn't take her long, and she didn't bring casseroles.

Nem-kee opened the box from Chicago, lifted out the contents and saw his original little thunderbird wood carving carefully cradled in bubble wrap. He laid it aside and took the packing away from the bags of hologram pendants. Something to show Annie.

She came in without knocking and plunked a bag of cookies on the table. "Eat 'em or wear 'em." She sat down, her ample behind overflowing the seat of the chair.

"Got something to show you." He poured tea, sat down facing her and picked up one of the bags. "These came; gonna sell them at the Jingtamok."

Annie took one of the bags and turned it over. "Your carving?"

"It's a hologram, copied from this." He held up the original little wooden thunderbird.

She opened the bag and took out the pendant, the gold filled chain sliding over her hand. "Nice! Never saw one like this."

Holding another pendant up to the light, he turned it around. The image was perfect, as if the original were embedded in the plastic itself. It had an iridescent quality, a rainbow of colors that shot out from the image, almost like the Thunderers themselves who flashed their eyes and made lightning.

Annie blew on her cup of tea. Nem-kee ate a cookie.

"I had a dream. Scared me." She told him about it. He nodded his head. When she had finished, he drank some tea. She waited.

"Enh. Yesterday morning I saw something." He told her about Shibizhee.

Her eyes widened and her hand trembled, making the tea in her cup slosh up the side.

"Things have been happening ever since the cave-in at the quarry," she said. "The kids say they saw white lizards. Folks have been seeing snakes....fish.... They're all white."

"Powerful," he said. White...a sign of power in any living thing.

"Shibizhee." She whispered.

"He must of come out of the quarry cave-in," said Nem-kee. "They could of come out with him... the old story about Nanabozho closing him up... he could of got loose..."

"Yeah. They must of come out with him...."

They talked about the old stories over a second cup of tea. Nem-kee finished off the cookies, and they were still talking when a call came for him about Jerry Higgins.

After he told Annie they sat in his kitchen on either side of his small worn table, aging hands around their empty cups, just looking at each other.

"Jerry shouldn't have done that," said Annie finally. "Dangerous."

"He didn't know any better. Who knows? Maybe it worked."

"I don't trust the situation. Sure, Shibizhee does good, but he can be really destructive, too. Can you do anything? Can we?"

Nem-kee leaned back, looked out the window and then back at the pendants on the table.

"Try to protect folks. I was thinking maybe these things... with the thunderbirds... kind of warn Shibizhee away from them... I think I called them..."

Annie picked up the pendant again, holding it up to the light so that the image was clear. "Might be a good idea to help the thunderbirds along some... Old Shibizhee can probably take care of himself."

They removed the hundred pendants from their little plastic bags and laid them on the table. Not sure that what they were doing would work; Nem-kee got the bag he used to carry his small drum and the pipe he was honored with by his teachers. To be a pipe carrier brought serious responsibility. He assembled the pipe and put sacred tobacco in it while Annie put bits of sage in a large abalone shell. He lifted an eagle feather from a small cedar box.

When they were finished with the blessing and request for strength, Nem-kee put away everything but the pendants. He fixed sandwiches and more tea, and they ate without talking. Annie sat back and folded her arms across her stomach.

Nem-kee looked out the window. "Want to take a walk down by the lake?"

"Sure." She stood up. He got two jackets and his baseball cap from the hooks behind the door. They took the narrow deer path to the lake.

When they came out of the trees into tall grasses and shrubs they walked on sand to the edge of the shore. The lake was just eating the edge of the sun. They sat on a large log and watched thin clouds of orange and pink above the horizon. Darkness came quickly, the rising moon hidden behind clouds.

"Do you think they will come?" asked Annie. "Will they know we need them?"

"They'll come." He spoke in an old man's voice, high and crackling slightly. The conviction was there. They waited.

Fog floated up from the swamps along the lake, lying in thin scarves swirling along the ground. Then long fingers of light began to show around the edge of the world, thrusting high, falling, and then thrusting again. The aurora borealis spread their wonder as they had forever here in the lake country. The lights were white, long thin shafts that danced and flamed up, then fell again. Nem-kee and Annie watched as bands of pulsing white lights reflected on the dark lake, rising and falling above the water.

Then the lights began dancing toward them, coming closer. Nem-kee felt his heart pound. They were coming - the ancients he had called with his mind with his prayers at the cabin.

The only sound was that of the endless waves coming and retreating. The white pulsing lights rose and fell, always coming closer until they were only a few hundred feet away, falling into the fog that surrounded them.

113

Annie gasped. "I heard of spirits dancing, coming to help....I never saw them."

Nem-kee began singing. His voice was soft, blending with the sounds of rhythmic plashing waves. The bands of light rose and fell with his song, taking color now, pale pink, blue, violet and green. Then they rose high and white again, and collapsed again into the fog.

Nem-kee's song stopped and his breath caught. The dancing spirits rose again, taking the shape of the ancestors. They danced in the old way, smiling, their faces kind and gentle. Their clothes were made of furs and leather, decorated with quillwork and beads. Their arms moved gracefully, feet hidden in the fog that surrounded them.

He glanced over to see Annie standing with her hands outstretched. He looked back and saw that one of the dancing lights had taken on the shape of an old woman, her face smiling, long braids lying on her deerskin beaded dress on either side of a rosette beaded in the shape of a star. His grandmother! She looked directly at him and he felt himself drawn to her. He started walking out into the water. Then her image faded into a single plume of violet light.

The ancestors danced slowly, moving back, gesturing with their hands in farewell.

Nem-kee backed out of the water in wet shoes and stood at the edge of the lake. Annie went to the log and sat down. He joined her.

He didn't know how the eagle feather came to lie next to them on the log. Nem-kee touched it when he put his hand down as he started to push himself up. He picked it up and held it before him as they walked back up the path to his cabin.

Going back into a building seemed strange for a few minutes. Nem-kee put the eagle feather on a shelf in his small living room. He took off his wet shoes and socks and put on a pair of slippers. They busied themselves with getting two more cups of tea. Neither of them spoke about what had happened.

She picked up one of the pendants and held it up against a light, turning it around.

"Oh!" Open-mouthed, she caught her breath.

Nem-kee looked at the pendant and saw the small thunderbird. Annie held the pendant steady now, but the little figure was turning, its wings lifting and falling, moving inside the pendant.

CHAPTER 17

The Coast Guard helicopter hovered over what was left of the Chiwaygan house. The early morning sun was just rising over the trees and cast long shadows on the devastation. Although Louie had to wait until the morning after the cave-in at Basil's home for a helicopter, it had arrived at first light. Without it, there would be no way anyone could safely inspect the area.

It would be two days before the Coast Guard Search and Rescue team could help. They were working on a shipwreck near Drummond Island; but the helicopter was available, so Louie and Chip were checking out the building. Louie asked Jack Derrick, the county sheriff, to come along. Louie hoped that Basil wasn't in the house, but if he was and could be reached they would attempt to find him.

"Glad you could come along, Jack," said Louie. His old friend the county sheriff had no jurisdiction on tribal land that was put in trust with the federal government, but they shared jurisdiction within the boundary of the original reservation that had been set up by treaty. They had a good formal and informal working relationship, unlike many tribes' with local authorities.

"Any way to help out." Jack Derrick was a bit on the portly side, but kept in good shape for his age. Since the days when he and Louie had gone to school together, his hair had gone gray. He was a big man and was wedged into the back seat of the helicopter, his shoulders turned sideways, looking down at the sinkhole below.

The Chiwaygan house looked as if it had been dropped from a height and crumpled. The sinkhole was large enough to swallow the house and at least a hundred feet beyond it on all sides.

"I sure hope Basil isn't in there," said Chip. "Doesn't look good, though. We haven't been able to locate him."

Louie grimaced. "Lorette was just talking to him before this happened."

"That looks like his car." Derrick pointed to a crumpled wreck half covered with soil and rocks.

"Oh. My God. He told her he was on the mainland. He's probably in there." Louie's hand gripped his seat belt.

Debris was strewn around the area, on the ground and limestone rocks.   Kitchen utensils, household tools and furniture, clothing, pictures, books, house plants - all of the things that make up a home and a life were scattered in the bottom of the sinkhole around the crushed dwelling. It was as though the house had exploded upon impact, tossing its contents in a wild jumble around the demolished structure.

Soil from the surface was still crumbling, pieces falling into the pit. Rocks and trees that had been on the surface had fallen around the house.

"I'll set down up top, not sure how stable it is down there," said the pilot. His skill was unquestioned, but he informed the other men as a courtesy. "There's cable in back we can use to climb down." The Search and Rescue team dropped down on cables from the helicopter, but it took training to learn how to do it.

Louie nodded absentmindedly. He dreaded landing and getting out to check out the house. Basil Chiwaygan was a friend, and this was a place he had spent many hours in over the years.

After landing a short distance away from the pit The four men got out of the helicopter, its blades still slowly swinging to a stop. The pilot helped them fasten the cable to a tree and toss it over the edge of the pit, and showed them the places in the cable to put their feet for climbing. He motioned for them to go on.

Louie could see that the pilot didn't want to look for Basil in the wreckage, and was busying himself checking the rotors and engine. Helping load a body into the helicopter was part of his job and the Coast Guard had picked up and delivered many injured and dead bodies over the years. Most of them were from islands out in the lakes, people who were too far from the mainland to get help in time.

"You'd better take this, let me know what you find." The pilot handed Louie a walkie-talkie. He had another one fastened to his belt.

Louie led the way down the cable. Derrick and Chip followed to what remained of the house. The exterior brick portion had tumbled like children's blocks, and there was brick, glass and mortar over the area. An interior wall supported by an I-beam had probably helped save what was left of the bedroom end of the building.

"Where should we begin?" asked Chip. He climbed over the roots of a small tree and came to a wall tilted on a sharp angle, one window open, jagged glass and torn curtains inside the opening. "Here?"

"Think I'll get some idea of the entire exterior before trying to go in, Chip. Might have some concept of whether it will cave in on us." Louie began walking around the remains of the house, testing the ground with each step, searching the area before disturbing anything. Jack went around in the opposite direction.

Chip followed his father. "This must have been the kitchen," he said, poking at the mass of wood and metal with a piece of broom handle.

The familiar metal canisters with their bright red designs lay next to the remains of the cupboards. Two family pictures in their glass and metal frames were tossed to one side as though in some domestic argument. Louie remembered seeing them on the wall of the dining area. He picked them up carefully, removed the pictures and placed them under his jacket before he walked stiffly through the ruin. "Susie will want these."

They circled the remains of the house and met Jack at their point of beginning.

Basil. Susie. All those years. Now, what? Nothing. Just a pile of rubble.

They came back to the open window. Inside were the twisted, distorted remains of what appeared to be a bedroom. Using the piece of broom handle to knock out the remaining bits of jagged glass, Chip stepped inside the opening under the angled ceiling. The floor gave a little as he walked on it. He called out to the other men "Coming in?"

Louie and Jack followed Chip inside and they duck-walked, bent over under the sloping ceiling. They had to support themselves with their hands as they balanced on the oak floorboards.

Bedroom furniture had slid to the end of the room, and a doorway at one side led to a partially flattened hallway. Chip looked through the opening. "I think that way is the bathroom. Pretty dark, can't see much, but I think I can get through."

Louie felt like he ought to be going ahead, but there was no room through the debris to get around Derrick, and Chip was already halfway into the hallway.

"Here's a light." Jack pulled a small but intense flashlight from his pants pocket, and aimed it into the hall.

"Be careful, Chip, it might cave in more with our weight," said Louie.

The boards beneath their feet creaked and shifted but held, and Chip squeezed himself down the narrow opening to the doorway of the bathroom that was angled but standing. Jack followed behind him, throwing the beam of light past them so that Chip could see where to step. Louie was still behind the others.

"In here." Chip motioned to the bathroom, and Jack aimed the flashlight so that it illuminated the tiled partially intact walls.

As Jack angled the light higher Louie heard him suck in his breath. The three men stared at the walls of the bathroom - the demolished bathtub- the broken mirror - a mass of bottles and cans. Blood was smeared on the walls of the tub. There were chunks of flesh on the walls. Large swaths of blood looked as though someone had used a giant paintbrush.

The body was on the floor, a man-shaped shadow in the poor light, half covered by debris. Jack handed the flashlight to Chip and reached down and gently pulled Basil's body out of the mess to the hallway floor. Chip pocketed the flashlight and helped Jack drag the body out through the darkened hallway into what was left of the bedroom.

"No!" Jack let go of the ankle he was holding, staring down at what was left of Basil Chiwaygan. He stepped back quickly, and Chip dropped the foot that he had been pulling on.

In the light of the bedroom, they saw that it was probably Basil, but it was completely devoid of skin. Just a mass of white fat with veins and arteries running through it.

The face was unrecognizable, eyelids and lips gone, the bone of the nose and ears visible. In no place was there any skin. The hair was gone, leaving the skull bald.

Chip turned and gagged. He put his hand out on the wall to support himself. Jack just stood and stared. He had seen too many car accidents to get sick any more looking at dead people. But this...

"What the hell?" Louie heard himself and felt his knees go weak for a moment. There was no skin on the body, but how could that be? How could a fall and cave-in cause something like this? When did it happen? Before the sinkhole caved in? During? After? It made no sense. If someone did this, was that someone still in the house somewhere, buried under the rubble? Or did that person get away before the cave-in?

Louie pulled his phone from his pocket and punched the speed dial for his office. "We found him."

=========================

As head of the Jingtamok Committee, sometimes Nancy Cloud felt as though it was too much work and trouble. But it was important to have a Jingtamok; it held the tribe together and brought in people from many Great Lakes tribes. It was a way of preserving the culture, and passing that along to the young. The feelings that were generated by the Jingtamok were what were important.

Nancy had coordinated the Limestone Point Jingtamok with other tribes so that it wouldn't fall on the same date as theirs. Traders and dancers traveled around, spending each weekend at a different Jingtamok in the Great Lakes. Dancers came to win prize money, and the traders depended on sales for income. The tribe charged entrance fees and table fees from the traders. She hoped that the tribe would at least stay within their budget this year.

She turned at the sound of someone calling. "Nancy! Come here, will you?" Sam Keshiawas was standing over by the arbor in the center of the dance arena by the loudspeakers. He waved her over.

She wondered what he wanted, and sighed as she got a bit out of breath hurrying to see what he wanted. She was no longer young, and was carrying a few extra pounds.

"What's this?" He pointed to something hanging from the arbor. It seemed to be someone's dance regalia, but was oddly shaped. Nancy reached out and pulled it away from the arbor pole so that she could see it more clearly. The regalia was a man's, beautifully beaded with old-time glass trade beads in turtle designs, a priceless costume one would only see in a museum. There seemed to be some kind of long thin wrinkled bag inside. She touched it and withdrew her hand as she felt the soft greasy object. Sam pulled it out from the regalia. It was in the shape of a person. The face and hands looked dried and wrinkled, and smelled like rotten flesh. She backed away.

"What the hell! Who put this here?" She looked at Sam, and saw he was pale, his eyes wide with shock.

121

Sam turned away, and then looked back at her, his eyes deep pools of horror. "Look again, Nancy."

"What is it?" Then she saw the hair. It looked real.

"I don't know who put it there, but I think I know what it is." Sam pointed to the top of the figure inside the costume, and she saw that the short graying black hair was real. The skin was a deep tan color. "Human skin."

Sam was one of the tribal deputies, and the police were pretty close-mouthed about the whole situation. But this was right in front of her. She felt her legs go weak. She put out a hand and grabbed one of the other arbor poles to right herself. She felt her asthma catch in her chest, and the wheezing that always accompanied it. She coughed, trying to ease the tightness.

As they backed away from the thing, flies began to hover over it.

"I'd better call Louie. Can you just stay here and see that no one bothers this?" Sam turned to go before getting her response. She looked at him desperately and nodded but she felt as though she might throw up. He went to the other side of the arbor, cell phone to his ear.

Sam came back. "Louie'll be right here. He's just leaving the coroner's office now. They found Basil's body in the cave-in at his house, and Louie had to sign some papers."

Nancy and Sam waited, guarding the thing on the arbor.

===========================

"Is it human skin for sure?" Louie asked, looking first at Sam and then Nancy.

"Evidently." Sam kept his voice low. "I told Lorette, she's already here."

Lorette came running out to the arbor carrying a blanket and a large plastic bag. "You'll need this." She gave the blanket to Nancy and stood away from the arbor, reluctant to go near the

122

grisly thing they were removing and wrapping. She had asked Nem-kee to help and he left his stand, carrying a large shell and small bundle of sage.

Louie helped Nem-kee light the sage and smudge the area to purify it, concentrating on the wrapped bundle. Then Nem-kee smudged Lorette, Nancy, Louie and himself. He put an arm around Nancy and hugged her. "You need to sit down. Come see me when you're done here."

Louie carried the wrapped flayed skin and dance regalia to the police car. Sam held the door open for him so that he could put the bundle on the back seat. The people around the Jingtamok grounds looked at them curiously, but held back from inquiring as to what they were doing.

"I'll be at the coroner's, and then I'll be back here to see if anyone saw or heard anything. See if you can find anyone that knows anything about this." He started the police car, looking straight ahead, his face grim. "We've got to get to the bottom of this. Too many people around, too many questions. It could cause some kind of panic."

"I'll see that things are kept quiet on this end," Sam volunteered. "We'll just kind of ask around."

"It would be best to say that someone was playing a joke, don't make it sound like a big deal."

"Right." Sam could be counted on to be laid back and not upset anyone. Lorette and Nancy kept things to themselves.

"See you later." Louie backed up, turned the car around and drove away with the skin of Basil Chiwaygan, on another trip to the coroner.

===================================

Dan Ebbot, the local funeral director and coroner was an old high school friend. Louie met him at the door of the basement leading to his work room. Louie looked and felt grim, stress showing in his rigid movements. Louie had never been

123

comfortable when he had to visit this part of Ebbot's workplace. He had visited John Ebbot many times as a kid, upstairs in the family apartment, but had always avoided the funeral part.

"I can't figure this out, Dan. First we found Basil's body with no skin on it, his house all caved in. Now this."

"Was it a cave-in like the quarry?" asked Ebbot.

"Yes, pretty much the same thing."

Louie walked over to a metal examining table and laid the blanket-wrapped bundle down carefully. "This was hanging up from a post at the Jingtamok grounds." He unwrapped the bundle and laid out its contents.

"I don't know what to make of this, John. Strangest thing I've ever seen." Louie stood back from the table, willing himself to stay in the room. He raised a thumb toward the elaborate regalia. "That outfit was with the skin. It's a very old one, traditional clothing used for ceremonies. In fact, I've never seen anything like it, except in museums." Ebbot hung the regalia on a clothing rack.

"Well, maybe you can find out more on the Rez. It's going to take a while here," said Ebbot. Wearing latex gloves, he began spreading the skin out on the table, starting the task of determining how the flayed skin was removed from the body.

"Right. Call me when you know anything."

Louis opened the door to the parking lot and welcomed the fresh air as he headed for his car. Too much happening. Was there a connection to this with what Nem-kee had told him?

CHAPTER 18

Confident that he could now travel about without problems, Mishipsea had explored the village in his man-form. He sat in the town restaurant enjoying his lunch. Once he determined that some kind of human identification was necessary, he used his powers to create the small plastic cards were required. As 'John Mishipsea' his story about being a descendant of one of the town's founders was accepted.

His previous visits to the island were in other forms - the ball of light that traveled quickly from his cave to Cathead Island, the bear that lumbered quietly in the wooded periphery of the Jingtamok grounds, and a quickly formed large quartz rock that lay on the beach overhearing songs of the young singers and drummers in the evening. As a small chipmunk he had watched the helicopter alight next to the sinkhole like a large dragonfly.

Removing the skin from the man was not difficult. As he had done at the museum, he shrank the body, increased the size of the skin and it slipped right off. Then he increased the size of the body. He felt his powers growing stronger with that action, releasing pent-up anger. For so long he had been entombed, and the frustration had been acute, demanding release. Once free of that torment, he was confronted with feelings of anguish over what the humans had done to the land and water. With the killing he felt a wash of pleasure, as if he had purified himself with vengeance.

Now, he felt at peace, able to take the human form comfortably. He ate the sandwich and french fries, sipped the well-sugared coffee, and smiled at the waitress as she came to refill his cup. He had learned to pick up the piece of paper on the table, take it to the cash register, and pay for his meal. There were many strange things that humans did. Learning about them had taken much of his time in the past few months.

As he went out, he saw the cork bulletin board with its ads and announcements. The Jingtamok poster in bright colors had pictures of dancers from previous years and basic information. He absorbed all of it in a second.

A long sheet of yellow paper had dates and times of the tribal Natural Resources Department community meetings about environmental issues. There was also a notice of a meeting of a local organization at the casino conference center regarding the invasion into Lake Michigan of Asian Carp. A picture of the intrusive fish species looked familiar, and he remembered seeing them when he was swimming underwater in his true form.

So it appeared that there were some humans involved with his concerns. As John Mishipsea, he might go to a meeting. He was tired of listening in on humans in the form of a lizard stuck to the window. It would be interesting to see how much of the information he had obtained on the computer would be discussed by the humans at that meeting.

Mishipsea took his time walking down the street to the marina. He passed two teenaged Anishinabe girls sitting at a small table outside the ice cream shop. They were both looking down at their cell phones, thumbs moving as they texted messages. Then both of them looked up and at each other and laughed. The actions of humans were often confusing, and that kind of behavior was a mystery. It had nothing to do with his concerns. Just another strange two-legged activity.

He got in his boat and started it up, aiming the prow toward Whitefish Island. About five hundred feet beyond the dock, the water began churning. His boat rocked back and forth as small whitecaps tossed it about. He clutched the seat with one hand. His other hand gripped the wheel. Bracing his feet and back, he kept himself from falling. "What...?"

Ahead, he could see large fish jumping out of the water, leaping higher than his boat. He tried to turn the wheel and avoid them, but it was impossible. The wheel wouldn't turn. He was surrounded by them. Water sprayed and his shirt was soaked as a large carp lifted out of the water and then came down with a huge splash next to his boat.

He tried revving up the motor but that was useless as well; it maintained an agonizingly slow speed. The churning water and leaping fish surrounded him as though moving with the boat.

An enormous Asian carp came out of the water directly in front of him and although he tried to duck, it hit him in the shoulder and fell to the deck. The boat motor stalled and then quit. The water around him stopped churning, and there were no more fish jumping. Silence.

Mishipsea spun around in the seat and looked down at the huge carp lying at his feet. "No!"

The head of the fish was flattened, and impressed on it was the face of Nanabozho. The eyes looked right at him, and one closed slowly in a devilish wink. The mouth turned up in a smile. Then the entire fish blurred and disappeared. Mishipsea could hear a faint sound of laughter echoing across the water.

The sky darkened, and he looked up to see a large cloud over the sun. A single sharp spike of lightning came down into the lake a hundred feet from his boat. He was drenched in a sudden downpour that lasted only a moment and was done. He wiped his face and looked at a clear sky. The cloud was gone.

A warning. His enemy was not a really a 'funny guy.' It wasn't a joke. Nanabozho had called on the sky forces. He would be a formidable enemy. Their next battle would happen soon.

============================

Tizbet and her mother left the hospital, stopped for lunch in town and then headed over to the Jingtamok grounds on the island. They parked behind the big tribal cultural center.

"Hey, Angie! How's Henry doing?" Annie bustled over to them, her hair pulled back in a ponytail, looking sweaty and disoriented. She had on an old pair of jeans and a wrinkled blouse.

"He's doing fine. We'll have to watch him around those young nurses. They've got him so doped up he's pretty silly."

Angie headed back to the kitchen to check the freezer and make sure that the buffalo meat was in good shape. "I'll just stay here with Annie," she said.

Tizbet saw Chip at Nem-kee's trading booth, a simple affair of three folding tables with an awning over them, folding chairs behind the tables. Although the Jingtamok wouldn't start that day, there were already things on the table.

Chip was adjusting the awning poles, pounding them in with a rock.

"Hi! How's it going?" She smiled at Nem-kee, who nodded to her as he laid out the black velvet cloths on which he would display the jewelry he had brought to sell. He had fastened two lamps on the awning poles, aiming bright lights at the hologram pendants. A few pieces of turquoise and silver jewelry and beaded pieces lay on either side of the pendants.

Chip stood up from his squatting position. "Got him all set up here." Chip came over to Tizbet and said to his great-uncle, "Do you remember Tizbet Mueller?"

"Sure do, hasn't changed much." Nem-kee put out one gnarled hand and took Tizbet's hand in it gently, squeezing ever so slightly. She returned the gentle pressure, the usual kind of handshake given by Indian people.

He looked at her critically. "Looks like a keeper, Chi'Pyan."

Tizbet smiled, but felt uneasy at Nem-kee's words.

"I'm thinking that she might be my best girl, what do you think?" Chip stood awkwardly, thumbs hooked in his jeans pockets. Tizbet stood, embarrassed, realizing that he was serious, and asking an elder for his opinion.

"You'd better hurry up, or I'll beat you to it. I think she likes me best." Nem-kee chuckled, and Chip laughed out loud. Tizbet flushed but laughed with them.

Tizbet looked down at the table and saw the necklaces with the crystal bubbles in which were embedded holograms of tiny thunderbirds. "Oh, how beautiful!"

She held one up to the light and was delighted as the iridescent colors shone out brightly in full sunlight. The image of the thunderbird was perfect, and she turned it this way and that, even turning it over and seeing how it was possible to look all the way around the tiny image.

"It's a thunderbird, made from one Nem-kee carved. Only he doesn't carve now, with his arthritis, so he has these holograms made up and put into necklaces. You know, laser three-D photography." Chip held one up to the light and turned it back and forth.

"You guys can keep those; wear them around, good advertising." Nem-kee motioned to them, and Tizbet immediately fastened the necklace and patted it on her chest, pleased with the gift. "They're fifteen bucks apiece, you just tell everyone that, okay?"

"Fine! Thanks!" Chip put his on, and they looked at each other. The necklaces were attractive, with gold-filled chains and settings for the images. "So let's advertise!"

"Sure! Thanks a lot, Nem-kee." Tizbet was surprised at the gift. She saw Nem-kee looking at them seriously, not smiling as he usually did.

"They should keep you safe. Stuff happening. Keep them on, both of you." He turned away and started unpacking another box, pointedly ignoring them, as though he had said too much.

========================

Deputy Lorna Mazur answered the phone. "Limestone Point Reservation Police." She nodded at Louie. "Yes, Mr. Ebbot, he just came in."

Louie picked up. "I'm afraid that it is the skin of Mr. Chiwaygan. However, I can't figure out how there isn't a single break in it anywhere. No knife marks, nothing." Ebbot's voice was usually low and somber, but now it was higher pitched.

"Well, the body didn't skin itself." Louie couldn't comprehend what he was hearing.

"I just don't know how. It seems impossible. Perhaps some new kind of technology."

Louie leaned back in his chair, stretching tired muscles. "Like what?"

"The skin was taken completely off the body somehow, just the dermis and epidermis. The layer of fat is undisturbed. The skin of the head and the hair are there, and the nails of the hands and feet. That is all a part of the skin, too, you know. Hair and nails, I mean."

Louie didn't respond.

Ebbot went on. "The entire skin was removed from the body evenly, not a millimeter of difference in the thickness at any point that I can determine. But there is no break on it anywhere that I have found so far, and that is also with microscopic analysis. Cursory, of course. I'll have to take more time. But it definitely is the entire skin from the body of Mr. Chiwaygan."

"Right." Louie wasn't surprised. But how could a body be skinned without a knife? "Could it have been done with a laser?"

"No. I don't think so. A laser cuts, too, it just makes more precise cuts. Of course, I could be wrong, or something I haven't found as yet. Perhaps something chemical."

"Well, if you come up with anything, give me a call."

"I'll do that immediately," said Ebbot. "I think we're going to have to call in an expert."

"Whatever you need, John. We can get someone but it might take some time."

Louie hung up the phone and then picked it up again. Something like this would bring in the very people he hated to deal with. The FBI had come poking around once before when there was a murder on the rez, and they took up most of his time just chin-wagging and treating him like some kind of country bumpkin. The longer he could keep them out of it, the better.

CHAPTER 19

Beanie was playing with other kids in an open park-like area west of the Jingtamok grounds; a field was rimmed with cedars. On the other side of the woods the waters of the big lake shimmered in sunlight. The voices of the children were high and shrill, excited about the Jingtamok, free to play until ceremonies and dancing began.

He had helped set up a net between two trees and organize a volleyball game. The kids were in jeans and shorts, many of them barefooted, wearing sleeveless shirts over smooth brown muscular bodies. Not all of them 'looked Indian,' and there was a wide range of hair and skin color. Beanie's cousins from Green Bay were only part Anishinabe, and had light brown hair.

Most of them had responsibilities at trading booths, or were dancers, and some had been up late the night before setting up camp. Not all of the children had arrived; some had to wait for parents to get out of work on Friday afternoon before leaving for the Jingtamok.

Beanie's older brother Mayn-gun, with his waist-length black hair pulled back in a ponytail was standing next to the net. The ball had gone to the back and he called to one of the Green Bay cousins, "Here, man!"

The white ball came flying through the air. Beanie ran toward it as Mayn-gun reached out to grab it, but the ball flew past him into the long grass.

"I've got it!" Mayn-gun ran after it and bent over to pick it up but straightened suddenly, clutching one hand with the other. "Aiee!" He looked up at Beanie, a confused grimace on his face. There was a blur of white in the grass and then it was gone.

"What's th' matter, bro?" asked Beanie.

The other children stood frozen in place when they saw the boy's hand dripping with blood. His face contorted in pain. "It was some kind of thing! Like a lizard or something. It bit me!"

He looked down at the deep teeth marks that were running with blood from his fingers and palm.

"Here!" Beanie pulled his t-shirt over his head quickly, and wrapped it around the bleeding hand. "Let's go see Mom."

"Lizards don't bite like that, not around here." An older girl that lived on the reservation spoke in a clear voice, and the rest of the children turned to look at her. "We don't even have lizards that big on the island. Maybe you cut it on glass."

"I don't lie!" Mayn-gun held his hand gingerly, keeping the shirt wrapped around it tightly. "That thing was about a foot long! It was all white, with black eyes and a red mouth and sharp teeth!"

"Well, something bit you, that's for sure!" Beanie steered his taller brother toward the Jingtamok grounds, looking back to shoot a glare at the know-it-all.

The girl stuck out her tongue at the boy, but followed them, glancing around carefully before putting her bare feet down in the long grass. The other children drew closer and went behind her, looking down as they walked across the field.

Beanie saw Sam Keshiawas at a trader's table and called out to him. "Hey, Sam! Mayn-gun got bit!" The other children stood back with the older girl as Sam unwrapped the shirt. The hand was still bleeding.

"Looks as though you ran into an animal or something. What were you kids doing out there?" Sam rewrapped the hand and put his arm around the boy.

"Just playing volleyball. I reached down in the grass to pick up the ball and this white lizard bit me." Mayn-gun's voice cracked in his excitement.

"We don't have white lizards with teeth around here." The older girl looked skeptical. "I think he saw something else. He's from the city. He don't know nothin'."

"I saw a white lizard! It had black eyes, a red mouth, and sharp teeth!" He was insistent, and half turned away from the girl, looking up at Sam. "I know what I saw!"

Beanie glared at her. "My brother don't lie."

Sam nodded, and looked around at the children. "It might be a good idea to stay out of that field until we find out what bit him."

He smiled at the children, who by now were restless, punching each other, wanting to get back to their play. "Don't you kids have something to do to help out around here?"

Two boys stopped their wrestling and grimaced. They followed the others as they drifted away to their respective families, not moving very fast. As soon as they showed up, there would be work to do.

Beanie looked back at the field. Something bit his brother. Something white with sharp teeth.

===========================

Tizbet worked alongside her mother in the kitchen of the screened-in open pavilion, stacking sandwiches on a large tray. The tribe was providing food for the people who were setting up things for the Jingtamok.

She caught sight of something white near her foot. "Now, did I drop one of these on the floor?" She bent down to see if a sandwich had fallen and pulled back quickly as two white legs retreated under a cabinet. A small animal? Had someone brought it into the pavilion?

She grabbed a long wooden handled frybread fork and slid it under the edge of the cabinet, moving it back and forth.

A large white frog jumped out into the kitchen, planting its webbed feet firmly on the floor, its head moving back and forth. It was at least two feet long and Tizbet saw its open red mouth and sharp teeth. Its dark eyes gleamed like two black marbles in its pale flesh. "A frog? With teeth? What the hell?" She had moved back away from the thing that was now the object of curiosity in the kitchen.

"Tizbet! Watch your language!" Angeline looked quickly around to see if any of the other women had heard her daughter.

One of the women grabbed a broom from the corner behind the door and came at the creature, ready to flatten it on the floor or sweep it outside. The frog jumped just then, leaped from the floor to the woman's wrist, and sunk its teeth into her flesh. She screamed and tried to shake it off, but it held fast.

The broom fell to the floor with a clatter, and some of the other women murmured or made high pitched noises as the woman tried to get free from the creature. "Get it off me!" She screamed, and flung her wrist against the wall and then the door, trying to get the frog to let go. "Get it off me!"

Tizbet was still holding the frybread fork. Her heart was pounding and she forced herself to remain calm. "Stand still!" She made a quick thrust and the fork went into the frog that was hanging from the woman's wrist.

It shuddered and dropped to the floor, followed by Tizbet who shoved the fork through it and into the wooden floorboards. The impaled creature lay on its belly, all four legs spread wide.

"Call Sam!" Tizbet shouted. One of the women went outside and ran across the Jingtamok grounds. Tizbet saw her talking to Sam, gesturing wildly, and then both of them came back to the pavilion.

Sam Keshiawas stopped short when he saw the enormous frog. He kicked at it with his boot, and it didn't move. He then pulled the fork free of the floor, holding the creature up to get a better look. Pale pinkish blood ran down from the holes made by the fork tines.

135

Tizbet felt a wave of relief as Sam took over the situation. She stayed back with the other women watching him hold the frog at arm's length.

Teeth on a frog? He shook his head. "Incredible!" It was the closest he had been to one of the white creatures.

One of the women brought a black plastic garbage bag to him, shaking it open so that he could drop the frog inside. Holding the bag, he withdrew the fork and handed it to Tizbet.

"You might need this again."

==============================

The meal had been served and people sat in small groups talking quietly. Already the stories about Basil's death and the white creatures had spread.

Some of the traders and dancers would come in later, driving long distances after they got out of work. A few dancers planned to wear their dance outfits to practice for the weekend dance competitions when things were less formal. There would be social dancing - round dances, the two-step and the rabbit dance - with couples dancing side-by-side holding hands. Much of the dance regalia was in luggage, encased in garment bags hanging up from canopies over places where their families sat, or in the recreational vehicles parked in the camping area. While people were eating, a group of elders and veterans congregated near the central arbor, led by Nem-kee, preparing to bless the grounds before things began. One of the drum groups started setting up their large drum with folding chairs around it.

Tizbet washed her hands at the stainless steel sink in the pavilion. She looked up and saw Chip talking with Sam Keshiawas and some of the younger men over near the woods. He turned and came back toward the pavilion, his face dark and serious.

She went out to meet him. "Hey, you look like a storm is brewing. What's up?"

"Dad is having the Security people patrol for those white reptiles. Sam is getting a group of the local guys together to try to keep them away from the area." He shoved his hands in his jeans pockets. The thunderbird pendant at his neck glinted. "They want us to help out."

"Are you going with them?" She put a hand to her neck, grasping the pendant at her own throat. Somehow, it gave her a sense of strength.

"I've got to go get some things in town, weapons and supplies."

"What do you guys plan to do?" she asked.

"Look for those white things that seem to be bothering people. Maybe see what we can find out about who or what..." He grimaced. "Sort of guarding the perimeter here. Protecting the crowd. It seems there have been more of them around the area."

"Can I help?" She wanted to reach out and touch him, to feel his arms around her. No. Yes. Damn. This whole thing was frightening. She was glad someone was taking action, but hoped he wouldn't get hurt.

"I heard that you already got one with a frybread fork," he said, smiling.

"That long handle helped. Hey, I'm serious about helping." She wanted to go with him. Be close to him.

"I'll let you know. We don't want anything that makes any noise, to avoid scaring people at the Jingtamok unnecessarily, so I guess it will have to be bows and arrows, maybe some pellet guns."

"Bows and arrows? You're crazy!" said Tizbet. "No, I guess that isn't crazy. I'm sorry. Shooting guns would make louder noises."

"I guess Sam has a few crossbows. He collects them. A lot of the guys have those fancy compound bows for deer hunting. Dad says he can get some arrows that have a small explosive charge and others that do a heck of a lot of damage."

Without realizing it Chip's voice sounded stronger, more excited, as though he were almost enjoying the challenge. Tizbet didn't miss the change in his stance, the way he held his head.

"Be careful." She did reach out then and touch him on the arm but withdrew it quickly. Since they had walked on the beach, he had been somewhat distant. Had she said or done something to irritate him? "Have you had anything to eat?"

"I grabbed a sandwich earlier."

She looked at his face. His dark eyes under the feathery brows looked tired but intense, and his mouth was set in a firm line. The black braids wrapped with red suede lay on his chest against the dark blue of his shirt, and she wanted to put her head there. It was getting harder to hold her feelings in check. Their eyes locked for a moment. Then he looked away.

"I'll see you later. Maybe you can talk to a few of the women and have them keep a lookout around the grounds." He turned to leave.

"Maybe I should just keep that fork handy!" She laughed, and was rewarded by a last smile before he walked away. He went past the men at the arbor, nodding respectfully as he headed back to those now gathered in the parking lot.

===========================

It wouldn't hurt to make a few prayers. Annie put her hand in her pocket, feeling the soft suede bag full of tobacco that had blessed. She closed the screen door behind her and felt the warmth of the sun on her face. As she turned the corner of the building, her eye caught a movement to her right, at the corner of the pavilion building.

A small white snake was just going into the grass. She walked quickly over to the spot where she had seen it, and parted the grass with her foot.

138

The snake lay still, and then quickly coiled itself and faced her. It lifted its head, and she saw its dark eyes and red as it opened its mouth, sharp teeth exposed. It darted toward her foot, but she pulled back, away from the threatening creature. The snake turned and slithered away into the grass. Annie stood transfixed for a moment, and then went back into the pavilion.

===============================

Chip and Louie followed Sam's van to the edge of the woods near the clearing. Sam had made another run over to the mainland. The van was loaded with additional weapons and gear. He had picked up canteens for water and a case of candy bars and trail mix. They might have to be out there for some time, and he didn't want anyone sneaking off. He also had small packets of tissues to use for toilet paper.

The other men and boys were assembling, and to Louie's surprise there were a few of the girls with them. Chip was even more surprised when he saw Tizbet walking with another girl across the field from the pow-wow grounds. They both carried a compound bow and quiver of arrows. She had her hair pulled back in a ponytail, and was wearing a pair of jeans and a dark t-shirt. The other girl was similarly dressed. Chip didn't remember her name, but thought she might be Lorette's daughter.

"Thanks, everybody!" Louie started right out, and the group came in close to listen to his instructions. "Sam here got some of the things you will need; there are camouflage outfits in the van, some that would probably fit those of you that don't have them. I recommend you wear 'em, it may make a difference." He looked around, and without counting figured that there were now about thirty young men and women, some carrying their own compound bows.

"I got some trail mix, canteens, a few things you might need to take with you, make it easier to stay out longer," said

Sam. "If you need to use the tissue paper, bury it. Also, if any of you were going to dance tonight, let me know now." He looked around the group. No one gave any signal that they wanted to leave, so he continued.

"I've got a map here of the area, so get geared up, and then we'll go over it." He gave his cell phone number and several entered it in their phones. "Set it on speed dial." After a few fumbles and muttering, they began moving toward the trucks.

"What exactly are we looking for?" the girl that had walked with Tizbet had a low voice, and several of the newer additions to the group looked up when she spoke. The rest of them were already going to the box of crossbows and gear.

"White reptiles, anything that might look like a white snake, lizard, frog, anything like that." Sam responded while handing out canteens. He had a keg of water in the van and would have them fill the canteens after the gear was passed around. "And of course, there's always the Shibizhee. He just might be out there." Sam's voice was sarcastic, and he grinned at the girl.

"Sure, Sam. Anything you say." She shook her head and her eyes showed her amusement as she took one of the canteens and a pack of trail mix. "And don't forget the meesee paper!" He handed her some of the tissue, and she shoved it in her pocket, laughing. Everyone knew what it was like to be out in the woods and need to go to the bathroom, and not have toilet paper handy. Several others checked their pockets.

===============================

Chip was over by the van, helping people fill their canteens when Tizbet walked up to him. She was wearing a slightly oversized pair of camo coveralls tied at the waist with a piece of rope. Her bow and quiver were slung over her shoulder. He filled her canteen wordlessly, and she screwed on the cap before speaking.

"Any chance we would go on this expedition together?" She spoke quietly, not wanting anyone else to hear the question, and hopefully not the response if it was negative.

He smiled at her, "Can't see why not." She nodded and went over to where Louie was standing, surrounded with some of the local people. "What happened to that frog we found over in the pavilion?" she asked.

"Dropped it off with Ebbot, for examination. Forensic evidence." Louie grinned at her. "He's going to fix it up with a little casket, got one of Kermit's suits to lay it out in."

Tizbet couldn't help a burst of the laughter coming out of her, and it felt like a release of pent-up tension. Several of the others had heard him, and joined in. She walked away, still laughing, to join Chip at the edge of the clearing.

======================

Tizbet followed Chip and Sam Keshiawas through the forested area between the Jingtamok grounds and Lake Michigan. Keeping their eyes on places where pale reptiles could hide and walking carefully, they skirted thicker stands of trees and bushes. Others walked quietly parallel to them at fifty foot intervals, keeping their voices low. The approaching sunset slanted beams of light through the trees.

Chip had a pistol-type triggered crossbow with a scope in one hand a quiver of short arrows tipped with explosive charges was slung over his shoulder. Sam carried a large crossbow with a nylon geared cranking device as a cocking mechanism and a large thick leather quiver with steel tipped arrows. Following behind them, Tizbet thought her compound bow that had only been used for target practice looked relatively cumbersome.

141

When Sam stopped to pull a bottle of water from his pocket to drink, Chip and Tizbet caught up with him.

"Do you really think this will work?" she asked. "Some people are pretty worried. After the guys came back to tell their folks what was going on... You know gossip. I just hope it doesn't spoil the Jingtamok."

She glanced up at Chip, and saw his jaw tighten.

"I'm not sure, but for now I'm going along with it," Sam said. "We've got to do something. Basil's death could have been accidental - except the fact that he was skinned."

"Minor detail," she said.

"See anything white and creepy in the bushes?" Chip asked Sam.

"Nope. All the tourists are over at the casino." Sam chuckled, and put the water bottle back in his pocket.

Tizbet pulled one leg up and stretched the muscle, and then did the same with the other leg. She was used to running, and the slow stalking of reptiles over uneven ground made the muscles in her legs tighten. "Hey, look!" She pointed under the ferns at the edge of a group of birches. "Is that a branch from a birch tree, or one of those things?"

Tizbet and Chip pulled arrows from their quivers and aimed at the possibility. It moved rapidly toward them, a large white lizard with eyes like black marbles stuck in the sides of its head. It opened its large mouth exposing menacing sharp teeth. A soft hiss escaped as its red tongue flickered.

Tizbet took a step backward. The thing stopped and closed its mouth. It came forward again. Chip released his arrow. It drove into the lizard and stopped the creature in mid-stride. It was only an instant before the explosive charge went off, and pieces of the reptile were blown outward.

Although there was only a sharp crack and a puff of smoke as the arrowhead exploded, Chip thought it possible that no one but them had heard it, but two boys on their left came through the underbrush. "Got one?"

"Yeah. A big lizard." Chip half turned toward them, already bringing another arrow to nock into his bow.

They went to the place where the explosive charge had gone off and looked at the bloody white flesh lying on the ground.

Sam pushed at it with his foot. "Well, that's one." He straightened his shoulders. "Good start. We don't have much light left, let's get cracking."

Chip stood for a moment looking down at the remains of the lizard. He had never enjoyed killing but justified deer hunting for the meat it brought to the table. This was different. He remembered the stories about any white animal being considered sacred. Had he just destroyed a spirit being? No one else seemed concerned.

CHAPTER 20

John Mishipsea sat on the Whitefish Island beach, next to him a balled up sandwich wrapper and pits from several plums. A half empty plastic container of Pepsi sat pushed into the sand.

A small red squirrel ran down the trunk of a pine and stood trembling at the base of the tree, its tail jerking as it eyed the plum pits. Mishipsea sent a thought of approval to the tiny one and it came toward him in start-and-stop-and-start movements. Finally, it reached the remains of the fruit and picked one up, nibbling on the juicy flesh.

Mishipsea waited until the squirrel dropped the pit and started on another to point at it with one finger. It fell over on its side. He pointed again. The small body lifted in the air and spun around, blurring until it was just a tiny whirlwind that lifted sand from the beach, spinning counter-clockwise to the left.

He dropped his hand and the squirrel fell to the ground, but now the small body was devoid of skin. The auburn fur lay next to it. Mishipsea smiled. He raised his hand and pointed again. The bloody flesh of the squirrel and the fur beside it lifted into the air and whirled in the opposite direction, clockwise now, to the right. His hand fell and the whirlwind stopped. The small squirrel fell to the sand, its skin returned.

Mishipsea lifted hands, palms up, and the squirrel moved, its legs pushing out. It rolled over onto its small feet and turned its head toward him. He sent a thought of gratitude to the tiny one. Its feathery tail jerked as it chattered disapproval. Then it grabbed one of the plum pits and stuffed it in its mouth and scampered back up the fir tree.

Mishipsea laughed. He stood up and gathered the wrappers. Tipping back the bottle, he finished the drink. Then the bottle fell to the ground as he grabbed his head with both hands.

The screaming in his mind that came from Cathead Island was like a spear thrust through his skull, and he felt his heart respond, pounding rapidly. One of his small spirit companions had been killed by a two-legged. Mishipsea stood and raised his arms to the sky, howling anguish.

===========================

Tizbet walked carefully, watching the ground ahead of her, raking the area with her eyes, remembering the times she had gone with her mother and aunt to look for morel mushrooms and berries. Like many of the women, she was experienced in looking for things close to the ground. The old patterns still existed to some extent with mostly men in the tribe hunting, but some of the women hunted now, and many of the men went berry picking with their families.

They walked cautiously, stepping carefully, moving almost noiselessly through the forest, Tizbet's movements fluid and soundless.

She kept glancing at Chip on one side of her and Sam on the other, maintaining her distance, watching for any movement that told her they had spotted anything. Then she saw Sam's lower lip extend and his head go back slightly. He was pointing with his lip, careful not to make a sudden movement with his hand or arm that would alert their prey.

They stopped at the same time. A large white snake was half-hidden in a patch of white flowered dutchman's breeches.

The mechanism on Sam's crossbow drew the bowstring back until it clicked in place. However, the tiny sound alerted the creature and it drew itself up until it was half hidden beneath the plants. Tizbet drew her bow back carefully. She and Sam shot nearly at the same time.

Both arrows pierced the snake. It writhed and curled on the mossy ground and then lay still. Sam walked over to it first, followed by the others. The arrows from the crossbow had gone completely through the creature, leaving two holes in its side seeping pale pinkish blood. Tizbet kicked at it with her booted foot and it didn't move. She bent over and stepped on the snake pulling her arrow loose, the body lifting slightly as the arrow was wrenched from it.

"Well, I guess that's how it's done." Sam pulled out his arrow, inspecting it before replacing it in the crossbow. "We'd better keep these things loaded; there might not be time ..." He followed his own advice and readied his crossbow for another shot.

The small black radio at his belt sounded and he answered. "Yo. Sam here."

"Boo-zhoo, nee-zhee. It's Louie. I've got another one." Tizbet could hear Louie's voice. It sounded scratchy on the old radio, and Tizbet eyed the instrument. The tribe could use updated equipment, but these seemed to be doing the job.

"Great! We just got two ourselves, a snake and a lizard. How are the others doing?" Sam grinned.

"I don't know," said Louie. "Sounded like maybe one of the pellet guns, I'm not sure."

"This is crazy-making stuff," said Tizbet after Sam put the radio back on his belt. "White lizards, snakes, frogs, a Shibizhee that skins people. This is just plain nuts!"

"So, do you have any explanation for it yourself?" asked Sam. "Got a better idea?"

"Well, maybe they got loose from a circus. Or a zoo." She searched for something logical that she could use as an explanation. "Maybe there's a lab someplace out here doing experiments."

"Not everything has a scientific explanation, Tiz," said Chip.

She didn't respond. They had their differences, and this was a big one.

Sam pulled a folded black plastic bag from his pocket and put the snake in it. He pulled it shut and slung the bag over his shoulder, holding onto the red ties. "Well, I'm going to keep on clearing these woods. How about you guys?"

"I'm ready," said Tizbet.

Chip nodded. Lifting one eyebrow, he said, "I forgot to ask, Tiz, were you going to cook that one for supper? Remember the old Anishinabe rule. If you kill it, you have to eat it!"

CHAPTER 21

After checking to be sure the building was in good condition Annie left the pavilion. The women that had helped were with their families, taking part in or watching the evening dancing.

Since many of the younger men and boys were out with Louie, a round dance was done primarily by women and children. One of the drum groups kept singing with a few women standing behind the men seated at the drum, singing with them. Some of the children danced by themselves, practicing for the contests the next day. There were too few men to do the two-step with their wives and girlfriends, so there was no two-step or rabbit dance for couples.

Annie found a seat near Lorette and her husband Stan Martine. Slipping her feet out of her shoes, she let the cool evening air take some of the swelling down. Although she brought her dance shawl, she didn't make any move to get up. Her thoughts were on Shibizhee. She wondered what should be done, knowing that the people needed to be protected.

"I don't feel so good about Tizbet and those other girls out there," she murmured to Lorette. "Why not just let the men and boys take care of those white things?"

Lorette smiled, "I guess some of the girls are better with a bow and arrow."

"Sure, but it just doesn't seem right." It was frightening to think of her nieces out in the woods chasing down such creatures.

"Don't worry; they can take care of themselves."

The dancing came to a close. The master of ceremonies bid everyone good night and the sound equipment squealed as it was turned off. Drummers began wrapping up their drums and drumsticks. People gathered their belongings and headed out to cars and campers.

Annie could hear an occasional muffled explosion out in the woods as charges went off that were fastened to arrows. It was better than gunshots, but it didn't fool anyone. Everyone had been talking about it. Yet no one seemed frightened enough to leave.

Nem-Kee called some of the elders together over by his stand. Annie joined them. He discussed in a quiet voice the situation as he saw it. He needed strength to help deal with the underworld forces represented by Shibizhee. Some of the elders listened and then quietly returned to their families, not committing themselves. Others quickly agreed to help Nem-Kee plan a men's and a woman's sweat lodge for the next morning. Annie said she would conduct the women's.

Annie walked to her car, shawl over her arm, keeping the fringe from touching the dusty ground. Like others who lived nearby, she was going home for the night.

Those who were camping had already lighted lanterns in their tents or turned on lights inside their RVs, and there was a lineup at the bathrooms. Some of the children played, running around the tents and buildings but few strayed out of lighted areas.

Annie drove carefully across the field that served as a parking lot, and bumped down onto the dirt road. She passed a group of teenagers walking together, laughing, heading toward the lake. "Don't have any sense at all, probably going to have a forty-niner anyway," she said to herself, wondering if she should stop and warn them.

Worry lay within her, so she stopped the car and backed up. The young people walked up to her car.

"Where are you going?"

One of the boys leaned over and looked in the window. He knew Annie, and smiled. "Down to the beach."

"You kids should stay at the park, stick close to your parents tonight. Don't go running around out in the woods." Annie spoke harshly.

"We're just going for a while, we'll make a fire." The boy looked irritated at her interference, but was polite to elders. "My mom said it was all right."

Another boy standing at the edge of the road grinned. "We'll stay close to the fire. Those white things would be afraid of fire, anyway."

Annie shook her head and said nothing. She drove on with her mouth set hard.

"Dumb kids."

===========================

Tizbet followed Chip up one of the dunes, fading evening light making it hard to see their way. She kept her bow ready. "See anything?"

"Nothing," he said. "We're almost to the beach. Might as well try to contact the others." He pulled a flashlight from his belt, and turned it on. The bright light made it seem darker around them.

"Yo!" Chip called.

Sam Keshiawas came through the woods at their right. "Ready to call it quits? I can't see good enough anymore. How about you?"

"Yeah. Might as well go get some rest," said Chip. "I haven't shot one of those things for an hour or so now."

Another group of hunters came out of the woods to their left. They talked for a few moments and agreed that it was time to call it a night. Louie came through the woods last, and told the hunters the latest theory from Ebbot and Teague about someone using a laser to remove the skin.

"I find it very difficult to believe that someone could do that good a job even with a laser - no breaks on the skin? It seems impossible!" Chip was careful not to disagree with his father, but had thought about the removal of the skin over and over and could find no sense in it.

"Well, if the scientists don't make sense, maybe someone else will," said Louie. "Nem-Kee wants all of us to get together for a sweat tomorrow morning, early. There will be one for the men, one for the women. Anybody that wants to."

There was silence for a moment. Then Sam grunted a deep sound of assent "Ah-hauw." It was echoed by some of the others who had come out of the woods and stood behind Louie. The purification and strengthening force of the sweat lodge was needed.

"What time?" asked Chip.

"Around six o'clock. Over in the woods where we got together. Some guys have been setting up the lodges. Get some rest. Long day tomorrow." Louie left, Sam behind him. The hunters melted into the darkening forest.

Tizbet and Chip stood together at the top of the dune looking down on the lake. The moon was just rising in the sky, the last of the sunset fading. Lights from the town across the bay seemed far away. Waves broke on the beach, making a quiet soothing sound – a contrast to their frantic search of the previous hours in the woods.

"It seems so peaceful." She moved closer to Chip, removed the arrow from her bow and put it back in the quiver. She leaned the bow against a nearby shrub. Chip set the safety on his crossbow, and put it down next to her bow. He turned off the flashlight and put it in his pocket.

She went into his arms gratefully, holding him close. They stood for a long moment before she moved back and he bent to kiss her. He cradled her cheek in his hand, and her arms went up around his neck. His mouth was a shock to her, urgent, demanding. She responded greedily. They both felt the need to be closer, to be a part of each other.

She pushed back away from him and saw in his eyes the same desire that she felt. "More." They kissed again, a sense of remembrance and familiarity merged with their present need for each other. She thought of her cabin, the privacy, her bed.

She took off the long-sleeved shirt that had been covering her arms from insect bites, and tied it around her waist. He tipped her head back with his fingers under her chin, and kissed her deeply. Then he bent and kissed her shoulder on the small black tattoo of a water snake, her clan symbol. Remembering, she thought of the time they had their clan symbols put on their shoulders - his a turtle, hers the water snake.

Then they heard the sounds on the beach, the kids laughing, running down the dunes to the hard-packed wet sand along the water. Chip turned, still holding Tizbet in his arms, and they saw young people running about, gathering driftwood. A large boy carried one of the drums, and some of the boys from a drum group went toward the others, their sheepskin padded drumsticks sticking up out of the back pockets of their pants.

"Looks like a forty-niner!" Tizbet spoke in a husky voice. She stood close to Chip, looking down at the kids on the beach. She smiled, remembering the forty-niners that she and Chip had attended in their youth. Not that they couldn't still go down and join the others. Some people in their twenties and thirties would probably make a night of it.

"Want to party?" Chip looked down at her. He didn't know what to expect of Tizbet, it had been so long.

"Sure," she said, slinging her bow over her shoulder." He picked up the crossbow and turned on the flashlight so that they could find their way to the beach.

Neither of them saw Muh-kuk-kee behind the group of white, ghost-like plants called "Indian pipes" and the thick shrub where they had leaned their bows. He looked at them, watched their lighted silhouettes as they walked away, and sent a strong message across the lake to Shibizhee.

======================================

Nem-kee walked out of the trees on the promontory that overlooked the bay and squatted down, his knees cracking. The sound of a drum and young voices from the beach below reminded him of the early years with his wife. She was gone now, walked on to the place where he would join her. Not so many years now, only a few left him in this life.

But he had a responsibility tonight, to call on the Grandfathers and Nanabozhoo - the earth spirit that he knew had returned. The underworld spirit – Shibizhee – was powerful. Too powerful. There must be balance between sky, earth and water. Something was not right. He could feel it tonight.

He opened the small deerskin bag at his waist and poured tobacco into a shell. From a cedar he pulled a small lacy piece off a branch, crumbled it, and added it to the tobacco. Sage and sweetgrass were in other pouches from his shirt pocket, and he dropped them in with the others. His old lighter erupted in flame with one flick of its wheel, and fragrant smoke rose from the shell into the night air.

He had brought no drum. The words he spoke were in the Anishinabe language. Ancient words asking for help from the ancient ones. He repeated his plea several times, watching the smoke rising up and hoping that he got their attention. Would Nanabozho hear? Would the sky forces hear?

Only ashes remained in the shell. He put them on the ground, pressing them into the earth with his broad thumb. "Ahaw." Then he waited.

===============================

Reddish-orange flames licked at the pieces of gray driftwood the kids had dragged over the sand. Chip and Tizbet sat by the fire, singing with the drum, an old forty-niner song. Chip sat in the sand near the fire, leaning against a large driftwood log. Tizbet sat between his legs, her elbows resting on his thighs. He let his fingers trail through her hair and felt its silky softness. They sang with the others, voices rising into the cool night air.

The drum was placed flat side down, four short legs keeping it off the ground; a large bass drum decorated with bright Indian designs. Strands of feathers and beads hung down at four places marking the four directions. This was not a special holy drum, but one that could be used for social occasions; the drummers would never use any of the special drums for a forty-niner. The boys sat around the drum on small folding stools, each with his own drumstick, hitting in unison, singing.

One girl sat by herself on a driftwood log, arms folded, obviously pouting, singing without enthusiasm. Tizbet leaned over and asked one of her cousins "What's with her?"

"Oh, she's a drummer in the school band in Detroit, and thinks only boys drumming is discrimination." Her cousin grinned. "She don't know shit." Women and girls had their own areas of power, and the separation of tasks and powers were maintained for practical and spiritual reasons, not to discriminate.

The high falsetto voices of the male singers blended in the five-tone pentatonic scale of the ancient people. The words were sung in English, a tale of love won and lost, pleading for the lost love to return - but reminding the lost one of other loves that could be had for the asking. Each verse was half-serious, half-joking, and as they finished several of the singers laughed. Another song was begun, and one of the drummers placed a small twig upright in the sand next to the drum. There were two twigs now; they would be arranged in sets of five next to the drum until forty-nine was reached. Some of the songs were traditional, sung in the Anishinabe language. Others were sung in English and were romantic or comical. The group started up a new song to the theme music of "Sponge-Bob-Square-Pants" and everyone laughed. The teenagers and young people seated

154

around the fire leaned against one another, or against driftwood logs half-buried in the sand.

Tizbet noticed that several of her cousins and other relatives were wearing little thunderbird pendants, gold chains glinting in firelight.

Her body against his warmth gradually relaxed. The song now was slow, steady like a heartbeat, an old melody in a minor key, words sung in the ancient language drawing the singers into a single entity. The melody repeated, and more joined in, drawn together. The music echoed up the beach to the dunes. And across the lake to Whitefish Island.

Tizbet sat staring into the fire, watching the burning wood glow red and yellow, pieces falling and spilling into each other. The steady drumming felt like her own heartbeat. Chip's hand cradled her face and brought it to his.

As she turned to him she saw a bright light coming toward them across the water. For a moment, surprise held her motionless. She pushed Chip away and jumped to her feet. "Look!"

A brilliant yellowish white orb moved rapidly toward them. It appeared to grow in size as it approached the shore, then hovered several hundred yards from the campfire, whirling and pulsing, lighting the entire area.

"What's that?" The girl from the city jumped to her feet. "A meteor?"

"Meteors don't float, they fall!"

Chip and the others were standing now, the song and drum forgotten.

"Some kind of fireball!" The orb moved toward them, showing no signs of changing direction. "It's coming at us! Quick! Run for cover!"

One teenager grabbed the drum and ran for the trees. He tripped and fell, drum and drumstick tossed on the sand just before the blazing ball brushed across him. Clothes and hair ablaze, he rolled in the sand and extinguished small flames on

155

his back and legs. The fireball raced across the beach, coming close to the others. Their cries filled the air.

A young woman carrying a blanket pulled it over herself and dove to the ground. She screamed, paralyzed with fear, unable to move.

The whirling fireball swept the length of the beach, slowed along the tree line, and spun out over the water. Everyone was running for the trees.

Tizbet ran with Chip to the boy on the ground next to the drum. He sat up and they saw the dark places on his back and legs where his clothing was burned off. "We've got to get him to a hospital. Now." She ran back to the campfire for a blanket to wrap around the burned youth that Chip was now helping stumble toward the woods. The fireball still whirled over the water.

As she bent to pick up the blanket, she saw her pendant swing down, gold chain reflecting the still burning wood. The little thunderbird within it sprang out into the air and hovered a few inches away from her face. It arched its back, fluttered its small wings and emitted a small but powerful screech like that of an eagle. Tizbet stood up, mouth open in amazement, watching it grow in size, and with a tremendous burst of speed fly off toward the spinning fireball.

Another object flew from behind her, like a small bird or bat. As it went past, it too screamed. Another little thunderbird that followed the first. Frozen in place, she looked out over the water and heard the cries of the small raptors as they grew in size and speed, announcing their entry into a battle with the ball of light. Others flew out, away from the people at the edge of the woods. She knew they were coming from the pendants Nem-Kee had made to protect the wearers.

Tizbet held the blanket to her, heart pounding, and ran to Chip and the young man now standing in the shelter of the trees. He had his cell phone at his ear, calling for help.

They turned to look back out over the lake. The moon had emerged from a break in the cloud cover, but its light paled in the brilliance of the fireball. Suspended over the water. it darted one way and then another, surrounded by spirit birds that dove in screaming and attacking.

========================

Shibizhee knew all too well the war cries of his ancient enemy. In his present form as a ball of light, he had his best chance of escaping or attacking them, and he whirled in a frenzy, compressing his power. Combat stirred his warrior spirit. He would destroy them all.

With a surge of energy he doubled in size. The small thunderbirds were thrust aside as he emitted his own ancient battle cry. His deep roar echoed off the lake and forest.

He released a bullet of fire at his attackers. They outmaneuvered its path. It missed its targets and hit one of the boulders along the lakeshore, smashing it to pieces in a blaze of molten rubble.

The thunderbirds flashed their eyes in unison, propelling small bolts of lightning toward him. Shibizhee again let go a bullet of fire. It grazed one of the small raptors and sent it spiraling through the air, screaming with pain, before it fell into the water.

==========================

Some of the youth began running for the parking lot. One boy called out, "What if it follows us and hits the cars? The gas tanks would blow up! Get back in the woods!"

Tizbet and Chip stayed by the injured man, half hidden by a large cedar.

The fireball had grown in size and Tizbet watched it plunge into the lake. A ring of water raised and splashed high and then fell, creating a circle of waves spreading out for hundreds of feet.

She hoped it was gone and turned to Chip, but then another roar echoed around the bay. Shibizhee emerged from the center of the circle of waves in his true form as a copper clad horned panther. He clawed at the small thunderbirds in the air above him.

Chip reached for Tizbet. She let herself be folded into his arms and watched the battle over the lake with her back firmly fastened to his chest.

A high pitched sound like a hundred sirens filled everyone's ears. Four huge black thunderbirds plunged downward with incredible speed. The shape of eagles with powerfully built bodies were the size of agile fighter jets. Flashing their eyes wide, the enormous warriors entered combat.

"The ancient ones! Nem-kee told us about them. They have fought Shibizhee many times," said Chip. "Nem-kee must have called them."

Tizbet couldn't speak. Everything she had been taught and believed had been challenged in the past few minutes. A little thunderbird came out of her pendant to fight the enormous ball of fire...A huge gleaming cat that rose from the water... there was no explanation. She shuddered, felt a chill wash through her, and pushed herself back against Chip's body.

The air over the lake was alive with streaks of fire and light like an intense electrical storm, interspersed with the piercing war cries of Shibizhee and the shrieking thunderbirds.

Shibizhee turned to meet the assault and batted at his enemies with sharp copper claws, teeth biting at them, an enormous cat fighting off the flock of deadly birds. His forked copper covered tail whipped about, struck one of the small ones, and sent it tumbling into the lake.

One of the ancient ones shot a bolt of lightning so bright that the human spectators on shore had to shield their eyes. It missed its mark and exploded in a volcanic-like eruption of fire.

But then a direct hit by one of the spirit raptors sent a piercing shaft into Shibizhee's side.

He fell and hit the surface of the lake with such force that the water spouted geyser-like as he disappeared beneath. The large thunderbirds now closed in over the area where Shibizhee had gone, ready to send a barrage of lightning if he emerged, but the turbulence settled.

"The big cat got hit, Chip! Those big bird things must have killed him!" Tizbet felt a rush of relief.

"Maybe. It would probably take more than that..."

The water returned to its gentle pattern of low waves as the thunderbirds circled, waiting, the hushed beat of their massive wings the only sound. They widened their sweeps over a larger area, but there was still no sign of him. Perhaps he was badly wounded, or even dead from the lightning bolt which had hit him, but they still kept a vigil.

"Is it gone?" Tizbet looked up at Chip. "What should we do?" She wanted to run, and she wanted to see what was happening. They weren't really safe, but the scene before them was so incredible...

"I don't know," he said. "Maybe hold on a bit, see if it's safe to get out of here."

The big thunderbirds were still circling over the lake. Tizbet heard some of the youth talking about the battle. Young guys. Trying to act like they weren't scared.

"Those were stealth fighters, man. Probably some military thing."

"No way. What about that cat or whatever it was?"

"It's done with holographic projection - virtual reality."

"Yah, some kind of war maneuvers. Probably army stuff."

"Maybe something else. My grandpa talked about some big cat in the lake."

"Yeah, some kinda spirit things, hey."

"Nobody will believe us."

159

Tizbet's eyes were drawn back to the water. Beginning as a dim glow on the surface, growing in intensity until it looked as though a great light was ascending from the depths of the lake, the water took on a golden color a half mile in circumference. It increased in luminosity, lighting the sky above to bring into full view the four large thunderbirds that now increased their speed to cover the illuminated area. The smaller thunderbirds whirled about the giant spirit birds, wings beating rapidly.

The young Anishinabe in the woods stayed close to the protection of the sacred cedars. Tizbet was stiff with fear and felt the hammering of Chip's heart as she pressed against him. Something was about to happen.

"Oh. Not again!"

===========================

At the top of the high dune overlooking the lake, Nem-kee watched the battle. He had not known if his plea for help from the sky forces would be answered. Something had called the thunderbirds. Nanabozho? His own efforts? The tiny thunderbirds had not been enough to defeat Shibizhee. Perhaps they had been heard, and the giant sky beings came to save them, not the humans.

The screaming eagle-like cries increased as the small and giant thunderbirds circled the lighted underwater area. The water began to churn. Steam rose as heat below hit the cooler air above, creating a cloud of fog and mist. The bubbling water became brighter and more turbulent. Shape-changed, Shibizhee now became dozens of small fire geysers that shot straight up into the air, - balls of light and fire of all colors and intensity. They charged directly at the massed thunderbirds.

Nem-kee stepped back on the sand. He lost his balance and felt one knee give out. He sat down hard on the sand, but felt no pain. Nothing seemed to be broken. He remained sitting, arms wrapped around his knees. Lightning flashes shot from the eyes of the spirit birds and fire shot out from Shibizhee lit the sky and shore as if it were daylight. One of the smaller thunderbirds was hit squarely, and plunged - a fallen warrior. Several others fell and slowly sank into the lake. Each time one of his creations was defeated, he felt it within himself and let out a soft "Unh."

The four large thunderbirds rose higher. Their wings beat rapidly, forcing great gusts of air to hit the fireballs and drove them downward. The action was quick and decisive, forcing the fireballs into the water where they disappeared.

An eerie silence followed and Nem-kee got to his knees, and pushed himself up with difficulty. Maybe it was over.

No. The surface of the water rippled in the moonlight. Small waves began lifting in a broad circle. Shibizhee broke the surface again in his lynx-like form, with a ferocious howling scream. His roar echoed to the sky and shore over the cries of the other combatants. His uplifted head was raised defiantly. The coppery iridescent scales of his body glistened, a princely warrior clad in his finest battle armor. He reached up, grasping at the smaller thunderbirds that darted away, avoiding his claws.

He spouted great jets of fire from his mouth at his attackers. They screamed and retaliated. Lightning flashed from their eyes. Then one of the ancient thunderbirds sent a bolt of lightning that made him twist and leap out of the water to avoid it. As he did, his underside was exposed and Nem-kee saw a tremendous gaping wound, dark with blood and torn flesh, the result of the hit that sent him to the bottom of the lake.

Shibizhee twisted and tried to leap out of the way of another lightning bolt. Then he dove into the lake, only a darkening shape under the waves. The water settled. He was gone.

Within minutes all of the spirit birds withdrew, a mass of beating wings going up into the air, then circling in a quiet sky under the bright moon and small scudding clouds.

==========================

Tizbet stood next to Chip at the edge of the woods, partly hidden behind junipers and cedars. "Do you think it's over?"

"Hope so."

"Those guys," she said. "They thought it was some kind of military thing!"

"Yeah, kids watch too much TV, play too many digital games. I think it was Shibizhee, Tiz. Something really big is happening."

"Well, we had better get him to a hospital," she said, kneeling to examine the boy now seated in the sand beside them. He was covered with the blanket, but she knew his burns were painful. He made a low groaning sound, rocking back and forth.

Somehow they stumbled through the trees to the parking lot. Chip helped the boy into the back seat, got in and started the car. When he turned on the lights, the parking lot and forest around it seemed darker. Tizbet's eyes adjusted slowly as she made her way around the car to get in the other side.

She was suddenly grabbed around her waist from behind. "Hey, what the hell! Let go!" Strong arms yanked her back through the cedars toward the beach. She tried to pull away, but whoever it was reached out with his foot to hook her ankle and threw her off balance. As she fell, she emitted a surprised scream which ended abruptly as her head hit a low wide rock jutting from the sand.

She felt herself being lifted, and tried to fight back, half conscious. Then the trees whirled around her.

==========================

Chip heard her cry out and turned off the ignition. He slid out of the car and looked around. He heard the sound of someone moving through the trees toward the lake, ran into the

162

cedars, and rounded a large boulder. Someone was going up the dune with Tizbet slung over his shoulder.

"Hey, what do you think you're doing?" he yelled. He ran toward them, but when he reached the dune, it felt as though the sand was pulling him into it. He couldn't move fast enough.

The man with his burden reached the top of the dune, silhouetted for an instant against the sky. He held Tizbet up above his head with both hands and then the two of them burst into twin balls of bright light. They whirled, spinning at man-height, and sped off across the water.

CHAPTER 22

Louie was heading bout to check on the Jingtamok grounds when Sam's voice came over the radio. "Dad! You there?"

He picked up the mike and answered. "What's up?"

"We've got a serious problem here. Kids had a forty-niner at the beach. Tiz and I were there. Pretty weird stuff; I'll tell you about it. Balls of light, a huge cat thing in the lake, big things, maybe thunderbirds fighting with it. One kid got hurt; we're taking him over to the hospital. I think the kids all went back to the Jingtamok grounds..."

"I'm on my way."

"Right."

Louie didn't want to turn on the siren or flasher unless he had to, there were too many people at the Jingtamok, and there had been enough strange business going on. Maybe he should talk to Lorette about cancelling the Jingtamok entirely.

He hadn't noticed any heavy lightning or thunder storm on the mainland, only some fog hanging in low areas as the night air began to take the warmth from the earth. He drove as fast as he could, pushing down on the accelerator, rising up in his seat a little as the car hit the rough dirt road. His hands clenched the steering wheel and he swore under his breath. More trouble.

Sam and Lorette were standing by a group of teenagers and adults in the parking lot behind the trader's stands. The arena was dark, overhead lights turned off; the only lights from small campfires and camping trailers. Louie pulled into a parking space, got out and joined them.

"Chip called. Told me some, guess I need to talk to the kids. See any more of those white reptiles?" Louie kept his voice low.

"Nope. Nothing since the afternoon, as far as I know. Everyone's keeping an eye out, though." Sam flexed his shoulders. He had been working at the Jingtamok grounds since early in the morning, and was dead tired. "If anyone has a problem, Elsie Cloud said she'd give us a call."

Louie grunted assent. "O.K., let's take this one at a time. I'll just have you sit in the police car with me and tell me what happened."

==============================

Tizbet's first sensation upon awaking was that she had a tremendous headache. Her skull throbbed with pain and she groaned. She opened her eyes, hands on either side of her head. The remembrance of being grabbed by someone raced through her mind as she tried to focus on her present surroundings.

She was lying on a hard surface. There was a ceiling of rock above her, dimly lit by a small fire off to her right. She sat up. It was definitely a cave, and a large one, just how big obscured in darkness. A large flat rock to her left had a desk lamp and computer on it. There were cans and packages of food, and bottles of water.

A man sat on a cut piece of log at the fire, someone she had never seen. Who was he? What had he done with her? How did she get here?

He saw her movements, stood and walked toward her, holding something to his side. "Come to the fire and sit," he said in a strong deep voice.

She was struck by his tone and the way he addressed her. He was definitely making a demand, but it didn't feel threatening. She also sensed there was something else about him verging on a request for help, a hurting - an unmet need.

She stood and balanced herself on weak legs, adjusting to the pain in her head. What she had thought were pale rocks

165

jumped quickly into her path, barring the space between her and the stranger. The pale reptiles she had hunted in the woods.

"Out of the way!" he shouted, and several small white lizards and frogs skittered to the side but kept their eyes upon her. "These are my companions," he said.

Oh shit. She had killed two of them. His little buddies. Whoever he was, he was probably really pissed.

The man was holding something to his side - a large piece of lichen through which blood had seeped, staining the moss-like bandage. It obviously hid a severe wound. He turned and walked to the fire and sat down, not looking at her.

She sat down on another piece of log across the fire from him and he began speaking.

"I am called Shibizhee. In this, my man form, I am John Mishipsea." He smiled and she saw that he was quite a handsome man, but obviously deranged if he believed what he just said.

"You are here because I have a need for someone to speak to the humans. It is what you would call complicated."

Tizbet felt anger rising, something out of a dark place inside her She didn't recognize the cave where she had found herself and her head hurt, but she was determined not to appear afraid. She got up and stood farther away from him. "I would very much like to go home. Could you arrange that?"

"That will not be possible right now, Tizbet." The man's voice sounded sad, and he looked weak, pressing the moss to his side. "We must plan, and it will take some time. There are many things to discuss."

"Well, mister, I'm not interested. It looks like you need to get to a doctor, and I'd like to go home."

"Yes, I was injured by the sky forces. There have been wars between us for a long time."

"Is that what they were? Sky forces? They looked like birds to me."

"Thunderbirds. Sent to punish me." He looked at her and then away. "Someone called them."

"Well, I didn't call them."

He obviously believed what he was saying. He looked sad and tired. Crazy people could be dangerous, so she decided to humor him and go along with his fantasy. "Why would the thunderbirds want to hurt you?"

The man looked down, staring into the fire. "I was angry and killed a human."

Killed a human? Oh shit. The murder! She had been kidnapped by a murderer! Chip had told her about the cave-in at Basil's house and finding his body... with no skin. She shuddered, a chill running up the back of her neck.

"You? You killed him?" She wanted to run, but didn't know where to go.

"I was angry. In my other form, my true form."

She had heard the stories about Shibizhee, but had dismissed them as mere legends. Now this crazy man who believed them had admitted to being a killer! "I really would like to go home now."

"I will not harm you. If we speak to the two-legged that called the ancient winged ones... He could call on much worse things that would destroy me. Perhaps you could speak to the humans..." He looked up at her. His eyes looked sad but kind. He smiled, and in spite of herself, she smiled back. Damn the man! He sounded convincing, and she was beginning to half believe his nonsense.

Of course, she had seen what looked like an enormous copper covered panther in the lake and Chip had called it Shibizhee. Some underwater thing, and this guy actually believed he was the spirit being. She looked around the cave. Where the hell was she? How did she get here?

Tizbet watched him grimly as he removed the pad of moss from his bleeding side and applied a new poultice. The dirt from the makeshift bandage had crusted the wound. He winced and beads of sweat stood out on his forehead.

"Why are you putting moss on that?" she asked, her voice echoing from the high ceiling.

"This moss has strength, it will kill infection." Mishipsea leaned back, breathing heavily as he pressed the moss against his torn flesh.

"It has dirt in it. Won't that make it worse?" Tizbet felt argumentative and angry.

"No." Mishipsea shut his eyes, leaning his head back. He suddenly opened them and looked directly at Tizbet. She felt a strange sensation of warmth. Her headache slid out of her head leaving her feeling as though a weight had lifted. Then he shut his eyes again, his breathing slowed and regular.

"What are you going to do with me?" Tizbet asked.

"I said before, I will not hurt you. It is important that I use you to talk to the others, tell them that they cannot have you back until they agree to keep me alive." Mishipsea's grunted slightly and closed his eyes with pain.

"Oh, that's just great! I'm a hostage!" Tizbet's voice was shrill. Her fingernails dug into her palms as she spoke. "You go around killing and then you don't want to have anyone kill you!"

Mishipsea grunted again. He hadn't expected the female to be so aggressive. Only the crackling of the fire broke the silence. Shadows of the two figures were thrown up on the walls and ceiling as the flames burned higher and then fell to embers.

He picked up a piece of firewood and laid it on the fire. "You probably don't understand what I really am, or my purpose here." He reached out and moved the wood farther into the fire. "Or do you?"

Tizbet stood up straighter, feeling cold night air on the backs of her arms. "I guess I understand part of it. I was there on the beach, remember? It wasn't exactly a natural situation. I really had a headache. Did you hit me with something?"

"No. You fell and hit your head on a rock," he said. "I wasn't trying to injure you. Is the headache gone?"

"Yes." How had that happened so quickly? Had he taken away the pain?

"Where am I?"

He smiled. "This is my home when I am in this form. They call it Whitefish Island."

"I'm on Whitefish Island?" She remembered coming over in a canoe with Chip when they were kids, but didn't remember any cave.

"We came here as round lights."

"Sure. Whatever." He probably had a boat. She was tired of humoring him. How in hell was she going to get off this island? Her parents and Chip must be going nuts wondering what happened to her.

"Sometimes when you change shape it takes a while to adjust," he said.

"Right. Awesome." Her sarcasm seemed to be lost on him.

"What you probably don't understand, is how important it is that I stay alive," he said. "Have you heard the stories about me, Tizbet? Do the Anishinabe still tell about how the world was created? About me?"

"Who are you, really?" she asked.

"I tell people when I am this form that my people began the town, that I am John Mishipsea."

"But..."

He looked at her and she felt as though he was projecting some kind of thought into her mind, although he didn't speak. *I am Shibizhee.* Her heart raced and she felt light-headed.

"They tell Nanabozho and Shibizhee stories in the wintertime, not now," she said. It seemed as though her voice was coming from her, but she wasn't sure if she was only thinking that she was speaking. The whole thing was unreal.

169

"Do you know why the stories are only told in the winter?" Mishipsea straightened slightly, his face taut with pain.

"Yes. Because the reptiles are sleeping and won't hear them. So that the reptiles won't tell the Shibizhee." Tizbet repeated what her grandmother had said, in the exact words. If this was Shibizhee himself, she was telling him something he already knew. She felt confused and foolish, and even questioned her own words as they left her mouth.

"Some of them believe that if you say the name of a spirit being, that it will come," he said. "The two-leggeds are afraid that I will be angered if I hear the stories of how Nanabozho and I fought, and how I was defeated by him." His face looked drawn now, but he smiled slightly. "It was a very long time ago, when the world was much younger."

"So would you be angry?" Tizbet felt as though she were floating now, somewhere overhead, looking down, watching herself. Her back ached from standing in one place for so long, and she felt herself brought back to reality. She walked over to the fire and sat down.

"No, not really." Mishipsea drew in a deep breath against the pain. "I am sad that the two-leggeds have forgotten my responsibility in the balance of life."

"You mean like the balance of nature - ecology, that sort of thing?"

"Yes, that is my purpose, to keep the fish, snakes, lizards, turtles, all of the underworld beings safe, and to keep the water safe. I was trapped underground for a long time, but when the ground fell, I was able to get out. Some of my companions came with me." He gestured with his free hand at the white reptiles that were now sitting quietly around the perimeter of the cave, their dark eyes alert, watching.

"The quarry cave-in? The white frogs and lizards, the white snakes...." Tizbet thought of how most people she knew reacted when they saw a reptile, and also of the many articles she had read about the effects of pollution on the fish and reptiles.

"People have really messed up everything, haven't they?" She saw her words reflected in John Mishipsea's face. He nodded bitterly.

"The humans have made a war against those I am responsible for; even their food is poisoned." Mishipsea leaned forward. "The insects which they eat are killed with poisons. And the ones that eat plants - the plants are poisoned." Mishipsea's voice was harsh now, and his eyes narrowed.

"Yes, I know," she said. "It seems as though people only want plants and animals they grow themselves, and want to destroy everything else. Thousands of species that have been killed." At least this conversation was reasonable, not full of superstitious nonsense. She hoped he could stick to it and not wander off into his fantasies.

"What gives these people the right to such destruction?" he asked.

"People control the earth."

"They destroy their own world," he said.

"It's wrong. Many of us know it's wrong. But we have little power to stop it." She hoped she could keep him talking rationally.

"So some two-leggeds have power and some do not?"

"There are laws," she said, "against polluting the air and water, wiping out species."

"Laws!" Mishipsea got to his feet holding his wounded side. "I hear this talk of laws, courts, police. I have done what you would call research about the laws. I have a computer. A man in the town showed me how it works. But the laws do not seem to work very well!" His eyes were cold, and the deep lines in his face seemed carved in stone.

"You have to have evidence that laws are broken. Solid evidence that can be used against the people that broke the laws." Tizbet again felt a sense of disembodiment as though she

171

were drifting somewhere overhead, watching her conversation with this strange man.

"What is evidence?"

"Proof that someone is breaking a law. You take a picture, time and date it, of someone polluting. Or you bring back some proof that is solid."

"I can bring proof! I can bring the dead ones! Their bodies lie on the beaches of the Great Seas. They lie dead in the forests." John Mishipsea had tears in his eyes now, and his voice was tight with grief. The man's pain and concern washed over her.

"You don't believe that I am Shibizhee."

"Well... it is a bit hard to accept..." She felt a stab of fear. This man had admitted to killing. No matter what his excuse, he was seriously deranged, and she was not safe with him.

"I can show you, Tizbet," he said. He stood up and motioned to one of the white lizards lying near the cave entrance. It ran toward him on its short legs and then suddenly lifted off the ground, whirling in a white blur. Suspended in air for a second, it suddenly dropped to the stone floor. The lizard was gone. In its place was a large green frog.

Tizbet's eyes widened in disbelief. It was a trick. It had to be some kind of magic trick. The man was simply some kind of magician.

"Perhaps this will convince you." He went away from the fire to the back of the high ceilinged cavern.

Mishipsea's shape blurred as had the lizard, increasing in size and whirling in the air. The spinning form plunged down and became a large copper-scaled cat with white horns. There were sharp protrusions along its spine, and its long forked tail whipped back and forth. The head turned toward her and she looked into the yellow-green cat eyes of Shibizhee. He bared his teeth and a noise came from his mouth that echoed from the walls of the cave, filling it with sound.

Tizbet ran to the cave entrance, hoping to escape. He reached out with one sharp-nailed paw and caught her around the waist, pulling her back. She screamed, but he held her and pushed her down, his paw on her stomach, pinning her to the cave floor.

Then in an instant she was released. She saw the large feline spin into a copper colored whirlwind. Out of it came the man John Mishipsea. He came toward her and put out a hand to help her up.

"It will take you a few minutes to understand."

She sank down by the fire. There was nothing to say. It wasn't magic, it was something else. It went against everything she knew, everything she had learned.

"So now do you believe?"

Tizbet couldn't talk. Her throat was dry and she felt like her tongue was sticking to the roof of her mouth. Her heart was pounding. She sat with clenched fists against her chest.

"I am Shibizhee. Can you accept that?"

She nodded her head. The fear she had felt before had grown to a massive fist that squeezed the breath from her and filled her mind. He wasn't a magician or a real person. There weren't supposed to be spirit beings, but he was something like that. Something else.

"I have powers, Tizbet. They could be used to make good changes if I am allowed to live."

She heard his words, but what she had just seen left her frozen, unable to speak. Her usual feisty sarcasm was gone, along with thoughts of humoring a deranged killer.

CHAPTER 23

Chip returned to the deserted moonlit beach and calm waters of Kitchi-gami. He plodded, one foot ahead of the other, gingerly stepping on huge rocks and sand. Something shiny reflected the light of the now smoldering campfire, and he walked over and picked it up. One of the hologram necklaces. No small carved image in it now, only a round circle of plastic. He put it in his pocket.

He walked on an angle up the dune that overlooked the lake feeling as though he were being pulled down by heavy weights. Anger and frustration still burned in his gut, and he groaned aloud. Tizbet was gone; someone had taken her. He had seen his father at the hospital, told him what happened, and hurried back to search for any evidence to suggest a way to get her back.

A man was standing on the top of the highest dune that overlooked the beach. Chip stopped and stiffened slightly, then recognized his great-uncle Nem-Kee. What was he doing here?

"Uncle!" He called out, and the old man looked down at him.

"Ahau. Chip, is it?" He didn't seem surprised.

By the time he reached the top of the dune, Chip was almost out of breath and stood bent over with his hands on the top of his legs for a moment.

"Did you see what happened?" he asked.

"Yes. The thunderbirds are strong, they fought the Shibizhee." Nem-Kee spoke quietly, looking out across the water. "I saw it. I was on the beach. The Great Lynx. He is here. Now. He has returned." Nem-Kee looked at Chip and then out over the water toward the islands.

"Well, I think he got Tizbet. I heard that he was a shape-shifter. Is that true?"

"Ah-hauw," said Nem-kee. "He is a spirit with that power."

"He was a man. Then I saw him turn into a ball of light when he took her."

"Did he turn her into a ball of light as well?" Nem-Kee asked sharply, his eyes meeting Chip's in a look of surprise.

"Yes. I saw two balls of light go out over the lake in that direction." Chip pointed and then looked down, not wanting to show his own depth of feeling.

"He has great powers. They can be used for good or for evil..."

"But why take Tizbet?" Chip brushed his hair back from his face. His braids had become loosened and one suede hair tie was hanging partly undone, his shirt streaked with blood from the man he had taken to the hospital.

His great-uncle answered softly. "Perhaps for a hostage. He wants something. He will use her to get his own way."

"Do you think he will hurt her?"

"I'm not sure. But he may try to use her to negotiate with us."

"Negotiate? Why? What can we do for him?" Shibizhee obviously had supernatural powers. How could mere humans harm him?

"Oh, call in the army, I guess. Missiles, radar, that sort of thing." Nem-Kee grinned. "At least that's what I've been thinking pretty hard on up here, sending thoughts to him, hope he is getting the message."

"How can that scare him? He seems to be able to do about anything he wants to! He could just leave here, go somewhere else."

"He can go anywhere. He has power over the underworld on this planet. But I believe that the Shibizhee is supposed to be mostly here in the Great Lakes."

The two men stood looking out across the bay. Chip's jaw twitched as he clenched his teeth in his anger. He pulled the necklace from his pocket and held it up.

Nem-kee looked over at the empty globe of plastic. "They did their job." His voice was soft, nearly a whisper.

"Yes, I saw them. I have a lot of questions, Uncle."

"There are some things you don't understand. We should go to my house and talk. You need to rest. Maybe get some grub."

They started walking toward Nem-Kee's cabin, accompanied by the sound of a whipporwill and the spring peepers.

The dunes flattened out near the trees, cedars with low bracken ferns. A path wound through the darkness; moonlight filtered through branches enough to see their way. Nem-Kee looked tired, bent over, one foot going after the other in a slow, old man's cadence.

"What'cha got to eat at your place?" Chip said behind him.

"Cold pizza. Thought I'd nuke you a piece."

"Wonderful."

Nem-Kee chuckled. "Might be something to make a hamburger, too."

Chip followed Nem-Kee, feeling his way past trees and shrubs. The high pitched sound of crickets hushed as they passed, and then began again behind them. He waited as Nem-Kee opened the door, went inside and flipped the light switch.

The cabin was small, made of squared off logs with white chinking, pine shelves and cabinets on the walls. A plain oak table sat squarely under a hanging lampshade made of pierced tin, oak chairs surrounding it. The kitchen was in an alcove with a refrigerator, cabinets and sink, a freezer, electric stove and microwave oven.

In the main room a woodstove sat squarely on its iron legs against a bricked wall. Plain pine doors led to the bedroom and bathroom. It was a house full of memories with pictures of children and grandchildren. Chip's graduation picture was displayed with others in caps and gowns. A small tribal flag had its place of honor and there were pictures of Nem-Kee with different notables -- a past governor, and a vice-president of the United States.

It was a house different from the newer homes on the reservation with their suburban similarity and newly manicured yards on paved streets. This was like the homes of those tribal members' grandparents. Nem-Kee's medicine drum leaned against the wall near the bookcase, and an eagle feather hung in the western window over a small wooden bowl of sage. Cabinets with glass doors held things made by his people, exquisite and perfect baskets, boxes, and bowls. It was a uniquely Indian home.

A bookcase held an assortment of books, mostly having to do with Indian history and law, and some on more current political issues. One shelf held copies of master's theses and doctoral dissertations about the Limestone Point Reservation and Great Lakes Indian people. Chip thought about the new curriculum for the school and how a treasure of information was right here in this small cabin.

Nem-Kee hung his sweater and baseball cap on a hook behind the door. He walked over to the refrigerator and pulled out a plate with leftover pizza.

"This okay, Chip? I think I've got some hamburger in here someplace, too."

Chip helped to get food prepared and on the table, and while they worked together, Nem-Kee talked. The story about Shibizhee was one that Chip heard as a child from his mother on cold winter nights. His grandfather had told some of the old stories about Nanabozho and the creation of the world. What he had not heard was that the Shibizhee was defeated and sealed in the underworld.

177

He realized that he hadn't had anything to eat since morning, and felt his anger subside a bit with the food, listening to Nem-Kee tell of how the Shibizhee escaped from the quarry, and the connection with Basil's death. They had finished eating as Nem-Kee finished with his story.

Chip carried the dishes to the sink. He stood for a moment looking out the kitchen window into the night, and then turned to his great-uncle. "That explains the lights on the beach, and the thunderbirds. He obviously is afraid of modern technology that we could use against him, using Tizbet as a hostage to bargain for his life. From what you just told me, I wonder if there could be more than that. Could he be bargaining for the lives of the fish and reptiles - the underworld life?"

Nem-Kee sat down at the table with his cup of tea. He looked up at Chip, his aged face serious. "Perhaps."

"We can't control everyone in the world that is polluting the environment!" Frustration rose inside Chip again.

"So we must explain that to him, somehow." Nem-Kee's voice was soft, barely loud enough to be heard.

"If he is all knowing, he should understand everything." said Chip.

"He isn't all knowing. All he knows is what he was created for - to take care of the water and the underworld creatures." Nem-Kee looked at Chip intently. "He is not some evil thing; he is a part of the circle of life."

Chip was silent. He felt only anger toward the monster that had taken Tizbet, as though he were bleeding inside with hatred and anguish. He didn't want to listen to the old man talk about the good points of his enemy.

"We'd better call your dad, and Annie. We're gonna to need some help." Nem-Kee reached for the telephone.

===================================

Chip went to the door of Nem-kee's cabin when he heard the cars pull up. Annie parked on the shoulder of the road. She was just going up the path to the cabin as Louie pulled into the driveway.

They walked up the path together.

"Come on in." Chip looked tired, but pleased to see them.

"Glad you could come over. I know it's late, but we sure have a problem here."

Annie gave Nem-Kee a sharp look as she took her usual seat at the oak table. She hung her shoulder bag on the chair, and scowled slightly. "What's all this about? Dragging a person out in the middle of the night? You know I like my sunrises, Nem-Kee 'Shko-day."

"Big trouble." Nem-Kee brought cups to the table and a pot of tea he had readied for their visitors. "You already know about Shibizhee. And those white snakes and lizards, and frogs. Well, those are his, too. Been down in a cavern with him for a long time, didn't get to the sun. Turned white."

Louie took a seat at the table and poured himself a hot cup of tea.

"Anyway, Nem-Kee was up there on the dunes," said Chip. "He called on some help from the thunderbirds. I guess some people will call it a meteor shower and lightning. It was pretty spectacular. But it kind of backfired."

Nem-Kee cleared his throat. "Shibizhee got Tizbet."

Annie sucked in her breath, her eyes widening, and she gripped the edge of the table so hard that her knuckles turned white. "What did he do with her?"

"I saw them turn into two balls of light, and then go across the lake," said Chip. "I couldn't tell where they went. Nem-kee thinks Whitefish Island. We should go get Tizbet back."

"Don't be a fool, Chip." Annie spoke sharply. "Shibizhee could kill you unless you know exactly what you are

179

doing. He isn't human, he's supernatural. He has great powers. You would have to be able to match him, use some powerful weapons." She looked at him intently, willing him to believe her.

Chip went to the table and sat down. "Then what? What weapons would work against him?"

"Cedar." Nem-Kee spoke softly, and the others turned to look at him. "He's afraid of cedar."

"The sacred tree." Annie spoke agreement.

"Sacred to the sky forces. But he only fears it because it is protected against the forces of the underworld. That's why I used it to make the carved thunderbirds." Nem-kee went to a basket on the shelf with pictures and took out several flat lacy pieces of cedar. He handed them out and nothing was said as they each put some in their pockets.

"They fought him good, uncle," said Chip.

Nem-kee raised an eyebrow. "Yes. But you forget something," he continued. "The Shibizhee was made at the time of Creation. He has a purpose, a meaning. His responsibility is to help maintain the circle life, the balance in life. He cares for the fish, the reptiles, the creatures of the water, and the creatures under the earth. Many living things are in his dominion."

"Think about it, Chip." Annie continued looking at the younger man. "What has happened to that dominion, why he's angry."

Louie suddenly straightened in his chair and put his cup down on the table. "Insecticides, herbicides, chemical dumps into the lake"

"Whole species are wiped out every year," said Nem-kee.

"How does he think keeping Tizbet hostage is going to change that?" Chip's jaw was set, and his fist on the table was clenched tightly.

"Maybe he wants to make a deal. His life for Tizbet's. So that he can continue taking care of his underworld." Louie spoke slowly, logically.

"Why does he think his life is in danger?" asked Annie. "I thought he was too strong for mere humans to threaten him."

Nem-Kee spoke again. "Before, that may have been true. But think now, what powerful weapons us two-leggeds have - bombs, missiles, radar, guns."

"We even have attack rifles at the police station," said Louie. "When we had a problem with drugs being shipped in on boats..." He glanced over at his son.

"I sort of projected thoughts of how powerful people can be at the Shibizhee," said Nem-Kee. "I think he can read thoughts, a kind of ESP kind of thing."

"Shape-shifter, too," said Annie.

"Yes. He can change into a man. I saw that down on the beach." Chip looked around and saw that the others believed him. "Then he turned Tizbet and himself into balls of light."

"He took her to Whitefish," said Nem-kee.

"We need to negotiate with him somehow." Annie reached for the teapot and poured herself another cup of tea.

"This is ridiculous!" Chip stood up and went to the window again. "We sit here instead of going and getting that monster! Tizbet might be hurt, or..."

"Don't think about it, Chip." Annie spoke sharply. "He won't hurt her if he wants to use her as a bargaining point."

"So what can we promise him? That nobody on earth will use insecticides or herbicides again?" Chip turned his back to the older people at the table. "Every time someone uses chemicals to kill weeds or bugs they kill the food of some reptile or fish. We all know that the stuff's in the lakes and streams, and our own water supply."

"And every time another species of fish or reptile or amphibian is killed off, the circle of life is destroyed a little more." Annie's voice was harsh.

181

"I'd say right now he's frustrated and angry," said Annie. "He's probably fighting back the only way he knows how."

"Maybe we could talk to him in his man form," said Annie. She was trying to find some way to resolve this situation without using violence.

"Whitefish Island is about the only body of land in that direction," said Nem-kee. That's the way Chip said he was headed with Tizbet. There's a cave over there, but not many people know about it."

"We could use the tribal boat," said Louie. He finished his tea and stood up. "I'm going to go down to the marina. Anybody that wants to come along..."

Everyone followed Louie out the door. Annie tried to keep up with the longer legs of the men as they went to the police car. "Middle of the night... balls of light... hostage negotiation..." she muttered to herself. Nem-kee helped her into the back seat and went around to get in the other side. Louie drove and Chip rode shotgun. Four against one, but not very good odds.

===============================

"I'll drive my own car, Dad. Just let me out at the parking lot by the beach," said Chip. Louie made no comment, and there was silence from the back seat.

He stood next to his car watching his father and the others leave for the marina. When he got in the car, he reached for the glove compartment and took out the locked case with his Glock. The gun was licensed, but he didn't have a state license to carry a concealed weapon. He was on the reservation, so state laws didn't apply. He put it in the back of his waistband after making sure it was loaded and the safety was on.

Gravel sprayed as he gunned his car out onto the shore road. His fishing boat was tied up at a small dock, and he cut the lights, coasting to the far end of the marina lot just before his father pulled up near the tribal pier. Annie was heading toward one of the porta-johns and the men were walking toward the tribal boat. He saw Nem-kee look over at him. His plan to secretly get over to Whitefish Island before they did obviously hadn't worked.

However, it looked as though he could beat the others to Whitefish Island where they thought Shibizhee had taken Tizbet. Annie would slow them down, and by the time they got their act together, he would be there.

The motor caught on the first try and he made himself go slowly until the boat cleared the dock. Negotiate, hell. He would get there and kill the son-of-a-bitch before any negotiating nonsense started. Even a spirit being would have to back off at gunpoint. Tizbet was too important to be used as a pawn in some kind of trading game.

He forced the small boat to its top speed. Clouds obscured the moon and he turned on the running lights and pushed the boat to the limit that the old engine could take, working the choke, urging the engine to go faster. It seemed like forever, but he neared the island and cut the lights, gradually letting his eyes grow accustomed to the dark.

A small boat was pulled up onto the beach. Thick vegetation surrounded a high outcropping of rock. He slid into the small bay where he and Tizbet had come as children.

He got out and pulled the boat onto the beach, sand and small stones scraping the bottom of the vessel. It was said that the island had been called Assinaway Island for the small stones that made up the majority of its beaches, but the state had named it Whitefish Island like they renamed most of the Anishinabe places. He walked as quietly as he could past the line of dried seaweed and dead fish that marked the last storm.

The beach was disturbed with footprints that led to the high rock outcropping. When he and Tizbet had explored the island, they hadn't found any caves, but he could see that they had missed what must be a cave entrance. The recent footprints led directly into a crevice in the rock.

Chip looked back across the water and saw his dad's boat coming, but it was still a ways off. He followed the footprints and pushed aside the bushes. A dark tunnel sloped downward toward a lighted opening. He stepped into the tunnel and drew his gun, flicking off the safety.

A rushing sound came from his right, and he whirled to face it. He saw something grey-white. A similar sound came from behind him. He turned around holding the gun protectively in front of him. In the near darkness he couldn't see what was making the noise.

The sound began again, and this time it seemed to come from the very ground itself, a brushing that signaled movement on all sides. Just then the moon emerged from its cloud cover and lighted the cave entrance.

He saw them. Several of the white creatures had him surrounded - frogs, lizards, snakes. He stood his ground and they held theirs. Shoot the gun? If he shot one, the others would attack. The things had teeth, and the thought of more than one biting him…

Chip felt his heart pounding in his chest, and a feeling of weakness in his lower body. This must be how guys crapped their pants in a war; just the fear itself seemed to make him feel as though he himself were running into the ground like a liquid. The gun in his hands felt as though it were made of lead.

The creatures blocked his escape back to the beach. He turned toward the lighted opening ahead. They retreated slightly to one side, making just enough room to pass, glaring at him with shining black eyes as he slid past them into a large cave with high gray stone walls and a smooth stone floor. A flickering fire and a small electric lamp on a large rock lighted the cavern. Two people were sitting on cut logs near the fire. One was Tizbet and the other the man who had stolen her. They both looked up as Chip entered the cave.

He wanted to rescue Tizbet, but to rush in and suddenly threaten with a gun seemed slightly ridiculous. Tizbet didn't seem to be in any harm. She appeared to be involved in a conversation. He kept the gun held protectively in front of him, the safety off, just in case.

"Chip!" Tizbet stood up, obviously glad to see him, but as she looked at the Glock in his hands she scowled slightly.

"Ah! Tizbet's friend. She was telling me about you." The man stood and walked toward Chip, smiling. He was as tall as Chip, dressed in a long sleeved blue shirt and tan pants. His hair was dark and pulled back in a pony tail that hung halfway down his back. The man from the beach. Shibizhee? Nem-kee said he was a shape-changer.

He stood in front of Chip, still smiling, his hand held out for the gun. He looked into Chip's eyes and the liquid feeling came back, but Chip fought it.

"I suggest you step out of my way and let her come with me," Chip said, his forefinger on the trigger.

"Please give me the gun, Chip. You don't want to hurt anyone." The man was serious now, still holding out his hand for the weapon.

"Oh, no," Chip responded sarcastically. "We wouldn't want to hurt anyone, would we? Or kill anyone? Or skin them?" He held the gun tightly, and saw Tizbet moving away from the fire toward the wall of the cave. Her eyes were large with fear and she shook her head in warning.

"There are many things you do not understand." The man's hand fell to his side as he realized that Chip would not give up the weapon. "Perhaps once you speak with me, you will know about my concerns."

"I know about your concerns. I just don't care for the way you've gone about calling attention to your problem." Chip kept the muzzle of the gun pointed at the man's chest.

"You give me no other way to protect myself." The man looked at him with sorrowing eyes.

185

Then the world turned upside down, and Chip found himself on his stomach on the floor of the cave, his hands tied behind his back.

===================================

Tizbet stood by the wall, her eyes still wide, not saying anything. The man was standing over him now, holding the gun in front of him with both hands. He put pressure on the metal and the gun bent easily, forming a U shape and then breaking in two. He took the two pieces and twisted them together, and threw the broken thing against the wall. It bounced off the stone and fell to the floor of the cave.

"Help your friend come closer to the fire, Tizbet." The man went over and sat down again near the fire, not watching as she helped Chip get awkwardly to his feet and led him to sit near the warmth.

Chip's hands were still tied behind him, and he bent forward slightly, his arms aching from the pressure of keeping them in one position.

"Will you try to harm anyone now, Chip? Your weapon is no good." The man's voice was soft, and he looked at Chip with a smile curling the corners of his mouth.

Chip shook his head. He refused to look at the man but felt the bindings loosen and slip off. There was no one behind him. The man had somehow removed the rope. He brought his hands in front of him again, looked down, and saw the red marks on his wrists. He rubbed them, looking over at Tizbet. "Are you all right?"

She sat down by the fire between the two men. "Yeah, I'm fine. I hit my head on a rock when I fell, and it hurt, but he fixed it somehow."

She reached for a long stick, used it to push a log back into the flames, and then laid the stick down carefully next to her. "This is John Mishipsea, Chip. He's been explaining about

186

the things that made him get angry - the pollution - the fish and reptiles that have been dying. Invasive species."

"Yeah, I heard about that already." Chip glanced at the other man who sat quietly. "Nem-Kee was talking about it at his house."

"He wants to negotiate with humans. Using me as a hostage." Tizbet's voice was clear and thin, a bit wistful, and she looked over at Mishipsea nervously. "I don't think much of that idea."

"Well, it looks like my rescue plan didn't work out too well." Chip grinned over at her, and was surprised when Mishipsea laughed out loud.

"Just don't try anything else. We can talk about this." Mishipsea stood up. He saw a movement at the back of the cave, and smiled widely as he saw the white reptiles that were coming through the passageway. "Ah, my poor companions!" He went to them, squatting down and touching the backs of the creatures, petting them gently. He picked up one of the lizards and cradled it in his arms, bringing it closer to the fire. "They had no sunlight, and lost their color in the cavern where we were imprisoned. Now, they are free!" He sat down, caressing the lizard, using one finger to gently smooth its back.

"Your companions are the fish and reptiles? The amphibians?" Chip watched the man as he caressed the rough skin.

"Yes." Mishipsea smiled at him. "In Creation, I was given the responsibility to care for them. To maintain the below-earth beings. To keep balance with the sky and earth beings." "All over the world?" Chip asked the question feeling as though he were talking to someone with a mental problem. Surely the man must be deranged.

"All over the world, Chip." Mishipsea smiled again. "I couldn't do my job very well closed up in a place deep in the earth but now, perhaps I can help again."

"Why are you here in this area?" asked Tizbet. "Why not somewhere else?"

"You do not appreciate the place where you live, Tizbet. It is one of the most beautiful places on earth. There are many lakes, inland seas, vast numbers of plants and animals, seasons of the year - so much beauty."

"You choose to live here in this place?" She tipped her head to one side slightly. "Or was it chosen for you?"

"I choose this place." Mishipsea put the white lizard down on the ground. It walked on its short legs to the back of the cave near the others.

The fire crackled and each of the people around the fire considered their own thoughts. Chip put his hands out to the warmth, looking at the orange and red tongues of fire as they ate the wood.

"Could you change them into regular animals?" Tizbet motioned toward the white reptiles and looked sharply at Mishipsea. "Wouldn't they be happier if they were normal again?"

Mishipsea's eyes crinkled in amusement. "Without teeth?"

"Yes. Without teeth!" Tizbet grinned at him, her own teeth white and even, and she smiled over at Chip.

"Yes. I could do that. Should I?" Mishipsea stood up.

"Please!" She laughed then, the low intimate kind of laugh that could turn Chip into a willing adventurer in their younger days. It seemed to have the same effect on the strange man.

John Mishipsea walked the few steps to the rear of the cave, bent down and touched a large white frog. As his hand moved over the creature, it changed color from white to a mottled green. The dark eyes became a pale green color, and it lost its fierce aspect. Mishipsea picked up the frog and brought it to the others. He carefully opened its mouth. "No teeth, Tizbet."

There was nothing but the tongue of a normal frog inside. He let the mouth close and put it down. It hopped away toward the opening of the cave, and then disappeared out into the night.

"Why not change the rest of them?" Chip looked up at Mishipsea. "If you can do that with one....."

"Yes, I could do that with all of them." Mishipsea sat down again. "Perhaps."

There was silence again around the fire. Only Mishipsea heard the sound of the tribal boat motor as it headed toward Whitefish Island.

===========================

When Louie drove Nem-kee and Annie to the marina and pulled up next to the tribal pier, he saw Chip's car glide to a stop at the other end of the parking lot. Just what he thought Chip would do, impatient and mad as a hornet.

There were other options. He could call for help on the mainland. They knew of the murder and the feds were already involved. He stood by his car for a long moment, hand on the cell phone in his pocket, lips tight together, eyes narrowed as he considered possibilities. Other law enforcement would just try to destroy a man named Mishipsea that was a murderer. Then he would change shape and there would be hell to pay. They wouldn't know about Shibizhee or the reason he killed Basil. They wouldn't be able to contain him, either. The fed would just bring in the big guns. Oh, they would mean well; they always did. He let go of the phone and took out the key ring, feeling for the boat key.

He cursed his son under his breath, taking it back in the next, accepting that Chip was only doing what he would have done himself at the same age. Nem-kee followed him down the pier, but Annie headed for the porta-john.

"I'll be there in a minute. Wait for me," she said.

"I'll wait." He went with Nem-kee to the boat and got it ready.

As Louie piloted the maddeningly slow old Boston whaler to the small island, he thought of the reports he had seen about reptiles. There had been a die-off of red-eared turtles in the southwest part of the state, and he had heard of wood turtles being decimated by human activity. Most people didn't see the research, just the media stuff about carp that jumped out of the water. And then there was the cement plant that used the limestone from the quarry...

He shut down his thinking and concentrated on getting to Whitefish Island. There wasn't any other body of land out there where Tizbet could have been taken, unless Shibizhee took her across the lake to Wisconsin. He couldn't see any lights from Chip's boat. Chip might already be there. Louie's heart gave a sharp jump thinking of what Shibizhee could do to his son.

CHAPTER 24

Louie saw the dark shape of Whitefish Island ahead, and cut the motor to let the boat drift in toward shore. According to Nem-Kee, Shibizhee could read minds, and had phenomenal ESP. If that was true, then he must know that Chip was coming to the island or was already there, and that Louie had arrived at the shore just in front of the cave entrance. There would be no need to try to take Shibizhee by surprise, because he could not be surprised.

He recognized Chip's boat and saw the other small motorboat next to it. He jumped out onto the pebbled sandy beach and tied the boat to a huge driftwood log. Nem-kee and Annie got out slowly, holding tightly to the railings on the side of the boat. They walked single file, wet shoes crunching stones, following previous footprints...

A bush blocked the cave entrance. Louie pushed it aside and the others followed him into the tunnel that led to the cave. A man was standing by the entrance; his dark silhouette was lit from behind by a fire that flickered on the cave walls. A woman stood next to the fire. Tizbet.

Seated at the fire was Chip. His son. He looked up. "Hey, Dad."

"Ahau, Louie St. Sable." The tall man standing between Louie and Chip spoke in a deep voice. He held no weapon, but had a large piece of moss held to a wound in his side.

Louie glanced at Tizbet. She stood with her arms folded over her chest. She did not speak or look directly at him.

"You are the father of this man Chip. And you are called Tikway-wenon Ininni, the man who grabs you?"

"Yes." Louie could see the man's face now. He had a tan complexion but no specific racial features. His eyes were pale green, and his long dark hair had a coppery color in the firelight, with two white streaks at his temples. This was the

191

man who had taken Tizbet, so he must be the one called Shibizhee.

Yes. I am Shibizhee. Louie heard the voice in his mind, but no one had spoken. So that was how he did it, pushed his thoughts into someone else's head.

"I call myself John Mishipsea in this form."

"In this form. OK. Whatever." Louie felt a surge of anger, but it was suppressed as though a hand pushed it down, causing him to gasp for air.

"So you take people. Do you wish to take me?" The man smiled.

"No. I wish to talk with you." Louie took a step forward, and Mishipsea stepped back, gesturing toward the fire. Nem-kee and Annie stayed at the cave entrance.

"Perhaps we could sit where it is warm to talk." Mishipsea walked over to the small fire and the cut logs that surrounded it. He sat down and motioned for them to join him. Chip and Tizbet said nothing and remained where they were.

Nem-kee and Annie came to the fire circle and sat. They looked at Mishipsea but said nothing. Annie pulled her sweater around her and clutched her purse on her lap against her stomach. Nem-kee bent over, clasped hands in front of him, staring into the flames.

"I'll stand," said Louie. He wasn't about to go along with the stranger's suggestions.

Tizbet came closer and sat next to Chip.

"Are you all right, Tizbet?" Louie's voice looked at the young woman sharply.

"I'm fine. Just wish I could go home, that's all." She smiled wanly at the policeman, still hugging her arms around herself. It was a bit cold in the cave even with the fire.

Louie saw several white creatures huddled against the back wall, their black eyes shining in the firelight. They didn't seem to be threatening, but he was apprehensive.

He looked at Mishipsea. "I came to ask you to let her

192

go."

"Yes. Your son here did the same thing." John Mishipsea looked up at Louie, smiling. "You know why Tizbet was brought here."

"I know that you're a murderer, and that you don't want to die for what you have done." Louie kept his voice low and even. He looked at the man-who-is-not-a-man, wondering what he looked like in his other form. Nem-kee had seen him, and the kids on the beach, but Louie had never seen him as the true spirit being.

"You know that I am very angry about what has happened to the water - to the life that is my responsibility. I punished the man who caused it." Mishipsea looked into the fire, and then at Louie.

"I understand your responsibilities, and your concerns." Louie walked over to the fire and sat down near the warmth. "You still had no right..."

"It has been explained to me by Tizbet that there are laws that say it is not right to kill a human." Mishipsea still looked into the fire, but then he suddenly turned. The depths of Mishipsea's eyes were like deep pools. They held no expression that Louie could read, and showed no sign of remorse or pleading. Louie had dealt with killers before, and it was as though this man was only analyzing the situation with no feelings except for his own interests.

"Yes, there are laws against killing someone."

"What happens to the human who kills another human?"

Louie explained in simple terms about laws and courts, feeling as though the information was pulled from his mind by the force of the other.

"Tizbet said that sometimes the person who kills is killed."

"Not here in Michigan. He goes to prison. But if a murderer fights the police and tries to get away, then sometimes the police use guns and he gets killed..."

"So you are here to take me away and put me in this prison?"

"No. You could get out of any prison. I am here to take Tizbet home. There been enough violence."

Nem-kee grunted. "He's right."

Mishipsea sat up straight and rocked back and forth, holding a piece of bloody moss to his side. He groaned a low sound that was close to a growl. Louie felt a chill of fear combined with a small surge of sympathy for the wounded man. Or was he really a man?

Annie said "Perhaps we could help you. You need that cleaned up and treated."

Mishipsea looked down at his side and over at Annie. "Are you a healer?"

"No. But someone could clean that out and put some medicine on it."

Mishipsea looked at the back of the cave. "Why are you killing my companions? That also is killing."

Nem-kee spoke up. "People are afraid of them. One of them bit a child."

"Another one bit a woman," said Tizbet.

"They only defend themselves," said Mishipsea. "You killed them."

"So what? You murdered a person," she said.

"Humans are more important?" asked Mishipsea.

"Leave it," said Louie. "We need to get Tizbet off this island. You need to let her go."

Mishipsea stood up suddenly and went to the back of the cave. He threw his hands up in the air and groaned aloud. Tizbet leaned closer to Chip and grabbed his hand.

Mishipsea turned toward them, his face stern. "I will do as you ask. But that man..." He pointed at Nem-kee. "He called on my enemy and the sky forces."

Nem-kee lifted his chin and looked away.

Mishipsea smiled at Tizbet. "Your son is a good person.

194

Tizbet is a good person. I am pleased that they put marks of a snake and a turtle on them."

Louie remembered the tattoos the kids had got when they were teenagers, their clan symbols. "Those marks are important," he said. "Tizbet is of the snake clan, and Chip and I belong to the turtle clan."

"Then you are also my responsibility." Mishipsea smiled.

Chip stood up. "We can take care of ourselves."

Mishipsea ignored him. "Your son had some trouble with his gun." He pointed at the twisted and broken weapon near the cave wall.

Louie looked at what was left of the gun and laughed aloud. All of his efforts to frighten Shibizhee were obviously in vain, if Chip's pistol had been destroyed so easily. It would take a lot more than small weapons to control him.

"What about them?" Louie looked at the back of the cavern where some of the creatures were sitting quietly. They moved occasionally, slightly, but were looking toward Mishipsea.

"I can change them - make them into what you consider normal animals. Would that satisfy you?"

"Certainly. At least then no people would be hurt. They would not be killed."

"So we have negotiated. I gave you what you asked. Now you give me what I ask."

"What about Chip and Tizbet?"

"They believed they were defending your people when they killed my companions. But they could help by speaking to other humans."

"You can speak for yourself," said Tizbet. Her voice was sharp, and Louie felt a stab of fear that she would be too aggressive. It didn't pay to rile up a spirit being, even if he looked like a man and had a wound in his side.

"How do I speak to humans about these things?"

195

Annie stood up. "You had better come with us."

"Why should I do that?"

Nem-kee walked toward him and put one hand on Mishipsea's arm. He spoke clearly with the authority of an elder. "If you stay here, you will not be safe. I called the sky beings and I can do so again... and there are other ways..."

"To destroy me. Yes. I know."

===============================

Mishipsea sat in the back of the tribal boat with Nem-kee and Annie, a bag of clothing at his feet. Chip and Tizbet followed in the other boat, riding the ribbon of moonlight to Cathead Island. As Mishipsea turned and looked back toward them, Tizbet saw his face and the two white streaks in his man's hair. She expected to see his green eyes reflecting lights from the boat, but they were dark. He was very good at maintaining the shape of a human, but she didn't trust that he would remain so.

===============================

The sun laid a scarf of sunlight across Louie's eyes. He threw his arm over his face and rolled on his side. Remembering the night before, his mind came alert in an instant. He wanted to shut it out, but thoughts of the past few days intruded. Chip would be up soon, and their guest John Mishipsea.

Louie had brought the man home with him the night before. When they got to Louie's place, Mishipsea was strangely quiet. After Louie cleaned and bandaged the man's wound, he looked about the house, picking up things and putting them back down. He asked a few questions and displayed curiosity about the kitchen and bathroom. Louie offered Mishipsea the spare room, but the man said that he would rather sleep on the living room carpet. Louie gave him a pillow and blanket, turned off the lights, and went to bed.

Louie lay there a long time before he got to sleep. He had never actually seen Mishipsea in his other form, but had no doubt that what the others told him was true. There had been stories about Shibizhee since he was a child, and Louie had accepted them as part of his culture and beliefs. Just knowing that an actual spirit being was here in his house was more than unsettling. His responsibility to somehow moderate the situation was an incredible task. That the spirit was acting reasonably from a human standpoint was not completely believable, and he worried that the whole thing was some kind of trick on Mishipsea's part.

He was amazed that he had slept at all, and forced himself to get up. He needed to get cracking. People would be waiting for him at the Jingtamok grounds. Should he take Mishipsea with him? He'd have to play it by ear.

Louie showered and dressed quickly. Chip was still asleep behind his closed bedroom door, and Mishipsea still slept on the living room floor. He went to the kitchen and started a pot of coffee, trying to be quiet.

What did Mishipsea eat? Bacon and eggs? Chip would want cereal, as usual. Louie missed going to the restaurant for breakfast, but had stuck closer to home since Chip arrived. He grunted disapproval as he put a bowl and cereal near Chip's place on the table. He heard someone flush the toilet, and a cough from the living room.

Mishipsea stood in the doorway to the kitchen. He stretched and smiled.

Louie poured himself a cup of coffee and then reached for another cup. "You drink coffee?"

Mishipsea walked over to where Louie was standing and bent over the coffee pot, smelling the steaming liquid. "This has a good smell."

Louie poured another and handed it to Mishipsea.

The man quickly put the cup down on the table. "It is very hot. I will let it cool."

"I'm gonna fix some breakfast," said Louie.

"Fix? Is there something wrong?"

Louie saw the look of consternation on Mishipsea's face. "Prepare something to eat."

"Oh! Yes. Food." Mishipsea sat down at the table. He reached out and picked up the box of cereal. "Is this food?"

Louie smiled, "Yes. Some folks like it. My son Chip, he eats that stuff. Rabbit food."

"You have rabbits? I do not like them very much. Especially the Great Hare."

"We don't have rabbits. I was just making a joke. That is called cereal, but to me it looks like something you would feed to rabbits."

Mishipsea made no comment, just looked inside the cereal box and then reached in and took out a handful.

He watched Mishipsea put some of the cereal in his mouth, chew and swallow. "This taste is sweet." He brought out another large handful. Louie remembered the Twinkie boxes in the cave. Evidently the guy liked sweets. It was something to remember in case he had to use the information later.

"I'm gonna fix bacon and eggs, and some toast," said Louie. He pointed to the toaster. The guy probably didn't know what it was. "I put bread in here and it makes toast."

"Let me watch you prepare the food." Mishipsea stood up, and the chair behind him toppled over on the floor. He turned quickly and reached to pick it up, looking embarrassed. "This seat surprised me!"

"You have to push it back first, and then stand up." Louie suddenly realized what a job it would be to help this strange man become accustomed to modern homes. That is, if Mishipsea kept his man shape and maintained his present attitude. He had never actually seen the shape-changing himself, and he sure as hell didn't want it to happen in his own house.

198

Louie was showing Mishipsea his egg-frying skills when Chip came into the kitchen. He grunted a greeting and poured himself a cup of coffee. "You guys getting into the cholesterol, huh?" He sat down at the table.

"Cholesterol?" Mishipsea asked.

"It's stuff in bacon and eggs. Bad for you." Chip grinned when his father turned, spatula in hand and glowered at him.

Louie lifted the eggs out of the bacon grease and laid them on the platter next to the fried strips of bacon. He plunked the platter squarely in front of his own plate and sat down.

"Is this food bad for me?" Mishipsea looked down at the steaming food. "You want me to eat food that isn't good?" He stiffened and backed away.

"Hey, I eat it. It tastes better to me than that stuff Chip eats," said Louie.

"You're coffee's getting cold, dad." Chip poured some cereal in his bowl and added orange juice from a cardboard carton. Louie knew that being lactose intolerant like most Anishinabe, milk gave Chip the runs, but the combination looked pretty foul.

"Is coffee bad?" asked Mishipsea. He sat down and watched as Louie loaded up his plate.

"Not if you don't drink too much. I drink it myself." Chip lifted his own cup, took a noisy sip.

Mishipsea tasted the coffee and quickly put the cup on the table. His jaw twitched and he was obviously making an effort not to gag.

"Here, I'll get you some water." Chip got up and brought Mishipsea back a glass of cold water.

"You eat the bacon and eggs, Louie. I'll eat this rabbit food." Mishipsea reached his hand into the box and took out

199

another handful. Chip gave Louie a look and Louie bent his head, hiding a grin.

Mishipsea suddenly stood up, reached behind him and pulled a billfold from his back pocket. "How much is the rabbit food, Louie? I can pay."

"No. You are a guest in my home. You don't have to pay anything."

"Oh. I am a guest." Mishipsea sat back down and helped himself to more cereal.

After they finished, Louie got up and put his dishes in the sink. As he came back, he looked out the glass patio door to the back yard. "Hey, John. I think you've got company." He pointed and the two men at the table turned to look outside.

White spirit creatures ringed the back yard just at the edge of the trees behind them. There was little movement, and they all faced the house, dark eyes staring. Louie and Chip were used to seeing wildlife around the house and froze in place, not wanting to startle them. The pale lizards, turtles, frogs and snakes stayed where they were, however, when Mishipsea slid the door open and stepped out on the porch. He made a low sound that resembled that of a large bullfrog, and then a high-pitched shrill trilling noise. The creatures turned and melted into the forest.

Louie suppressed his thought of the hunt and the sharp teeth on the ones he had seen near the Jingtamok grounds. But had they actually attacked anyone? Every time someone was bit, the animals seemed to be protecting themselves. He felt his gut tighten. It was important not to let your enemy know you were frightened. He had learned that the hard way. He made himself relax and take a sip of his coffee.

Mishipsea sat back down at the table. He smiled. "They were concerned about me."

Louie didn't know what to say after what he had just seen. "Well, I've got to get going to work. I already got cleaned up. Who's gonna be first in the shower?"

"I can wait," said Chip.

"Shower?"

"A bath. Wash yourself. Clean your body. Take off the dirt." Louie wondered how much explanation would be required if he had to keep the guy around. He had work to do. There was a lot going on this week, with the Jingtamok and all the tourists.

"I clean in the lake."

"There's a shower in the bathroom. I showed you last night. You can take off the bandage from your side and I will help put on a new one." Louie felt impatient but was trying not to show it. He also tried not to think about the last time Mishipsea had been in a shower, in his other form, in Basil's house. Or what had happened to Basil.

Mishipsea followed Louie in the bathroom and watched a demonstration of how the shower worked, the soap and washcloth process, and what to do with the towel. He pulled his shirt over his head and pulled off the gauze and tape. The wound was now crusted with a dark scab.

Chip had told Louie about the battle and how the huge creature was struck by what he called thunderbirds. Perhaps this was why the man was so subdued. It looked severe, although Mishipsea hadn't complained.

"The sky spirits have great force. They made this." Mishipsea looked at Louie with a wry smile. He dropped his pants to the floor, sat down on the toilet seat and began taking off his shoes. As he bent over, the wound opened slightly, letting a trickle of blood run down his side.

"You ought to have a doctor take a look at that."

"Doctor?"

"Medicine person." Louie was at a loss. He didn't want to have to explain the whole damned medical profession to the man.

"I make medicine. I put plants on wounds. There is strength in plants." Mishipsea looked casually down at the wound. "It'll heal soon. I wasn't strong last night. Now, I'm stronger."

Louie went out of the bathroom and closed the door on the naked man. He smiled as he thought about how well preserved Mishipsea was for someone that had been alive since the beginning of the world.

============================

John Mishipsea came out of the bathroom, his dark hair with the two white streaks still damp. His face was smooth with no facial hair. He smiled broadly, his teeth white and perfect. Laugh wrinkles appeared next to his green eyes. Chip had given him a pair of clean jeans and a tan knit long sleeved shirt. He wore moccasins over bare feet.

"This is much better. I do like the shower."

Louie started to say something, but the phone rang. "St. Sable here."

It was Annie. "Is that John Mishipsea still at your place?"

"Sure is."

"I assume he's still a man."

"Yup."

"Not a bear or a lizard?"

"Nope."

"Nem-kee called me, wants me to come pick him up at his place. Then we'll be over to get John..."

Louie wasn't about to ask why. He needed to get some things done and was tired of baby-sitting someone that was clueless, even if he was some kind of spirit thing.

He turned to his guest. "Annie and Nem-kee are coming over to pick you up. I guess they want to see you."

CHAPTER 25

After the other men left and hot grandfather stones were replenished, Nem-Kee sat in the sweat lodge with John Mishipsea. The lodge was filled with steam and he tossed a handful of leaves on the rocks, sending up a sweet and pungent smell that permeated the air. The men breathed it in deeply.

Outside, Annie watched the fire and beat slowly on her small hand drum, singing a prayer that repeated with slight changes each time it was sung. The sound filled their ears as the steam and the scent filled their lungs. For a long time, the men did not speak.

Nem-Kee had felt the fear in the other man when they entered the lodge and fought to keep the feeling from himself. What if this shape changer became angered by memory or thoughts? What if he changed himself back into the Shibizhee or the bear, or even a ball of light? What if he tried to turn Nem-Kee into a ball of light as he had Tizbet?

He drew on his own strength, calling his guardian spirit to help him and on the sky forces that were his totem. Gradually, he felt Mishipsea's anxiety dissipate as the spirit in human form relaxed in the healing steam. Twice Nem-Kee threw back the lodge covers, letting the steam escape. Twice more he put the covers back over the lodge frame, poured water on the rocks, and tossed healing herbs on them.

Mishipsea spoke, "There is much in my heart."

"Yes. And in mine." Nem-kee had not expected Mishipsea to share thoughts with him, and was pleased.

"I dreamed last night. The Great Spirit came to me speaking of my responsibilities to the underworld beings. Many of them have died in the modern world, gone forever like my great ones the people call dinosaurs. He showed me the streams and waters of the world. I smelled the stench of the factories and their exudates into the air and waters. I saw dead fish lying on the banks of the rivers, their eyes staring. I saw my cherished ones coated with black oil, dying in the waters and on the beaches. He showed me the poison in the earth itself, leaching into the forests from fields covered with chemicals that kill insects and plants - the food for my reptiles and amphibians. He asked that I work to protect them, keep true to my ancient purpose."

Nem-kee waited for Mishipsea to say more, but he was silent.

"Let's pray for guidance, then - for direction." Nem-Kee closed his eyes, bathing himself in the steam. He concentrated on his prayer, gradually losing his sense of self in the lodge, feeling himself flying out over the land, looking below at the beautiful earth. From a height, it looked pure. The poisons that worried Mishipsea were not discernible.

While Nem-Kee's spirit went somewhere else, searching for a solution, Mishipsea sat breathing shallowly in the nearly unbearable heat. Outside, Annie drummed, keeping up the steady singing.

"Yes! I think that did it!" Nem-Kee spoke. "Might have an answer or two. Need to talk about it, contact some folks..."

He completed the ceremony to end the sweat and the two men came out into the cool air, blankets wrapped around them. Annie laid aside her drum and gave them water.

One large white frog sat quietly hidden behind a nearly translucent Indian Pipe plant and bracken fern. He grunted his approval.

========================

John Mishipsea drank deeply from the bottle of water that Annie handed him. He watched her as she bent to put her hand drum in a soft suede bag. She had good broad hips, a full body and a kind face. If he were a human, she was a woman he would want to be with. His responsibilities would never allow for that, and yet in this man form in the past, he had women in his bed. Annie was probably not the kind of person with whom he could spend a single night of pleasure. He pushed the idea aside.

"I will think about this, Nem-kee," he said.

"Ahau." Nem-kee picked up his clothes. "I will let you know what is possible that may help you."

Mishipsea knew that he could communicate with Nem-kee without the devices humans used. Although the thoughts sent by a human were not as strong as those sent by his small white spirit beings, he would know when Nem-kee wanted to see him again.

He walked away from Nem-kee's sweat lodge and into the trees that sheltered the clearing from lake winds. Once out of sight from the others, he rolled his shoulders and threw his hands up to the sky. The scab over the wound in his side pulled and he winced. Dropping his arms, he rocked back and forth a few times and then spun around, whirling until he was only a spinning shaft of light that compressed into a bright pale yellow brilliant ball. The ball of light whirled for an instant and then shot out across the lake to Whitefish Island.

Hovering over the beach, the whirling slowed and descended to the sand. The shining orb spun once and then Shibizhee emerged in his true form, copper scales gleaming in sunlight. He reached with one paw to his side at the place where the wound was exposed, its copper scales curled from the heat of the lances of thunder fire. He thrust one paw into the damp sand at the edge of the lake, scooped out the wet earth and slapped it on the wound. The curled scales began to flatten, and small thin new scales slowly protruded from the wound. He tossed back his head with its gleaming white horns and gave a deep purr of satisfaction.

After sinking down onto the warm sand and small rocks of the beach he rolled over onto his back, paws stroking the sunlit air. He writhed back and forth a few times, twisting in the

205

sand enjoying the impromptu back scratch. Flipping over onto his feet, he stood shaking himself, flinging sand in all directions.

He waded out into the water and pulled out a paw full of water plants. He thrust them into his mouth and although there was a faint tinge of chemical in the leaves, it was better than human food. Except for the sweet food, of course.

He lay down on the softer sand near the cave entrance and let himself relax, needing to think about how to deal with the humans. It would be difficult to deal with the impatient Louie, but Nem-kee had shown an understanding and desire to be helpful. There was so much to do to repair the destruction made by people over the past few hundred years. It would be helpful if he could learn more about what had happened to the insects needed for food for his beloved ones. Probably he could find out in the computer.

His great yellow-green eyes began closing and there was a slight rumbling in his throat beginning a satisfied purr. The sun slipped downward gradually toward the blue line where the sky met the water of the lake, and he slept.

It was night before he awoke. He saw the fireflies lifting and falling around him. He stood up, coppery scales shimmering in moonlight. Then his true form faded and became a yellow-white ball of light floating over the beach. It began shrinking until it was half its size, then half its size again. It whirled around dancing with the fireflies, and shrank yet again. Now a tiny bit of light, it shot out where fireflies were gathered in a clump of beach grass, diving and weaving among them, alighting on a plant stem and then going on to another. The cloud of fireflies rose into the air, flickering against a backdrop of a million stars in the dark sky.

=========================

John Mishipsea walked into the police station the next morning. Louie looked up from his desk, trying not to show his surprise and the feeling of unease that tightened his stomach.

"Hey, John." Louie put down his pen and stood up. "What's up?"

"There is a meeting about the lake and water today. I saw the notice at the restaurant. I would like to go and listen to what the people talk about."

Louie hadn't planned on attending the meeting, but he definitely wanted to keep an eye on Mishipsea. There was no telling what he might say or do. "Sure. We can do that." He brought up the tribal meeting schedule on his computer. If they took off now for the casino conference center, they could make it to the Interagency Natural Resources meeting.

What next? The man could read, used a computer, and now he wanted to go to a tribal meeting. But he could still change his shape into anything he wanted, and he had killed Basil.

So Louie would go to an environmental meeting with a murderer. Great. But there was no point in attempting to arrest him for that. How to keep a spirit in jail had not been part of his training for the job.

They took the police car over the causeway to the mainland. The day was warm with a clear sky dotted with a few small puffy clouds, and the water was calm. A buzzing sound and flashing red light on the dashboard indicated that Mishipsea's seat belt wasn't fastened. Louie pulled over to the shoulder and stopped the car.

"You have to buckle up your seat belt." Several minutes later, after a lengthy explanation and discussion, the seat belt was still not fastened, and they rode the rest of the way to the casino with the buzzing and flashing light. Mishipsea sat rigid, not speaking. He looked out the windows with great curiosity, but his hands clutched at the seat beneath him, white-knuckled with tension. Then Louie remembered that this must be the first time Mishipsea had ever ridden in a car or other motorized vehicle.

With his long dark hair pulled back, a tan short-sleeved knit shirt and black jeans, he would hopefully look similar to others at the Great Lakes Protection Coalition meeting on the mainland.

The road into the reservation casino complex was paved, lined with elegant street lights and formal landscaping. Large trees and natural woodland vegetation had been left standing around the parking lots. There were inviting paths through the woods at intervals. Any cables for electricity and communications had been buried. The massive casino building with its arched portico over a four-lane entrance drive dominated, half hiding the parking structure and hotel/conference center area behind it.

Louie pulled up in a Tribal Vehicle Only parking area. He didn't get out of the car at first, letting Mishipsea get a feeling for the place.

"There will be people here that feel the same you do about the water and land. They care for the fish and reptiles, John. They want to help."

Mishipsea looked over at him with a wry smile. "Of course. And you think I must trust these humans. After they have destroyed so much..." He looked away.

"Not these people - others. These men and women have a certain amount of power to repair the damage and prevent other problems. It is too late to change everything about what has been done so far. They don't have that kind of power." He unfastened his seat belt, pulled the car keys from the ignition and put them in his pocket.

"I will introduce you as a consultant, someone with special interests and expertise, asked to attend by the tribe," Louie said. He started to get out of the car, and Mishipsea copied his movement, finding the door handle with some difficulty.

They entered a side entrance to the conference center and Louie walked up to the reception desk. A young Anishinabe man in a jacket with a tribal logo embroidered on the pocket was sitting at a computer and looked up smiling. "Can I help you?"

"We're here for the environmental meeting," Louie said.

"Oh, you're a bit early ... first ones to arrive. You might as well go in, Lake Huron Room." He lifted the telephone on his desk and punched one button. "Louie St. Sable is here, with a guest." He replaced the receiver.

"Fine." Louie motioned for Mishipsea to follow him to a large conference room. Bookshelves of texts and professional journals lined the walls. A table to the left of the door had a coffee maker and cups, and a large tray of glazed and chocolate donuts. The long pale wood conference table in the center was circled with comfortable chairs. Hanging from the ceiling over the table was a construct of deer antlers and energy saving lighting. Pictures on the walls were a combination of navigation maps of the Great Lakes and colorful photographs of underwater scenes.

"What are those books?" Mishipsea, using his chin to point in the Anishinabe way he had seen with Louie, indicated the books and journals on the shelves.

"Writings about the water and the land ... the fish and animals ... things that live on the earth. The people who work here and those coming to the meeting have probably read much of what is written in them. Some of them have studied the problems that exist in the water and have written about it." Louie pulled a book from one of the shelves and handed it to Mishipsea.

Louie wondered just how much he understood. "Excuse me, John. I'm going to go to the bathroom. I'll be right back."

===========================

Mishipsea stood looking for a moment at the books. His image faded, blurring and whirling. A small yellow-white ball of light appeared, floating in the air at a man's height where he had been standing. The orb went up in the air to the first shelf, hovering there for a moment, and then sped rapidly through each of the shelves of books and journals, back and forth until all of them had been included in the absorption of their contents by the mind of the Shibizhee.

The ball of light again appeared at man's height and the human image of Mishipsea took shape again. When Louie re-entered the room, the man was standing next to the table of donuts, selecting one and picking it up. He popped it into his mouth and stood smiling and chewing. "Good donuts, Louie."

===========================

Louie poured coffee for himself and Mishipsea, adding plenty of sugar to the other man's cup. He took a donut for himself, and indicated a place at the table where they could sit.

The sound of voices came from the hallway, echoing in the vaulted space. A group of men and women came in, talking among themselves. They knew each other. Greetings and joking filled the room. Nearly all of them were non-Indian, but there were a few Anishinabe tribal representatives as well. Louie was glad to see that, he hated to stand out as the only Indian in a room full of white people.

Ben Sturgeon, a member of another tribe south of the Limestone Point reservation came in and sat next to Louie. As Chair of the meeting, Ben asked each person to give their name and organization.

There were fourteen around the table, representing the non-profit Tip of the Lakes Watershed organization, the Lakes Watershed Protection coalition, the Cathead Bay Protection group, the Great Lakes Conservancy organization, state and federal natural resources departments, and tribal natural resources representatives. Louie hadn't attended a meeting before, but had met some of them and knew that they were dedicated to keeping the Great Lakes and their tributaries as pristine as possible. They fought against corporate interests, corrupt politicians, and the general apathy and greed of much of the population.

Mishipsea was introduced by Louie as a consultant brought in by his tribe to attend the meeting. No other explanation was given, and there was little curiosity about his presence, as there had been many others who came to these meetings for various purposes, some of them providing assistance, others not.

Several projects were reported on by those who had been successful in obtaining grant monies. The Clean Water Act provided legal authority, and monies came from the Environmental Protection Agency, donations from non-profit organizations and corporations, and from tribal casino enterprise grants. A Coastal Management program was underway, and there was ongoing surface water quality monitoring which provided valuable data.

"How long does this go on?" murmured Mishipsea.

"Until they're done," said Louie. He could see that his companion was getting restless.

The reports continued. Hazardous waste removal, pressures on industries that dumped waste, fines levied against those refusing to comply with guidelines. It went on and on.

Mishipsea stuck his long legs in front of him and leaned back, clasping his hands over his head and stretching. Louie thought he could hear something approximating a low growl coming from the man. It had a distinctly feline edge to it. He nudged Mishipsea in the rib with his elbow and the sound stopped.

A young woman representing a federal agency that worked with farmers talked about the problem with ponds filled with runoff from herbicides. When Mishipsea spoke up, Louie

211

straightened in his chair and caught his breath. What the hell had he been thinking, bringing the guy to this meeting?

A small woman in a tan state Department of Natural Resources uniform had just said: "There must be some kind of decontamination process...."

Mishipsea's voice was deep and grabbed the attention of the participants. "I believe there is a solution. I read about the use of micro-organisms in Malaysia which was quite effective in removing pollutants. A multiculture of anaerobic and aerobic beneficial microorganisms was placed in mudballs that were thrown into polluted ponds. Perhaps some of you read that article – it was presented at the 2010 International Congress on Environmental Modeling ..." He looked around the table and leaned forward as though he was waiting for a response.

Everyone around the conference table stared at Mishipsea. No one said anything.

Then a young man in a tan Department of Natural Resources uniform cleared his throat. "Mudballs? Never heard of that one." He laughed, and several people in the room chuckled and smiled.

The woman who had talked about the ponds went on talking as though Mishipsea hadn't said anything. Everyone turned and focused their attention on her again, ignoring Mishipsea.

Louie heard the low growling sound again and pushed his chair back quickly. "Excuse me, I just got a call. Gotta go." He pulled his cell phone from his pocket and held it to his ear as though someone was talking on the other end. "Yo. I'm on it." He shoved the phone back in his pocket, stood up and motioned for Mishipsea to come with him.

===========================

On the drive back to the island Mishipsea was quiet, looking out the open window of the police car, his head turned away.

Finally, Mishipsea spoke. "Microorganisms eat up mercury and other chemicals. The University of Denver used them on sacred objects that are being returned to the tribes from the museums. They eat up the arsenic, lead and other things that were used to prevent insects from destroying the objects."

"Yes, I heard about that, John." Louie drove slowly, remembering that Mishipsea had a computer. How much 'research' had the man sitting next to him accomplished?

"I do not like the people at that meeting." Mishipsea looked at Louie for an instant and turned away.

"They were very rude to you."

"What was the reason for that?"

"Probably they think they are important, and they don't know you. They have college degrees, and they think that anyone who is involved with them should declare what their credentials are before talking to them."

"That is a very strange way to act, Louie."

"Yes. Some of the people you will meet went to college for a very long time and have doctoral degrees. Everyone seems to think they are more important than other people, and that they know more than others."

"I do not have a degree, Louie. Do you?"

"No." Louie thought about his years in the military, working with the tribe, helping his family and the people on the reservation. "I guess I have a doctorate in hard knocks." He chuckled, grinning.

"I will make the mudballs myself, Louie."

"Just let me know when, I wouldn't mind throwing a few of them at something besides a pond."

===============================

Mishipsea waited until he had walked part way down the road from the St. Sable house before entering the woods that led to the lake. Just before he came to the cedars where he could see the water and sky through their branches, he stopped. His man form faded and the yellow-white ball of light emerged, floated in the air and then moved silently, avoiding the cedars to hover for a moment over the lake. The golden ball dropped and pierced the water, disappearing beneath the waves.

CHAPTER 26

Finding the laboratory where the micro-organisms were created was not difficult. Getting in was another thing. It seemed like a good idea at the time to simply shape-change into a small white insect and ride in on the back of one of the worker's white lab coats. Placing himself on the woman's shoulder, Shibizhee-now-bug thrust his six legs into the fabric. One of the other workers saw him, and lifted his hand to slap the small intruder. The woman backed up, surprised, and while they were laughing, Shibizhee crept up under her collar, hiding until he got inside the building.

She sat down on a stool in front of a large machine and he emerged, spinning himself into a tiny ball of light that sped through the computers absorbing necessary information. Gathering the needed micro-organisms was somewhat more complex, but he shape-shifted into a bee and loaded up his legs with the minute bits. He escaped to the outside without incident.

He flew up through the mountain air over Denver and whirled, a tiny blur of light that sped skyward. Less than an hour later, he reached Whitefish Island and transformed himself again into a bee with the micro-organisms firmly riding on his hairy legs. Inside the cave he headed for the large rock and landed on a clean plastic plate.

Shibizhee-now-bee brushed his legs together and released their burdens. He whirled around, a tiny blur of pale yellow and black, and then spun himself out again into the man John Mishipsea.

He picked up the plate, carefully slipped it into a gallon sized plastic bag and zip-locked it shut. With his powers, he could create enough micro-organisms to test them in the local bay. The people at the meeting had ignored him, but he knew how to clean the water in the Great Lakes, and if they wouldn't cooperate, he could do it himself.

His small white companions huddled together at one side of the cave. They seemed to be communicating with each other, but they blocked him and he was unable to penetrate their thoughts. They had their backs to him. He looked at them for a moment, wondering at their unusual behavior. Then he remembered that he needed to locate a source of mud for the mudballs. He turned on the laptop computer and accessed the Internet. Soil survey maps were easy to find and he located several thick mud swamps.

First, however, he needed to help the micro-organisms multiply. They must be fed. He opened a box of Twinkies, and after putting one beside the laptop for himself, he crumbled the rest of the treats and dropped pieces into the bag.

More moisture. He unscrewed the top of a bottle of water and sprinkled a bit into the bag. He drank the rest himself, washing down his Twinkie.

It would take time for the tiny life forms to multiply, so Mishipsea turned off the laptop and lay down on his improvised bed. He rolled over onto his side and within minutes was asleep, only a slight purring sound echoing in the island cavern.

The sun was a pale rim of gold on the horizon when Mishipsea came out of the cave   carrying the plastic bag filled with a creamy substance. He put it inside his shirt and stood still for a moment before bringing his arms in close, whirling rapidly like an ice skater, making the sand at his feet fly out in all directions. Forming himself into the bright ball of light that was a tiny twin to the massive sun rising over trees to the east, he lifted into the air and shot out across the bay to the mainland.

When the spinning Shibizhee ball of light hovered over the swamp, a large red-winged blackbird clinging to a branch of a Russian olive tree rose from his perch and flew off to land in a lower branch of one of the tamaracks.   The ball of light spun around a wide open area of the swamp in spiraling rings.

With each circuit, sparks of light spread out and fell into the mud flat, every tiny glittering bit carrying micro-organisms that would devour unwanted substances. After the whirling ball of light tossed a final shower of sparks, Shibizhee compressed into a single orb that whirled in a giant circle around the swamp, making the tamaracks bend away from the glittering surface.

Dark bubbles began rising in the wet soil as though heat was coming up from beneath, roiling and tumbling, tossing bits of moss and fungi up into the air. The bubbles lifted, breaking free from the mud flat, spinning into the air in a multitude of balls of glittering moist earth. They rose into a huge cone of mud balls that followed the spinning ball of light out toward Cathead Bay.

The whirling balls glittered in the light of the rising sun, lifted and then dropped suddenly, falling into the water with tiny individual splashes, creating thousands of miniature whirlpools.

In seconds, the water calmed.

===============================

Shibizhee rested on the sandy beach, his copper scales reflecting the rays of the noonday sun. His pale companions came out of the cave and made their way toward him. Muh-kuk-kee - the largest white frog - hopped across the small pebbles and sand to sit before him. Its thoughts went into his mind like sharp nails. The others stayed back, white turtles, snakes and lizards, and smaller white frogs. Their black eyes looked toward him and he could read their echo of the message being sent by their envoy.

They had decided among themselves that it was time for changing and Shibizhee was enveloped with their plea to be changed into common beings. He was filled with the weight of their unspoken cries. They weren't safe in their spirit forms. He should not allow them to endure the wrath of humans. They needed to camouflage themselves. They needed a chance to live as others of their kind.

He lifted his massive copper-scaled head, white horns gleaming in sunlight. Shibizhee stretched out one shining paw and touched the large one. He stood up on his thick legs and walked to the others, touching each one gently.

Muh-kuh-kee changed first, his coat gradually taking on a mottled dull green color, his eyes the yellow-green of his species, and when he opened his mouth, the sharp teeth were gone. Tipping his head to one side, he looked at Shibizhee and then turned and hopped into the lake.

Shibizhee watched the others as they completed their transformations and went toward the water. They didn't look back. It happened so quickly. After millennia, they were released. The last of them went under the surface.

He threw his head back and let out a low yowl of lonely despair, dug his sharp copper claws into the sand and thrashed his tail about, whipping it through beach grasses. His isolation was a dark empty place in his gut.

He could follow them into the lake. He started to walk into the water and then stopped, waves covering his feet. No. He turned and went back to the beach. Small wormwood plants had begun to grow near the cave, and he grabbed one paw full and then another, shoving them into in his mouth. He lay chewing, waiting for the calming effect to set in.

The sun was high now, and he could hear rhythmic drumming coming across the water from the direction of the Jingtamok grounds. It was starting.

===========================

It was almost time for the Jingtamok to begin when Shibizhee crossed the bay as a small ball of light and landed in a tall pine at the edge of the grounds. He turned himself into a tiny red squirrel. He could see nearly the entire area from his perch, and lay down flat on the somewhat prickly limb, avoiding a slight oozing of sap from one branch.

The humans had arranged everything in a circle, the Anishinabe sacred shape. In the center was the arbor made of cedar posts, with cedar branches laid on top. Beneath it were the drum groups, five of them for this Jingtamok. The men and boys around them were talking among themselves. Shibizhee spotted the microphones at each drum group and the big speakers standing next to the raised platform at the edge of the dance arena. Just what he expected – technology and tradition.

He climbed to a higher spot. He could see better, and there was less sticky sap to contend with. There were a lot of humans below, all around the earthen dance circle sitting on chairs and benches, standing, talking and laughing. In the open area behind the onlookers a long line of colorfully dressed dancers waited for Grand Entry. Shibizhee saw the hundreds of cars and trucks parked in neat rows in a nearby field, a large area with campers and tents, and three tall white tipis.

He settled himself down again, belly on the limb and small legs hanging down comfortably. There were things to do, but he wanted to see the humans for a while. The mudballs were in the bay, hopefully working. Just cleaning up the water in the bay was not enough, but it was a test to see if the mudballs would be effective. If it worked here, he could use it in other parts of the besieged planet.

However, he had listened to some of the young people talking about pollution of the air with smoke in restaurants. One of them said that non-smoking in one end of the restaurant was like only peeing in one end of a swimming pool. He thought that trying to clean up Cathead Bay when it was connected to the larger Lake Michigan was probably a good comparison. His efforts in Cathead Bay were just a test of methods in this new world. But it was probably like peeing in one end of the pool.

======================

Nem-kee came out into the dance circle wearing his usual old beaded deerskin loin cloth over his gray pants, and his comfortable shoes instead of moccasins. Over a dark shirt, he had on a heavily beaded vest with an American flag on either side in front, and a traditional eight-sided star design on the back. He wore an eagle feather headdress that stood up on the back of his head. His movements were stiff but not like those of most old men. He walked proudly, even more erect than usual, and went to a spot just in front of the head dancers carrying a small drum and drumstick, and a small medicine bag.

===========================

Neewin and Beanie were trying to be patient while their mother finished the last touches on their dance regalia. One of Neewin's leggings kept slipping down his leg because he had pulled too hard on the leather thong that held it to the Spandex shorts under his tunic. His mother sighed and finally reached for the duct tape.

"That itches!" he complained.

"Tough. Get used to it," she said. "You should have checked it out ahead of time."

"Too busy scarfing down fry bread," said his brother, grinning.

The legging held, and she pulled the tunic down over the emergency repair. "Good. You look really fine." This was a big compliment from his mom, and he smiled up at her, keeping his mouth closed over his missing front baby teeth.

"Wait!" She put out her hands and held them back. "Nem-kee's gonna bless the arena. Stand still. Show some respect, hey." The boys waited, watching as their great-great-grandfather walked into the empty dance circle.

===========================

220

Nem-kee began dancing slowly and then bent low, striking the small drum, singing softly, speaking to the forces that would protect the people at this gathering. He asked the spirits to bless the earth and the people on it, and keep them safe. He thought about Shibizhee and the events that had occurred in the past few days.

As he completed his circle, he finished the prayer and the song that carried it. He went to the place where Annie and Lorette were sitting on chairs under a blue plastic awning.

"Migwetch," said Annie, handing him a bottle of spring water. "Take a load off." She motioned to the chair next to her.

"Just a minute. I'm on again pretty quick." He took a long drink of water and leaned back.

The tiny red squirrel high above him in a tall pine tree chattered approval and then spun in a small whirlwind that glowed pale yellow and brightened. It hovered over the tree and then shot across Cathead Bay in the direction of Lansing and Michigan State University.

==============================

A small dancing mayfly hovered above the doorway to the science lab where sea lamprey pheromones were being synthesized. Shibizhee-now-mayfly had read on the internet that testing proved female lamprey were attracted to the pheromones and would follow them anywhere. Getting into the lab was going to be difficult, however. The nature of the research inside was such that temperature, humidity and any possibility of contamination was eliminated. Even an entity as tiny as a mayfly was unwelcome. He had to change himself yet again. He rode into the lab as the period at the end of a sentence on a paper carried by a graduate student.

It took some time to locate the place where the pheromones were stored, and he discovered that he would need

221

to transport the precious attractant in liquid. Improvising, he became Shibizhee-now butterfly, and inserted his long proboscis to insert into the tiny vial to suck up the precious attractant.

Once he was back in his cave, he could replicate the substance and use it to lure the female sea lamprey to his planned destination.

===============================

Tizbet and Chip sat under a dark blue canopy held up with aluminum poles, relaxing in folding chairs. "Hey, look at Yvonne and Jason," said Tizbet. "Wow. It must have taken years to do all that beadwork!"

The handsome couple stood just behind Nem-kee and the other flag bearers, waiting for Grand Entry. They were obviously the head dancers, Sam Keshiawas's son and daughter-in law, old friends of Tizbet and Chip. Tall and slim, in regalia heavily beaded in turquoise blue, red and black, they were impressive. Yvonne Keshiawas wore a white doeskin dress with a long skirt and sleeves, hair ties with mink trim and large beaded barrettes on her heavy black braids. She carried a beaded bag in one hand and a feather fan in the other. A turquoise and black shawl was draped over one arm, and her moccasins and leggings were heavily beaded with intricate floral designs. She wore a beaded cradle-board on her back with their new baby tightly wrapped inside.

"I think Nem-kee must have given Jason that otter fur medicine bag. It seems like he used to carry it before he made his new one," said Chip.

Jason Keshiawas wore a beaded tan deerskin vest and loin cloth over dark shorts. His leggings had bright floral designs that matched his wristlets. His dance regalia was traditional, with a bustle of turkey feathers and a deer hair roach headdress. One eagle feather stood up on the headdress and bobbed as he moved. He carried a feather fan and the otter fur

222

bag. Deer hoof rattles on his ankles and copper bells fastened just below each knee would emphasize his dance steps.

"Mom told me that neither one of them plans to compete this year," said Tizbet. "Why is that?" She knew the prize money was substantial, and the young couple could probably use it.

"I guess both of them have won so many times, they're giving other people a chance," said Chip. "Maybe there isn't room for all their prizes combined, since they got married." He chuckled, and Tizbet smiled. She felt so good being here with Chip, with the tribe, friends and relatives. The Jingtamok only lasted two days. Not enough time. She had to carry the feeling inside her for an entire year when she lived so far away.

"I've been thinking about your suggestion that I apply for a teaching job here," she said.

"Great! I've been hoping..." He reached over and lightly touched her hand. It wasn't appropriate to give her a big hug here at a traditional event, but maybe later...

===============================

Shibizhee-now-squirrel deposited himself once again on a topmost branch of the pine tree. He had helped himself to a bottle of sweetgrass perfume from one of the booths at the Jingtamok and emptied the synthesized sea lamprey pheromones inside. He had already checked the situation in the Atlantic and discovered that there were plenty of male lamprey in their places of origin. They would have to be destroyed, but he hated to see them go to waste. Finding a factory that made cat food in Michigan was not as easy as he had expected. Finally, he located one over the border in Indiana.

He wanted to see more of the Jingtamok before he tried becoming the Pied Piper of female sea lamprey. It looked like something was happening down below at the entrance to the dance circle.

223

He flattened himself out again on the branch that gave him a clear view of everything below. This was the wrong kind of tree for pine nuts, and for an instant he wished he had some of the sweet morsels. Then he flipped his brushy tail up over his back and concentrated on the interesting behavior of the Anishinabeg.

Nem-kee waited with other veterans at the head of the long line of dancers waiting for Grand Entry to begin. The master of ceremonies was a large Anishinabe man dressed in a sport shirt and jeans with a long graying ponytail and a broad smile. He stepped up to the microphone on the grandstand and blew into it a couple of times, looking over at a teenage boy who was handling the sound system. The boy nodded and the man began speaking. "Well, let's get started. We want to welcome all of you to the twentieth annual Limestone Point Jingtamok. That's our word for what is also known as a Pow-Wow. The Limestone Point drummers are here."

A drummer tapped lightly on the big drum circled by men sitting in folding chairs, each one with a large drumstick padded with sheepskin.

"We've got the Chicago drum here, too." Another group beat a short response, the men seated around that drum dressed the same as others, in jeans, long sleeved ribbon shirts, some wearing cowboy hats; others wore baseball caps with Native American designs.

"The Lac du Flambeau drum finally got here, I see." The men at that drum pounded rapidly, and there was a trickle of laughter from the spectators. Nem-kee chuckled and began walking with the other veterans toward the flagpoles at one side of the raised platform. The banners of the United States, Canada, Michigan, POW/MIA and the Limestone Point Reservation were evenly spaced in flagpole holders.

The traditional long staff with eagle feathers fastened down its length stood at the end. Nem-kee lifted it and settled the end into the pocket of a belt he wore around his waist to help carry it. He held tight to the heavy flag, straightened his back and turned with the others to go back and stand at the head of the line of dancers. This was probably the last year he would be able to do this, and sweat had already begun sliding down his cheeks.

The master of ceremonies spoke again. "Ladies and gentlemen, would you all please stand for the Indian Flag Song. For those of you not recognizing it, this is our national anthem." The Limestone Point drummers began, the heartbeat of a people, sound that wove the people together. They sang in high falsetto in the Anishinabe language. Everyone stood quietly until it was done. A small older woman went to the microphone. She said a prayer in the language, her voice strong and clear over the sound system.

The procession began. Nem-kee marched out first with the other flag bearers. Yvonne and Jason Keshiawas with their tiny baby followed, feet sliding across the ground in measured dance steps. The long line of dancers moved behind them into the dance circle, moving clockwise on the grassy ground of the arena.

Shibizhee-now-squirrel watched the dancing for a while but started getting restless. The Lac de Flambeau drummers played and sang a traditional honor song for veterans. He saw old Nem-kee go around the dance circle once and then walk off to sit beside Annie under one of the canopies. Tizbet went over to sit with them while Chip joined the other veterans. He danced next to Sam Keshiawas and his father Louie. One young woman walked behind them, bouncing a bit on an artificial leg. Her face was badly scarred on one side, half hidden by her long black hair. Other dancers came into the arena and followed the veterans.

It was time to collect the pheromones and gather the female lamprey. Without females, the males would just die off naturally. The small squirrel spun in a reddish blur and then

225

compressed into a pale yellow ball of light that shot through the air toward the cave on Whitefish Island.

============================

One worker at the pet food plant in Indiana saw the massive whirling tornado coming toward him and ducked into a doorway. There had never been tornados in his part of the state before, and there had no warning on TV or radio. He reached for his cell phone and dialed 9-1-1, but had a hard time describing what he was seeing.

"It's a tornado. All of a sudden. I'm out at the plant..." His hand holding the phone dropped to his side as he watched the strange tornado. He felt no wind, and the rest of the sky was clear. His heart beat fast and loud in his chest and he stood open-mouthed.

It was coming closer, a spinning cloud that looked as though it had picked up thousands of small eels or snakes, tails whipping about. The cloud hovered over an empty grain silo. The roof of the silo blew off and flew into a nearby field and the funnel of writhing flesh dropped into the silo without a sound. A few small wriggling creatures slid down the rounded side and fell to the ground.

The man waited, scanning the sky for more tornado action. There was still was no wind. He went over to the silo and stood looking down at three dying sea lamprey. Since he lived inland in an area where there were few lakes, he had no idea what they were. They looked like fat little snakes. Darnedest thing.

"Yes, sir. Can I help you?" He looked at the cell phone in his hand and put it to his ear.

"I don't really know, ma'm. I guess not." He closed the phone.

The boss would be asking a lot of questions. The big question in his mind was whether cats would eat snake meat.

==============================

Shibizhee sat on the beach of Whitefish Island in his true form, listening to the sound of drums coming from the Jingtamok. There was so much to be done yet. The amount of trash under the water of Cathead Bay was incredible. Getting rid of invasive species and cleaning the water was one thing. Little by little, his experiment with the bay would tell him if the same approach would work on the larger bodies of water. The debris underwater made him feel physically ill. He couldn't stand the taste of the water. And there were all the bottles, cans, fishing equipment, sunken boats... the garbage was massive.

He discovered at the grocery store that the beer and soda cans and bottles had value, that the store would give people money for each one returned. Yet there were thousands of cans and bottles in the lake. Humans had thrown them into the lake instead of getting money for them. Just another thing he didn't understand about these new two-leggeds.

He rolled over onto his back, sliding his copper scales back and forth on the sand, stretched, and then jumped to his feet. There were nets in the lake. They could be loaded up with cans. He ran to the water, his shining back reflecting light for a moment before diving down.

Toby needed a beer. They didn't allow it at the Jingtamok, and Louie had his deputies watching for booze and drugs. Since losing his job at the quarry, he'd been hitting the sauce pretty hard, but he figured he deserved a little something. He drove his truck over to the store and picked up a six-pack and headed home. His wife and kids would be fine. The kids had wanted to get something to eat and he bought them all frybread and corn soup. He'd come back to the Jingtamok later and get them.

His truck rattled down the rutted driveway and he swerved to avoid hitting a couple of his chickens. He got out and started to reach in the truck bed for his six-pack when he realized that there was an enormous pile of empty beer and pop cans and bottles in the back field. It was higher than his house trailer. He didn't drink that much. What the hell?

"Holy wah!" He left the beer in the truck and trotted past kid's bikes and toys to stand at the fence. Someone had dumped a treasure on him. After scrounging for work since the quarry closed, he had barely made ends meet. There must be thousands of dollars in returnables. He was rich!

Toby threw back his head and looked up at the sky. "Mee-ee-ee-gwetch!"

===========================

Annie and Lorette danced together, movements liquid and graceful, carrying their shawls. Annie wore her old long green dress, the appliqued designs on it edged in sparkling beads. Lorette had on her usual dark blue Jingtamok skirt and tunic top, and wore her long dark hair up in a tightly braided bun with a big round beaded barrette firmly fastened to the back of her head.

"Look at those kids dance. All that energy." Annie moved well herself, but she couldn't keep up with the children. She thought the tiny ones were amazing, dressed in miniature dance outfits that were replicas of their elders, copying their movements as exactly as their little legs would carry them. They danced seriously, following the older children or moving up to dance near their parents. The little girls bounded up and down with complex dance steps, and the boys bent and looked from side to side with the jerky movements of the animals they imitated. One little girl had to keep hitching her small shawl up over her tiny shoulders. The older girls held their shawls out and whirled around like bright butterflies.

"Let's get Angie out here," said Lorette. "She's been over at the hospital and then cooking. Take her mind off

228

things." She headed over toward the place where Angeline was sitting.

"Hey, girl, get out here. Shake a leg." Lorette grabbed her sister's hand and pulled her to her feet. Annie opened up her shawl and put it around Angeline's shoulders.

"Oh, I don't know..." Angeline looked tired, but she didn't sit back down. "Oh, okay." She joined her sisters and they went back into the dance circle, moving together in the slow measured steps, careful not to bounce and make their breasts wobble. That was something they had seen women from other tribes do and they considered it shameful.

============================

The small red squirrel watched the three women slowly moving together as the younger dancers followed. He flattened himself down again, legs hanging down on both sides of the branch. His eyes closed and he curled his tail over his back. Time to take a little nap. He dug his paws into the branch beneath him just a bit. No point in falling out of a tree. The sound of drums washed over him, the heartbeat of the Anishinabe. Maybe they weren't all that bad... Maybe he could put up with them... Maybe...

CHAPTER 27

Lorette came to Nem-kee's trader table under its canopy. She sat down on one of the folding chairs, her shawl with the long fringe folded in her lap.

"Sold all of your necklaces?" she asked.

"Yup. I guess the word got out." He reached into the small cooler next to him and got out a can of root beer and handed it to her.

"Migwetch." She popped the top and took a long drink. "I've been thinking."

"That sounds dangerous," he said.

"I think that the quarry was a big mistake. Shouldn't mess up the land. It came back on us people." She drank again, and put the can on the ground next to her chair.

"You got that right."

"I think the quarry cave-in and Basil's house falling in that sink hole were just a warning. I shouldn't have listened to Basil and those developers."

"Enh," he agreed.

Lorette watched the young dancers as they talked, the youthful bodies in colorful regalia moved rapidly. They were the ones to be concerned about – what kind of world were the elders leaving behind? The teachings Nem-kee had been given and taught her said that planning should be carried forward to the seventh generation.

"There's been a lot of short term gain here for the tribe," she said. "I've seen a lot. I take responsibility for things that have gone on here. Me and the Council. We wanted to do everything fast, keep up with the rich white people."

"We got a pretty strong wake-up call," he said. "That Shibizhee – Mishipsea guy – scared the crap out of me and a lot of others."

"What do you think he's going to do next?" Lorette looked over at Nem-kee and saw his jaw tighten. "Have you talked to him?" She knew about Tizbet's rescue and the events that followed.

"He talked to me some, at the sweat lodge."

"What did he say?"

"He seems concerned about the water, the fish – reptiles – amphibians. His responsibility. He's pretty upset, wants to do something about it."

"Do you think he'll hurt anybody else?"

"I don't know."

They sat for a few minutes. Nem-kee got up, his knees cracking slightly.

"Guess I'll shake a leg for a while. Help yourself to more pop." He walked away.

Lorette finished her root beer and followed him out into the dance circle. She put her shawl about her shoulders so that the long fringe came down nearly to her ankles, and half danced over to join one of the older women. They danced companionably without speaking. The music seemed to fill her, along with the sense of responsibility for her people. She was just one of them now, losing her usual feeling of separateness. A good feeling, being a part of the people.

Shibizhee-now-squirrel woke, sat up and looked down on the dancers and traders. People were lined up at the food booths. The signs on the booths advertised blanket dogs, corn dogs, Indian tacos and buffalo burgers. There were several booths selling corn soup and frybread.

He was hungry, and the smells coming from below made his stomach growl. He leaped from branch to branch down the tree and ran across the campground area into the woods.

The transformation into John Mishipsea only took seconds, and he still felt hungry. He checked himself, brushed his hair back into a neat ponytail and tucked his shirt into his jeans.

He saw a large rabbit hiding inside the hollow of a fallen log. It huddled there looking directly at Mishipsea. Was it him? The Great Hare? Nanabozho? No. Too small.

He walked between tents and campers. Food cost money. He reached into his back pocket and pulled out the leather wallet.

Chip and Tizbet were sitting at a picnic table next to one of the food concessions. As Mishipsea walked toward them, Tizbet looked up, a surprised expression on her face. She said something to Chip and he turned around.

"Hey!" he said. "You decided to come."

"I wanted to see this Jingtamok," Mishipsea said.

"Sit with us," said Tizbet. Her eyes were wary, and he could tell that she was afraid of him. He looked at what they were eating. Something in small white plastic bowls.

"What is that?" He pointed to their food.

"Corn soup. It has some potato, meat, corn and beans in it," she said.

"They sell it here," said Chip. He pointed to the trailer next to them with an open window and awning. Signs indicated all their offerings.

Mishipsea bought himself a bowl of the soup and a piece of frybread. He came back to the table and sat down. The food was good and he ate without talking. Tizbet and Chip waited for him to finish before they spoke.

"Dad said he took you to some kind of environmental meeting," Chip said. "How did it go?"

"Not good. They are too slow. What they do is too complicated," said Mishipsea.

"Like how?" asked Tizbet.

"Too many rules and regulations. Nothing gets done. All they do is run experiments and come up with ideas, but there is little action. They need money to do everything," said Mishipsea.

While they were talking, there was a slight tremor in the earth under them, and the coffee in Chip's cup sloshed up the side. Tizbet grabbed the edge of the picnic table and gasped.

"What the..." Chip swung his legs over the bench and stood up. Mishipsea did the same, as did Tizbet. The three of them had difficulty keeping their balance and held onto the table for support.

"An earthquake?" said Tizbet.

The drumming stopped and the arbor poles and roof swayed and collapsed, covering the drummers. Several men and boys crawled out from under the cedar branches. Dancers in the arena were running or lying on the ground. The canopies over the trader's booths were shaking and some of them were tumbling down, covering the people and their wares. Sound screeched from the speakers at either side of the high platform and then stopped. People were crying out, yelling and screaming. Food stands shook violently and one small trailer exploded. The woman inside came falling out of the doorway screaming, but unhurt.

"Lie down!" said Chip, throwing Tizbet to the ground beside him. Mishipsea was already down, on his stomach next to the picnic table.

"He is very angry," said Mishipsea.

"Who?" asked Tizbet.

"Nanabozho," said Mishipsea. The warnings had been real. He had not imagined it. The Great Rabbit was back, truly. The messages on his laptop computer were real. He had ignored the earlier warnings. Nanzbozho had sent them. The great earth spirit was challenging him, coming for him again.

The ground continued trembling. Then there was a sound like rushing wind that howled and filled the air with a roar like a thousand angry bears. Then, as quickly as it had begun, the trembling stopped.

People stood singly and in groups. Where before the dance arena was full of dancers in colorful regalia with onlookers and traders in street clothes around the periphery, now the area was a wild mixture of everyone seeking out their families.

Chip and Tizbet got to their feet and stood next to Mishipsea. The area was a shambles, as though a giant had taken the entire area and shaken it, throwing everything down in a fit of anger.

"Holy crap!" Chip pointed to the causeway - or where the causeway had been. The road to the mainland had disappeared. The water of Cathead Bay had merged with Lake Michigan in one broad stretch of water that was still choppy.

"He has done this. He has awakened and returned," Mishipsea said.

"Who? "asked Tizbet.

"Nanabozho," he replied.

"Why?" asked Chip.

"He is angry that I escaped." Mishipsea clenched his fists. This meant another war with his ancient enemy. Could they never have peace between them? Would there never be balance in the world again? Must he always be confronted with obstacles? First the humans, and now this. He turned and looked at Chip and Tizbet.

"He wants to punish me for what I did to his brother. He wants to put me back beneath the earth. I must go. Humans are not safe around me."

He didn't bother to hide his transformation this time. He simply whirled rapidly, a blur and compression into a ball of white light, and sped across the bay toward Whitefish Island. He didn't see the expression on their faces as they watched him go.

===========================

The glowing orb circled Whitefish Island and hovered over the beach in front of the cave entrance. As it spun and expanded, Shibizhee emerged to stand on the sand and pebbles. He looked across the choppy waves of the lake toward Cathead Island and saw smoke and flames rising over the burning houses in the small town. He should never have allowed himself to get involved with the humans. Nanabozho would only take out his anger on them as well. Their ongoing battles should involve

234

only themselves, not others. But no. His enemy had called on the sky forces.

He shape-changed into John Mishipsea, strode across the beach and into the cave. Without his companions, he was alone. The place seemed cold and empty. He sat down at the computer and nearly lifted the cover, but checked himself. With one swipe of his hand he dashed the device across the cave, and it hit the stone wall and fell to the floor. His howl and the loud hiss that followed echoed from the cold limestone.

He stood, feeling himself changing. In his true form he would be too large to get through the opening to the beach. The anger was taking over. His fingers were already arching into claws. The floor of the cave began shaking and buckling and threw him to his knees. A cold wind blew in from the doorway laden with pebbles and sand that struck him like pounding fists and needles. He gained his feet and held onto the limestone rock wall as he staggered to the entrance. Not again. Nanabozho would not trap him again.

Large chunks of the ceiling tumbled down, crashing around him as he made it through the opening. Plants and shrubs on the beach swayed violently, and a tree ripped from its roots slid down the hill above him. The boat he had pulled up on the shore rocked back and forth and slid into the water as the earth beneath it lifted and fell.

His hands and feet were copper-clad claws He arched his back and felt the sharp spikes emerge; fell to all fours and lifted his head back, huge head and horns once again that of the great copper lynx. He turned his huge body and in one smooth leap he was in the water, disappearing under the waves.

Shibizhee surfaced a few hundred yards from shore. As his head emerged he looked back to see Whitefish Island shaking with a tremor that leveled the rocks and trees. Then the entire island was sucked down under the water as though being pulled down in a massive vortex. It was gone.

He kept his head above water and turned to the place where the causeway had been. Nothing but the roiling waves of the lake. Turning again, he saw that Cathead Island remained, but it was cut off from the mainland.

Shibizhee needed other underworld spirits to assist him. He sent out a call and dove down to the underwater tunnels that would take him to them.

===========================

The tunnel was dark but Shibizhee's feline eyes could see clearly. He swam underwater for many miles and finally came out in a familiar subterranean cavern, emerged and pulled himself up by his claws onto the broad shelf that led to his old friend's lair. The archway into the cave was rimmed with shining silver. Ganoozow-makwa, the Long-Tailed Bear of legend stood on his enormous back legs, his thick white body taking up most of the space. "You escaped. That is great news, my friend." The corners of his mouth lifted, exposing large copper canines. He ambled majestically toward Shibizhee, his long copper tail waving in the air behind him. A wide purple and white wampum necklace nearly covered his neck and shoulders.

"I come for your help against Nanabozho. He is angry that I am free now. I have taken on my responsibilities again, but he keeps causing problems."

They spoke for a long time and planned what to do next. Ganoozow-makwa was anxious to begin immediately, but there were others that needed to be contacted. Underworld creatures were numerous. The Memegwesiak mermen and merwomen had powers that would be useful.

"Have you considered asking Mishi-ginebig?" asked Ganoozow-makwa.

"Yes, but I'm not sure where that old underwater serpent is. It's been a long time," said Shibizhee.

"He would be quite helpful if you could get Nanabozho to suck in the poison from his breath. Even a spirit being could sicken just with one dose. Like rotten eggs. It's pretty foul stuff." Ganoozow-makwa waved one paw in front of his muzzle as though he were smelling something malodorous.

"If I remember, he is pretty fond of sumac," said Shibizhee. "At least it hasn't been pushed out by all the invasive plants. I can't believe how many strange things are growing on the land and in the water. There are masses of little trees that the humans call 'Russian olive' and big pink things they say are loosestrife. I managed to get rid of a couple of things in the water, but there is much more work to do."

"I have been told about this," said Ganoozow-makwa. "So you are going to clean things up. Try to change what the two-leggeds have done?"

Shibizhee looked down, realizing that he sounded more confident than he felt. "I shall try, my friend. But I cannot do all of this alone and fight Nanabozho too."

"It seems to me that the old serpent is sleeping in the south somewhere. One of the Memegwesiak told me about it some time ago," said Ganoozow-makwa. Shibizhee knew that the shape-changing mermen and merwomen were usually seen along river banks, but they occasionally ventured deep underground, following the water into the earth.

Shibizhee left knowing that he had at least one ally, and there could be others. Once he reached the surface, he headed for Cathead Island. He remembered seeing a good stand of sumac in the woods near Annie's house.

CHAPTER 28

"Are you all right?" asked Louie as he walked toward Chip and Tizbet over the uneven ground.

"Yes. How about you?" Chip brushed dirt from his clothes.

"Fair to partly cloudy." Louie rolled his shoulders and put one hand behind his back where he was pretty sure a bruise was going to let him know about it later.

Louie looked around the Jingtamok grounds. People were setting up their canopies and talking in small groups. The speaker's stand had collapsed and the center arbor was a pile of poles and cedar boughs. "The causeway is gone. Thank goodness the power cable is buried, still seem to have electricity and water."

"How about communications?" asked Chip. He dug his cell phone out of his jeans as he spoke, flipped it open and tried his speed dial.

Tizbet looked down at the pocket in her long skirt and pulled out her phone. It was buzzing and vibrating. "Hello?" Her eyes met Chip's and they both burst out laughing.

"Yah, Dad. Phones work."

The next hour was a flurry of activity around the area. Most of the traders picked up everything that had been tossed to the ground and shut up shop. No one would be buying anything fancy. Only the ones that had food booths set up as best they could. People had to eat. Dancers took off their regalia and packed it away. People wandered around looking for family and friends, talking and shaking their heads in amazement at what had just happened. Louie checked out people around the arena.

Louie found the community building with its kitchen and dining space was still standing, as were the bathrooms. Some of the siding had peeled off, windows were broken and shingles from the roofs lay on the ground but the walls and roofs were intact. Louie headed over there to check out the kitchen equipment. The last thing they needed now was a fire. He glanced up to see if the water tower on a hill on the other side of the island was still standing. It appeared to be stable and the cell tower was intact. He sighed with relief.

"Have you seen Lorette?"

"Not yet. I'll see if I can find her." Chip took off on a search, his long legs going over the lumpy ground so that he looked like a sailor negotiating high seas. His arms were out on either side as he tried to keep to his feet and move quickly at the same time.

Louie's cell phone demanded attention. "Yo. St. Sable here." It was Lee Kinwah up in Thunder Bay again.

"You got a minute?"

"Not exactly. We just had a slight earthquake here. Lost the causeway to the mainland. Damndest thing, Lee." Louie kept walking. "What's up?"

"Another earthquake or something. You know the Great Serpent Mound down in Ohio?"

"Yup. Been there." Louie paused just outside the building and tried to open the screen door with one hand while holding the phone to his ear with the other.

"Well, it's gone. Flatter than a pancake."

"Holy crap." Louie gave up on the door and turned around. "Another earthquake?"

"They say not. Some of those Shawnee down there are freaked out completely. Saying that Mishi-ginebig has gone missing."

"You have got to be kidding."

"No. On my mother's grave, Louie." Lee's voice was firm and serious. "My great aunt lives down there, and she's not one to be very funny. Called me up just a while ago."

Louie didn't say anything for a moment. He felt like he needed to sit down. He leaned back against the wall of the

239

building. "Kind of strange that these earthquakes are happening. Are there any other places? Anything on the TV?"

"I'm going to check it out with the seismologists up here. We've got some calls in."

"Good idea. I'll do the same."

He finally got the screen door open and threaded his way around tables and chairs that had been flipped every which way. "Anyone here?"

A hissing sound came from the kitchen. The big gas stove was tipped; a front burner losing gas was filling the area with fumes. He kept his mouth shut, not breathing, and ran over to turn the handle. It wouldn't move. He pulled the big stove out away from the wall, felt a burning sensation in his back but ignored the pain. The gas connection was intact, and he grabbed the flat handle and twisted it shut. The hissing stopped.

Pans and kettles were all over the floor of the kitchen and cooking utensils were spilled across the room. The big double sink was still standing and he tried to breathe only shallowly as he turned one of the faucets. A clear stream of water came out. Great! Something works.

Outside, he drew in a deep lungful of clean air and wondered if his house and the police station were still intact. He needed to get someone out to the rest of the island. There were people out there in their homes, tourists in the town, probably a couple thousand souls that were his responsibility.

Lorette was coming toward him across what had been the arena. She had one grandson by the hand and her dance shawl was slung over her shoulder. What she wore primarily was an extremely concerned and angry expression. No time to think about spirits. Time to get to work.

===========================

Annie saw John Mishipsea stride up the path to her place, cross her yard and take the steps two at a time. She came to the screen door. "Ah-nee, John."

He only nodded; his face grim and his body rigid. "I need to get some of your sumac."

"Help yourself. I've got a gunny sack here someplace, you need that, too?"

"Yes." He didn't look directly at her, just focused somewhere to the side of her face.

"Time for a cup of tea? I just made a pot."

"Yes. I am thirsty."

She opened the door and he followed her into the kitchen. "Have a seat. Hungry?" She went to her old gas stove and stirred a pot of soup.

"That would be good. I can pay you for the food."

"No need." She lifted the teapot from the back of the stove, brought it to the table with two cups and poured their tea. "You look like a man on a mission."

"I did not make the earthquake, Annie."

"Your old buddy Nanabozho?" She dished up his soup and set it on the table in front of him with a large soup spoon.

"Yes. He was attacking me. Your old buddy Nem-kee is responsible. He called Nanabozho. And the sky forces."

"He is Nem-kee Ish-ko-day, John."

"Yes. Thunder fire. When the Thunderers flash their eyes."

She sat down, picked up her cup, blew across the rim and took a small sip. "I was with him."

He sucked in his breath and his brows rose in surprise. "You called them?"

"We were afraid of you. We thought you would start killing people."

"I only killed the bad person that was responsible....."

"Yes. In some ways, I don't blame you now. We didn't know what he had done."

241

He began eating the soup and neither of them talked until he finished. She sat sipping her tea, looking out the window.

He pushed the bowl away. "My island is gone. Nanabozho destroyed it."

"Whitefish Island? Gone?" She hadn't heard about that. She had seen the causeway collapse and sink into the lake. Annie and many others that lived on the island had gone to make sure their houses were still standing. Annie had walked home, found her house intact and called Lorette. Apparently the quake was small and most of Cathead Island was untouched.

Mishipsea got up and paced around the room as they talked, and Annie sat patiently waiting for him to calm down. Finally she gave up. It wasn't going to happen. He was just too upset.

"Where are you going to stay?" she asked. "With the island and your cave gone…"

He stopped pacing and looked at her, his face a blank. Evidently he hadn't thought about that.

"Why don't you stay here with me, John?" she offered. It would be easier to keep an eye on him, and she had a few ideas of her own. "I have a spare room, and perhaps I can help you."

"What about Nem-kee? If you do that, he will be angry. He wants to destroy me."

She thought about that before responding. Finally she spoke. "He doesn't want to destroy anyone. He just wanted to rein you in some. You were so disturbed with the pollution and all the strangeness now…"

"He did too much, Annie."

"Yes, and I helped him." She got up and took the cups and bowl to the sink. "I'm half to blame."

"I can do much good for the water and all those in my care," he said. "Humans will benefit from that."

"I know that now." She sat back down at the table. "You know, when I was a kid, Lorette and I had matching t-

242

shirts. Our mom wrote on them with some kind of marker thing. Hers said 'Did it.' Mine said 'Overdid it.' Looks like I haven't learned much."

"You are like those humans at the meeting. You mean to do the right thing."

"You don't trust me. I don't blame you. But take me up on staying here. I don't bite." She broke out in a full guffaw. "But you do!"

"I won't bite, Annie." His face was serious. "Not you."

"Well, let's go get some sumac. You might tell me what you want to use it for...."

===========================

Nem-kee and Beanie took apart the poles of his fallen canopy. They folded the plastic and stuffed everything in a large green canvas bag, folded up the table and chairs and stacked them in a neat pile, the empty necklace cases on top.

"There, done. Migwetch."

Nem-kee walked with one hand on the boy's shoulder to the men's bathroom. He carried a small sports bag with his regular clothes. They passed two veterans at the demolished speaker's stand folding flags and stacking the flagpoles. "Might as well get this dance stuff off. You go see if your mom needs anything." He patted the boy's back affectionately.

"She said to help you," the boy said.

"Well, I don't need more help. So scoot."

Nem-kee stood in line to go into the bathroom, but the younger men in front of him waved him on in ahead of them, showing proper respect. He thanked them and entered the building. Other men and boys had the same idea and were removing their regalia, carefully placing feather bustles and beaded buckskin clothes in bags and cases. The place was crowded, but they made room for him.

243

When he came out, the soft shushing sound of wings drew his attention upward. Eagles were circling the Jingtamok area, coming lower and closer to the humans than Nem-kee had ever seen. Several landed in the tops of pines.

"Guess they're having a meeting," said one of the men in line for the bathroom. There was a ripple of laughter.

High above the trees, more eagles circled, their wings tipping back and forth as they floated and then pushed down hard to lift again. Nem-kee's regalia bag slipped from his hand and dropped to the ground. He felt a chill go up his back. Men standing in line for the bathroom had their heads back looking up.

"Holy wah!" said a man Nem-kee recognized from the Keweenaw Bay reservation in the Upper Peninsula. "Never saw nothin' like that."

Nem-kee felt his knees go so weak he could barely stay upright. He sucked in a breath and felt dizzy, then caught himself, forcing strength into his body. This was not good.

One by one, the eagles on the trees lifted into the sky and circled with the others. High pitched screeching from dozens of the huge birds filled the air with sound. Then silence.

The men looked around at each other and up again at the circling birds. There were so many, a swath of brush strokes, white of their heads and black and white of their wings making a staccato pattern against the cloudless blue.

One of the thunderbirds flew away from the group, headed west. Nem-kee estimated that it was just over the area where his and Annie's houses were when the raptor shot a bolt of lightning from his eyes, turned and flew back to the others.

With one quick movement the enormous circle of wings whirled, lifted higher and higher, and compressed into a single dark spot. The spot disappeared. They were gone.

Nem-kee headed over to the community building. He had to find someplace to sit down. Maybe Annie was home. He was out of breath and his legs felt like they would barely hold him. The uneven ground was a challenge, but he made it to the building. The tables had been set up and a number of the elders sat together at one side. Annie wasn't there. He collapsed onto a bench and dropped his bag next to him. He hated to use the cell phone in his pocket and took out his reading glasses so that he could see the numbers.

She answered on the first ring. "Who's this?"

"Nem-kee. I saw one of those thunderbirds shoot down some lightning, looked like it was over there."

Her voice was higher than usual. "Right behind my house. Just about got that Mishipsea guy as he was leaving."

"Any damage?"

"None to speak of. Looks like they are gone from here."

He leaned back and felt himself go limp with relief. "Here, too. Well, take care."

"You too, old man." She hung up.

"Nem-kee, were you there, did you see those eagles?" one of his older cousins asked.

He simply nodded. No energy left.

"What do you think all that means?" asked another. He shrugged and shook his head.

"Bad medicine if you ask me," said the first one. Nem-kee just sat, wanting to somehow melt down into a pile of ashes. Everyone was going to expect him to interpret the strange thing with the eagles and the lightning. His mind was completely empty At times like this it would be a very good thing to be a shape-changer. He could see himself as one of Shibizhee's small lizard forms right now, just sitting here and nobody asking him to come up with anything wise or profound.

========================

John Mishipsea ran through the woods behind Annie's place, a gunny sack full of sumac leaves and roots over his shoulder. The bolt of lightning had just missed him. He looked

245

up and saw the huge thunderbird return to the others who were still circling the island.

Everything around him seemed so peaceful. The birches with their little thunderbird markings had just begun to leaf out. Bracken was coming up, unfurling in the warmer air. Small yellow and white wildflowers dotted the carpet of green underfoot. He paused at the edge of the trees, stepped out onto the sandy soil of the high dune overlooking Cathead Bay, brought the bag of sumac down to rest on his feet, and spun himself into a round ball of light that rose up over the bay and shot down into the water.

Within minutes he was in the river tunnel that led to Ganoosow-Makwa's cavern. He emerged as himself, holding the bag of sumac in his teeth as he loped through the silver-rimmed entrance. The great white bear was sitting in his usual place, lounging against the back of the massive stone seat. He grunted a welcome and gestured to Shibizhee to come forward.

"Our friend is coming very soon." He offered Shibizhee a place to rest on a low ledge near him. "I see you brought his gift."

Shibizhee dropped the bag on the floor, climbed up on the ledge and lay down, resting his head on his paws. "Changed shape so many times, I could use a rest."

"Yes, it does have that effect." Ganoosow-Makwa snorted a laugh.

A deep roar echoed down the tunnel outside the cavern, faint at first and then louder until it seemed to fill the space. Ganoosow-Makwa covered his ears with his enormous white paws. His copper claws glinted in the faint light from the greenish luminescent fungus on the cave walls. Shibizhee felt as though the sound was inside his head, and his ears throbbed with the vibrating noise.

Both spirit beings got up and ambled through the doorway to the ledge next to the river outside. The sound stopped. Water churned and splashed up onto the ledge, wetting their feet. An enormous head shot out of the river and Mishi-Ginebig slithered up and out, onto the ledge. Shibizhee had only seen him a few times in the past and for a moment was awed at his size and radiance.

The giant serpent was covered with iridescent scales that glowed, giving off multi-colored opalescence in the dim light of the cavern. Two short shining horns rose above his head and flattened, cobra-like projections on either side were adorned with amethysts and opals. One huge diamond was embedded between his pale purple eyes.

"Welcome, brother," said Ganoosow-Makwa. Shibizhee managed to emit a low purr of approval. This was a formidable being indeed. He felt his claws curling in anticipation of added strength for a battle with his hated enemy.

"I have been sleeping for some time. It is good to know I am needed. Shibizhee caught the smell of the serpent's breath and nearly gagged. He controlled himself, but backed away a bit. Ganoosow-Makwa looked over at him, his copper incisors clamping down on his closed mouth, suppressing a smile. The serpent hissed a long satisfying sound of pleasure. His long red tongue darted out to test the air around him.

Shibizhee and Mishi-Ginebig followed the huge white bear into the cavern. Over the next few hours they listened to the story of Shibizhee's recent difficulties with Nanabozho, and his plan to have a final battle to settle their differences.

"He has the Sky Forces on his side, brother. The thunderbirds are powerful beings," warned Mishi-Ginebig. His long body curled and uncurled nervously.

"They use eagles, hawks....you could breathe on them," suggested Shibizhee. That breath would probably kill anything.

"Come with me," said Ganoosow-Makwa. From his laid back position on his chair, he rolled down onto all fours and led the way to the back of the cavern. He brushed aside a thick hide curtain and held it as Mishi-Ginebig slithered through into a wide tunnel. Shibizhee followed the others down a slight slope into another cavern the size of a stadium. It was lit on all sides by torches set against the rock walls. Shibizhee could not see the height of the dark ceiling above him.

Hundreds of white bears looked up at them as they entered. Some were sitting or standing, others tumbling and wrestling. They were smaller than Ganoosow-Makwa, and none had long tails. Each wore a thin silver band around his or her throat. The wrestlers stopped and pulled apart as they saw their leader.

Ganoosow-Makwa spoke to them in their own language. His deep voice echoed off the walls and bounced off the ceiling, resounding in sound after sound that duplicated itself many times. When he was finished, their response came back, hundreds of times over and over. Shibizhee felt as though he were covered in layer upon layer of the low growling of bears. The copper scales on his back lifted in the wind that blew out from their throats. His heart beat hard, and its warmth filled him.

Shibizhee lifted his head and opened his mouth, teeth gleaming in torchlight. He uttered a leonine roar of thanks and heard it echo through the cavern. He rose up on his hind feet; a copper clad lynx rampant, and pawed the air in triumph. His army would be great and would defeat the one who killed his beloved mother. He would at last taste sweet vengeance.

Mishi-Ginebig's voice reached Shibizhee as the serpent hissed a promise to bring his own minions to the battle. Shibizhee held his own breath somewhat but had to take in a whiff of the poisoned sulphurous vapor before he roared gratitude.

Plans for the battle went on for hours. The serpent left first, slithering down into the water, tiny bits of rainbow colored mist rising up as his long body disappeared under the waves. Shibizhee stood on the ledge and then whirled into a glowing yellow orb that circled the massive white bear once, hovered over the river, and then plunged into its depths.

================================

The ball of light came up at Cathead Bay on the path to Annie's cabin. John Mishipsea walked through the birch trees, wildflowers and grasses to her porch steps. A thin haze of smoke rose over the building, and he could smell food cooking as he came to the door. He opened the screen door and stood in the doorway.

"Just made pot roast, John." Her voice came from the kitchen. "Take a load off." She came in, carrying a bowl in both hands, one forefinger curled around a large ladle. He walked in and waited for her to put the bowl on the table.

"You look like the cat that swallowed the canary," she said.

"Canaries are very small, Annie," he said, smiling. "I will swallow larger prey."

CHAPTER 29

Nem-kee walked the road from the Jingtamok grounds to his cabin. Now that things had settled down somewhat, he wanted to be sure he still had a cabin. His legs didn't seem to be working quite as good as usual, and he heard his kneecaps crack with each step. A few clouds had gathered overhead, and just as he made it into his yard, drops of rain left darkened spots on the sleeves of his shirt.

The cabin seemed to be intact. He grabbed the railing and climbed the steps, feeling like he was hauling a heavy weight. He was totally pooped. Cave-ins, earthquakes... what next?

Just as he finished a hot cup of tea, he heard the ruckus outside. Crows. Someone coming? Nem-kee drew back the curtain at the kitchen window. The rain had stopped, but the tops of the trees by the lake tossed in the wind. He got up, opened the screen door, went out on the porch, and watched as the sky darkened and then brightened. A single streak of lightning came down in the distance. There was a low rumble of thunder. The crows were still yakking about something over by the lake.

Nem-kee walked across the clearing behind his cabin. A large horned owl swooped past flying low and then rose to land in the branches of a tall pine. Crow sounds seemed to come from the narrow strip of forest between his property and the dunes, but they stopped as he walked into the shadows under thick pine branches. As he stepped out onto the sand of the high dune overlooking the bay, the sky overhead darkened. He looked up and saw them coming – hundreds of hawks and eagles crying out, raptor voices shrill, filling the air with sound. They came in a wide swath of wings. He grabbed the trunk of a small birch.

On the beach below him, a tall man stood facing the bay, dressed only in a tan loin cloth, holding a long plain wooden bow. A quiver of arrows was slung across his back and a war club dangled at his waist. His hair was black and hung past his shoulders. The man turned and looked up at him.

Nem-kee heard the voice in his head. "I said I would return when the people asked me to come. You called, Nem-kee." How could that be? The man's mouth didn't move, yet his voice was clear. He must be some kind of spirit. Was this Nanabozho? Nem-kee held tightly to the tree and felt his heart pumping in his chest.

The eagles and hawks flew in a wide circle over the place where the man stood. As Nem-kee watched, the man lifted his arm and raised the bow toward the sky. A single shaft of lightning crashed down into the lake. Two more bolts of blinding fire came down from the sky on either side of him. The birds kept circling, not scattering as they should in the face of danger.

Nem-kee called out "Are you Nanabozho?"

The man nodded his head. The voice came again. "I am here to fight for you. My old enemy will be defeated."

For a moment Nem-kee wished he were younger and stronger. He would like to be able to join this great spirit, to fight with him. But he had met that underwater cat spirit in his man form, and knew his concerns about how humans had messed things up. It was too confusing. He felt torn between helping Shibizhee and preventing him from causing more problems.

Having this great spirit being respond to his call was a great honor. No. It was incredible. The handsome muscular man on the beach was walking toward him. A finger of cold fear ran up his spine. A fight? Some massive battle between the two old enemies? Good grief. Someone probably would call up the military. The entire island could be destroyed.

"Be careful," he called out to Nanabozho. "Humans are different now. They have powerful weapons. They could possibly destroy you and your enemy."

This time he saw the man's mouth move and heard his deep voice. "Humans are my friends. I taught them how to survive, gave them fire…"

"They have taken the knowledge you gave them and made powerful guns and bombs. They could destroy the entire world."

The man tipped his head to one side and his smile was bitter. Nem-kee could sense the anger and determination of the powerful spirit. The raptors overhead circled silently, and the wind caused by the downward beat of their wings rippled the surface of the lake. Nanabozho slung his bow over his shoulder and raised his arms, motioning them away. They turned in a cloud of dark and light wings and flew off. Nem-kee watched as they disappeared over the horizon, leaving Cathead Bay silent and still.

Nanabozho turned and walked up the dune. "We must speak together," he said. He kept walking, taking the path to Nem-kee's cabin and the old man meekly followed.

It was a long evening and night as Nem-kee sat at his kitchen table across from the tall man with distinctive Anishinabe features. They spoke of many things, and the weight of guilt that Nem-kee carried grew heavier as the hours wore on. He had brought the spirit back with his entreaties. Whatever happened next, he carried a heavy load of blame.

They drank coffee that Nem-kee brewed in an old fashioned percolator on the gas stove, and ate scones that one of Nem-kee's grand-daughters had brought over.

"You could try communicating with Shibizhee. Maybe work things out," said Nem-kee.

Nanabozho lifted one buttock from the wooden chair and farted loudly. He laughed when Nem-kee visibly flinched.

"He changed himself into a man. I spoke with him," said Nem-kee, thinking of the time he spent with Mishipsea in the sweat lodge. "He got pretty pissed when he saw what the humans have done to things that are his responsibility to maintain. They have done really bad things to the environment, messed up the water...."

Nanabozho laughed and farted again. "You must really like that killer, old man. He is a killer, you know. He killed my brother!" he shouted, pushing back his chair. He stood up and went to the doorway as if to leave. Nem-kee felt the anger and grief as though it was his own.

The shape of Nanabozho was dark against bidossigay - the pale coming light of dawn. Trees and the single cell tower on the island were silhouetted behind him against the sky. He raised his hand, and a bolt of lightning hit the tower. He turned and smiled wickedly. "The humans will not find it easy to call for their weapons."

Nem-kee said nothing. He was exhausted from lack of sleep, and his stomach churned from drinking too much coffee. There was no reasoning with this one.

"So Shibizhee thinks he can defeat me? I will put him back in a hole in the ground. He will never escape. I will tear those shiny copper scales from his back, pull out those horns from his head, and rip him apart. My friends will fly away with all his parts and scatter them to the four directions. Then I will have peace."

Nem-kee sat stunned at the sharp edge of hatred in the voice of the tall handsome spirit. He was too weak to rise as he watched Nanabozho stride back to the table and stand over him. "You asked me to come. You asked me to help you. I have returned." He turned and walked out the door.

Nem-kee got up from the table and watched the lithe muscular figure run across the open clearing and enter the forest. The old stories about Nanabozho came back to him. He was supposed to be amusing by playing tricks and making people laugh. He was supposed to be wise and create good things.

The evening and night had been a disaster. The two opposing forces would come together in battle, and it seemed that nothing could stop them. What would happen to this place if it were the scene of such a horrible thing? There would be nothing left. They would destroy each other and everything around them. He must see Annie. There had to be some way… something they could do.

===========================

Louie gave up on his cell phone and sat in the harbor using the radio in the tribal Natural Resources boat. The Coast Guard was already up to speed on the situation at Cathead Island. He climbed out of the boat to the somewhat wobbly pier and hiked back to the police station. As he came in, he asked his deputies if their cell phones were working.

Sam got his out of a pocket and flipped it open. "Nope."

"I've got some battery left, but no signal," said Lorna. The land line cable must have been cut in the earthquake. I think they laid the cable along it under the rip-rap stones on one side of the causeway. Evidently it went with the causeway.

"Sam, would you mind going back down to the boat and calling the Coast Guard again?" asked Louie. "They might be able to get divers to lay another land line cable."

"You got it, boss." Sam headed out for the marina.

Louie needed check in with Lorette. "Anybody know how to send smoke signals?" Lorna just shook her head.

Louie grabbed his jacket and pushed the door open with the flat of his hand, letting it slam behind him. He got in the police car, started it up, and checked the gas tank. Half empty and no way to get fuel out to the gas station on the island. He turned on the police radio, got nothing but static. However, by scrolling a few minutes, he finally raised an inland state police post. With state cutbacks, so many of them had closed. He must be picking up a satellite or mainland tower.

The commander at the National Guard training center at Camp Grayling assured him that they were working with the Red Cross to send out food and supplies. Louie arranged for a dropoff point at the Tribal Center parking lot and went back into the police station to ask Lorna to round up a couple of trucks for pick up and distribution. She said that several men and women had offered to drive and check on island residents.

"Make sure you keep track, write everything down. We need to know the whereabouts of everyone on the island," said Louie. Lorette had already sent word by runner that people up at the campground that needed it had been provided with shelter by island families, and she had a list of who was staying with whom.

The sound of Sam's ATV taking off for the marina echoed the rumble from Louie's stomach. He needed to get something to eat and drink before he fell over. A couple of people were just going into the restaurant, and he trotted double time across the street. Even a sandwich would help.

The place was in semi-darkness, the only light coming through the large plate glass window. He saw Chip and Tizbet in a booth at one side, and Chip slid over to let Louie in.

"What's with no lights?" he asked.

"Did you ever figure out what happened to that George guy?" Louie asked Tizbet.

She burst out laughing. "He embarrassed himself, took off for home once they let him out of the bar." Tizbet retold the story, glad for something to talk about that wasn't focused on the less amusing things that had been happening.

The waitress brought two plates with cold sandwiches and potato chips and two cans of cola and put them down in front of Chip and Tizbet. "Just give me the same and two more to go," said Louie. He checked his cell phone again. Dead. Crap.

255

"As soon as I'm through here, Dad, I'm going over to see if I can help out at the marina. We're going to need boats." Chip took a big bite out of his sandwich, chewed, and held it out in front of him. "Peanut butter and banana. Yum."

"That's the menu. No refrigeration. Elvis special," said Tizbet, picking up her own sandwich and licking around the edge of the bread. "You did ask for the lunch special, didn't you?"

The waitress brought Louie's meal and he ate without comment. Food was food. He had to get back.

As the door to the restaurant closed behind him, he saw a small crowd gathered around the back of a car next to the police station. Toby was standing by the opened trunk compartment. Louie walked over to see what was going on and heard the chuffing of a small yellow gas powered generator. A cord ran through it up to the trunk into the end of a power strip. Several cords ran from the power strip to cell phones, laptops and I-pads lying in the trunk. A tall teenaged boy pulled out a cord and reached in his pocket. Toby held out his hand, and a five-dollar bill was slapped into it before the boy turned away. Another kid plugged a cord into the empty socket.

"Hey, Louie. Only five bucks a charge. How 'bout it?" Toby shoved the money into his pocket.

Louie just shook his head and kept on going to the police station. There was always someone who took advantage of a bad situation. No law against it. He could see one of the kids already playing a game on his I-Pad.

"You kids should be helping out instead of standing around playing games," said Louie. One of the dark haired tribal kids looked embarrassed and motioned to the boy next to him. The others just looked at Louie defiantly and walked away. Louie shook his head in disgust.

"Get back here!" He herded six of the boys into the station. Runners were needed to carry messages, and it was time to set an old communication system in motion.

"I got you some help, Lorna," he said. "Runners. Put them to work. Let Lorette know what's going on." He dropped the bag of food on Lorna's desk. "For you and Sam."

Louie heard Sam coming back and went outside. Thunder sounded, and a shaft of lightning came down in the bay, followed by two more simultaneous branches of silver. A light wind pulled at his shirt. The sky darkened, and a few drops of rain hit the ground and made dark spots on his sleeves.

Sam followed Louie into the police station. "There are guys down there getting their boats ready to go for supplies, take anyone over to the mainland that needs to go. Setting up a shuttle service."

"Write it down, send one of these kids up to the campground," said Louie. "Have another one inform Lorette. And I brought you some lunch."

"We've gotta get someone out there to check on the elders. The food guys are just too slow." He reached in the bag and drew out a sandwich. "What? PB and monkey food?"

"I like it. Elvis was my mom's dreamboat." Lorna opened her can of soda. "Got a note from Lorette out at the Tribal Center. She says if you are in contact with the Red Cross, ask for blankets and pillows. And insulin." She handed him several sheets of paper with the tribal logo at the top. Lorette's messages.

Louie ran his finger down the list of campers, recognizing several names. Retirees up from the cities downstate. Quite a few were elders. With diabetes high in the tribal population, there would be a need for insulin, for sure. "Who's Lorette's pony express guy?"

"Beanie on a bike," said Sam. "Lorette's been putting kids to work, too."

One of the boys Louie brought into the station snorted: "Beanie-on-a-bike. New name for you." Beanie punched him on the arm. The kids all laughed.

257

"You guys cut it out," admonished Lorna in her mom voice. "We've got to make sure the elders are taken care of. Get over here. I've got things for you to do."

Sam balled up the paper from his sandwich, aimed it at a wastebasket, and missed. Lorna sighed, rolled over in her office chair, picked it up, and pitched another shot that made it in.

"She needs the exercise," said Sam, making it out the door before she pitched another ball of paper at him. Louie followed him back outside. He got back on his ATV and started it up. "I'm going back to the marina."

It was now raining, and didn't look like it would let up soon. He went back into the station. "There are some ponchos in the locker. See that the runners wear them."

Lorna got up and headed for the back room. "Got it." She would hold down the fort.

Louie went back out to the tribal police car and started it up, letting the engine charge the battery, not bothering to turn on the wipers. The radio worked, and he called in the message for blankets and insulin.

The next half hour he spent on the radio with the Army Corps of Engineers in Detroit, working on plans to have a temporary pontoon bridge installed between Cathead Island and the mainland. With the economy the way it was, what seemed temporary might have to hold up for a while. They asked for information and promised that someone would be coming out within the next few days to assess the situation.

There really wasn't much he could do now but coordinate everything. Not much chance of any crime happening, unless you considered that underlying chill of fear that kept Louie's nerves on edge. The whole thing began with Mishipsea… Shibizhee… and now others…

It was one thing to make do and joke about Elvis sandwiches. Electricity and phones would be restored. They would get the sinkhole at Basil's fenced off. A pontoon bridge would be built. People would be fed. These were things that

258

could be handled. Everyone pitched in when there was an emergency.

But how would people – the tribe – Louie – handle a situation where angry spirits were causing the whole thing? And what if it got any worse?

=======================

Nem-kee only woke up once in the night to use the bathroom. Might as well check on the weather, so he stepped out on the porch. The floor boards were wet and water dripped from the eaves into the bushes. He stuck out a hand to see if it was still raining and caught a fine mist in his wrinkled palm. Still dark out, and he was still pooped. He went back to bed.

Someone was knocking on his door. He got up and pulled on some jeans and a t-shirt.

Annie's car was in his driveway and she stood on the porch in a wet bright yellow raincoat. "How ya doin'?"

"Don't know yet. Need coffee. How's by you?"

"I've had that Mishipsea guy staying with me. He got up early and took off. Madder than a hornet. Says he's got help lined up, gonna take on Nanabozho." Her voice was tight and higher than usual.

"Watch it, gal. I think we got ourselves into a kettle of crap here. Should have left good enough alone."

"I feel like I've been run over by a ten ton truck. Wound up pretty tight," she said.

"Too tense, huh?" Nem-kee kept the phone by his ear, hitched up his jeans, and aimed himself toward the percolator.

"Too tents – a tipi and a wigwam." She tossed out the old joke and laughed. "I'm a mess."

"Makes two of us." He got coffee started on the old gas stove.

"I can see Mishipsea's point. People have really messed things up, the way he sees it."

"True enough." She kept talking about the environment and he kept uh-huh-ing. She needed to get it off her chest. Once she got started about invasive species, she just had to keep talking until she ran down.

The percolator was burping now, fresh coffee smell seeping out from the old aluminum lid. He got two large mugs out of the cupboard.

"Well, I figure that there's gonna be a big whoop-dee-doo between Shibizhee and Nanabozho, and it's gonna happen pretty soon. I just got a feeling, Annie."

She said: "Maybe something would calm them down. Get things back to what passes for normal around here."

"We need to get some help. Can't do this alone." He poured the coffee.

"I'm thinking the same thing. Been contacting the women who might help."

He didn't ask who she was calling. Probably women of her Bear clan, others that were more traditional-minded. The women got together by themselves once a month and had their own private ceremony. Strong women. Not a bad idea.

Not that many people really knew what was going on with the spirit beings. What men could he recruit that would understand? He started making a mental list. There were Thunder clan men on the island, and some that had come up from downstate.

His mind kicked in finally, and they headed out to recruit reinforcements.

The rain had stopped, and the sky cleared over the bay, with only a few small white clouds off to the west. Shibizhee surfaced near the place where Whitefish Island had been and sent out his challenge. He knew Nanabozho would get his message. Time for a faceoff. Time to show that old braggart what he was up against.

He dove to the place where he loved to swim, under the surface but above the old shipwrecks and debris that humans had dumped in his beloved lake. Green tendrils of plant life brushed against him in the middle place, and he passed schools of fish that gently swung away. A thought ran through his mind as he stroked, pulling on the water with copper paws. There should be some middle place like this where there was no conflict. Where life could be serene again as it was in the past.

No. He shook off the thought, baring his teeth at giving into weakness. It was time to confront his enemy. To bring the underworld forces here and have it out. Call them together on a battleground. He swam steadily toward the western end of Cathead Island.

===========================

After making his rounds recruiting help, Nem-kee drove back to his house. He heated up a cup of coffee in the microwave and took it out to the porch. His rocker was still damp, but he sat down anyway and blew across the cup to cool it. He was disappointed. Not all of the men would help out. Just some of them. It had taken some time to explain what was going on, and what he wanted to do.

That conversation with Bobby was the worst. Most of them had just been noncommittal if they wouldn't help. Not Bobby. Pitched a hissy.

===========================

"What th' hell, Nem-kee. I been puttin' say-ma in the lake for the last forty years for that big cat."

"I know, tobacco gifts every time you go fishing. I understand." Nem-kee tried to calm Bobby, but his nephew tended to get loud.

"I been fishin' that lake and puttin' up with all the fed shit and all the DNR shit, and all the tribal tree-hugger shit..." Nem-kee knew that tribal fishermen had gone through a lot over the years, and just trying to make a living for their families was more than a challenge. Most of them lived on food stamps.

"I just thought we could have some kind of ceremony here, sort of try to calm things down here…"

"That big cat has been good to me, Nem-kee. Times I thought I wouldn't make it. He came through for me. I sure as hell ain't goin' against him now."

===========================

Nem-kee got himself something to eat and walked once around his yard to blow off steam, ignoring his cracking knees.

Well, he did what he could. So far, it looked like about twenty-five would show up. Chip offered to help build a fire. They would meet here, in Nem-kee's back yard. He started taking dried wood and kindling out of his woodshed, walked it over to the fire pit and covered it with a plastic tarp. Might rain.

The big round grandfather stones he used in the sweat lodge were off to one side of the fire pit and he left them for Chip to move. Pretty heavy business now, lugging rocks around. He dug in his pants pocket for the little soft suede bag of cut tobacco and sprinkled some on the grandfathers, speaking to them in Anishinabemowin. All the help he could get.

"We gotta at least make an effort here," he said to the grandfathers. Maybe they could convince those spirit guys to set aside their differences. Make them see that what they were doing could have terrible consequences. You get the underworld spirits and the earth and sky spirits at each other, and all hell would break loose. Supposed to be in balance, help each other out.

Annie drove back into his driveway, got out of the car. She came out to where Nem-kee was standing by the fire pit.

"You have any luck?"

"Some. Guys are comin' over later. Chip said he'd help out."

"I got some of the women coming. But even if they are Bear clan, not all of them wanted to go along with it. They figure if I'm siding in with Shibizhee, they have more ties with the other side. Even though water and women are part of each other..."

"Same here. You should have heard Bobby rakin' me over the coals. He's been giving say-ma to Shibizhee for good fishin'..."

"I don't see this as exactly taking sides. We just need to get through to them that we can't take any more. They are just thinking of themselves," she said.

"Maybe we ought to do some planning." Nem-kee had a thought about lunch and wondered if Annie had the same idea. He could maybe drop a hint. "I'm getting a bit peckish like them Englishers say."

Annie laughed. "I know about how you get peckish, old man. Let's see what you've got around here for chow. Sit tight."

Nem-kee watched Annie bustle around his small kitchen pulling cans and boxes out of the cupboard. Nice. Sometimes he missed his wife. His son. Both gone. This was one of those times.

============================

"That wasn't half bad. I won't ask what..." said Nem-kee.

"Just a little road kill and pasta. Nothin' special." Annie's eyes sparkled. "Gotta do somethin' with dead skunk."

"Yeah, right." The impromptu goulash had really hit the spot.

They took fresh cups of tea out to the porch and sat in the wooden rockers that Nem-kee had made years before. He could hear his knees crack in time with the chair's squeaking. His tea sloshed a bit, but he made it to his mouth without dumping it down his front. Tea, coffee, living on caffeine. Too much going on. Need to cut back.

"Wish things would get back to normal." said Annie. "It's been makin' me so darned antsey. One thing after another, and just when you think it's settling down, something else happens." She shuddered a little, her shoulders jerking, put her tea cup on the porch railing.

"Your idea for the women makes good sense. I've got some guys coming over later." Nem-kee got to his feet and looked down at her. "Ever try predicting stuff?" He bit his lower lip and took a deep breath. "With stones? Try to see how this will all turn out?" He needed to give her something else to get her mind around.

"I heard about it," she said.

He led the way out to the field behind his cabin. Annie followed. "What are you up to?"

"Telling the future with stones. My grandpa showed me how."

He moved faster than she expected considering his age, and she was huffing a bit as she made her own way through the trees down to the beach. At the bottom of the dune, they crossed the wide flotsam of driftwood and dried seaweed that held bits of shell and dead fish.

The sand beyond had been washed clean by waves. At the water's edge, a rim of water-worn rocks were dried by wind and then wet again as wave after wave splashed over them. Under the water, more small pebbles and rocks lay in the pale sand. Nem-kee leaned down and picked up a handful.

"We'll need quite a few, so fill your pockets," he said. Once they had what he considered enough, he trudged through the sand to a large driftwood log.

"Here, just spread them out in a circle." He emptied his pockets and started a circle of small pebbles. She filled in the circle with the rocks she had gathered. "Now, just have a seat."

264

Nem-kee spoke the words his grandfather had taught him and asked Annie to repeat them. "You have to do it ten times," he said.

"Right." He could hear the skepticism in her voice. Probably she thought he'd be asking her to pee on a dishcloth and bury it at a crossroads at midnight, or some such nonsense. Well, at least it would keep her from being so blasted negative. They needed to keep up their courage.

He kept repeating the chant, Annie echoing. As he finished the last repetition, a large white raven flew over their heads and landed at the far end of the log. It tipped its head back and forth and then just sat there staring out at the lake. Nem-kee didn't move. More mischief? White – the sign of power. A spy? Nem-kee felt a chill run up his back and the back of his neck. Annie was looking the other way. No point in scaring her. He didn't say anything about the white raven.

"Look!" Annie pointed at the circle of stones. They were vibrating, each one tossing up bits of sand around it. Nem-kee watched as the stones lifted in the air and began spinning a few inches off the ground. He never saw this with his grandfather. He expected some kind of message, some prediction like he had asked for. Not this. The raven. Maybe the white raven was doing it.

They stood up as the whirling stones lifted higher in the air, now just in front of them, and then moved out away toward the water. What had been dull gray and white stones turned into blue, pink and purple colored streaks of light, a circle of color lifting higher. They separated into tiny bits of fragile, gossamer wings, moving up and down rapidly, rising into a wide circle of small butterflies. A light wind blew in from the lake and caught them. They rose up in a cloud that hovered and then blew out over the lake.

Nem-kee and Annie sat back down on the big, gray driftwood log.

"Well. That was interesting," said Annie.

265

"Yup." Nem-kee had no idea what had happened. It sure wasn't a prediction. Or was it? Did he just think he had any control over anything that the spirits decided to do? If that was the message, he got it. Humans probably didn't stand a chance at changing anything if the spirits got it in their head to do something.

"Well, we might as well get ready anyhow," he said.

"Won't hurt. Might help," said Annie. She didn't sound very confident.

===============================

The white raven watched as they walked back down the path to Nem-kee's cabin. It rose on strong black wings and circled the beach. Its cawing was strident and then changed to the echoing tones of Nanabozho's laughter.

CHAPTER 30

Annie and Tizbet led the way down the path beside Cathead Creek on the western end of the island, followed by Lorette and Angeline. They wore long skirts and ribboned tunics that came to their knees. Annie carried her small hand drum and a short soft, suede-tipped drumstick. A braided leather string fastened to her medicine bag trailed out of a side pocket. Lorette carried two colorful wool Pendleton blankets in her arms, and Angeline wore a backpack with things they would need for the ceremony.

A few fishermen had been there earlier in the spring for smelt and salmon runs. They all stopped each time Tizbet picked up a bottle or can left beside the path, grunting in disgust as she plopped another can into her bag. They came out of the shaded creek bed onto a wide sandy opening devoid of plant life. Here, the creek ran off in different directions through shallow winding troughs to the big lake. Raised ledges on either side of the creek were covered in beach grasses moving in the wind. Annie's eyes picked out familiar lacy wormwood and winding wreaths of beach peas as she led the way to a shallow rock-lined fire pit.

"Just dump your stuff here. Tiz, see if you can get a fire started. There's some birchbark in your mom's backpack. I'm gonna go get me some peas." Annie put her drum and drumstick down, pulled a couple of wadded up plastic bags from her other pocket, and climbed the slight rise. Might as well get some wormwood too, while she was at it. Take some home. She gifted the plants with tobacco and filled two bags in the time it took for Tizbet to start a fire, while Lorette and Angeline roamed the beach area for driftwood.

Voices from farther up the creek carried down to the women on the beach. Bear Clan women, most of them relatives, came with their hand drums and blankets.

"Ah-nee nee-zhee-kwayak!" The white-haired woman in the front of the line called out a hello to women friends. Annie responded in the language and half slid down the embankment to the beach. Tiz waved a greeting and began spreading out the blankets for places to sit.

Annie counted nineteen women in all. She explained what was needed, women's strength to ask for peace between the strong forces that threatened their island and perhaps the entire area. A battle between the underworld, earth and sky forces could have enormous repercussions not only here at Cathead Bay, but on a world-wide scale.

"The last thing we need right now is another earthquake," said Lorette. "I'm convinced that it wasn't some freak of nature."

"Too much has been going on since the cave-in at the quarry," said a young woman with long brown braids. Annie knew that her husband had lost his job and now worked for half as much money doing custodial work at the Health Center.

"That started it, and I've heard stories about the Great Lynx," said another woman. "They say he got out, and he caused a lot of stuff. And that he's royally pissed at people."

"Killed Basil, is what some say."

"My husband says he's a good spirit, helps out the fishermen."

"Not what I heard. He eats children and white dogs."

"I heard that he helped out Jerry Higgins. Cured him."

Annie put up her hand to stop the opinions that were coming fast and furious. It took her the next half hour to explain the situation clearly. Finally there were no more questions. They just sat staring at her, and she felt as though she were being impaled with twenty-two sets of eyes. Thank goodness there wasn't even a word for interrupt in the language. If this had been a bunch of white women, she'd be here 'til next week.

"Well. That's it." She waited.

Two women got up from the blankets and stood at one side. The older one spoke. "You're just siding in with that guy who says he's really Shibizhee. I've always been told to watch out for that sort of thing. My family is Bear Clan, and maybe that means I'm supposed to help him out. But my husband is Thunder clan, and so are my kids. I'm leaving." She walked away back up the creek path, the younger woman trotting along behind.

"Anyone else?" Annie waited. No one. "Well, guess we'll just get the show on the road here. How many drums?" Fourteen. She stood up and tossed a piece of driftwood on the fire. "Here's how it goes."

Annie led with her clear voice, singing each phrase and then waiting while the others echoed it. Her steady beat on the small drum was picked up by the others who kept time with her on their drums. The heartbeat of sound lifted above the women seated on blankets around the fire. Repeated over and over, with each phrase a slight change in melody or words, the sound rose above the beach as the sun gradually slid into the west where lake met sky. Thin layers of cloud turned yellow and orange, then pink and purple as the lake ate the sun. A cool breeze lifted the hair of the singing women and ran chill fingers down their necks. Their cross-legged bodies warmed the wool blankets but the sand around them lost its heat.

A light fog began rising over the waters of the creek tumbling into deeper water. Moisture settled on their hands and faces as they chanted. Annie felt her shirt growing damp and clammy, and she twitched a little with the chill, but kept drumming and singing.

Annie brought that part of the ceremony to an end. She sat for a moment, resting, and then got up.

"Time to take a break." Angeline took bottles of iced sweet tea out of the backpack and passed them out. Plastic baggies with the sacred plants were opened and their contents poured into four wooden bowls near the fire pit. Sweet grass. Cedar. Tobacco. Sage.

Some of the women walked down to the lake and talked quietly among themselves. Others went up the embankment and gave tobacco to the wormwood plants before taking feathery leaves and rubbing them together, breathing in the pungent healing scent. They came back to the fire and made gifts to the spirits by dropping small bits of sacred plants in the flames. Annie gathered them into a circle, shoulders and hips nearly touching, hands clasped together. The drums lay silent on the blankets behind them.

Annie backed away, and the others followed. Then she took a step forward again and so did the other women. Back and forth, and a new song began. Old words. Old melody. The ancient five-tone pentatonic notes that would reach the ears of the spirits and call them. Old words that asked for pity on humans. Ancient Anishinabe words that begged for mercy from raging spirits threatening chaos. Old songs sung by strong Anishinabe Bear Clan women facing dangers and retribution by those same spirits. The women circled and walked forward and back in a dance passed down through generations of women at this same place. They sang in the words and sounds of their ancestors.

The spirits responded. Annie caught the movement out of the corners of her eyes but didn't turn. She kept up the dance and repeated the words in the song, sensing the coming of others just behind her. Across the fire, behind the women on the other side of the flames, she saw them.

Rising and falling like the Northern Lights, a second circle danced just behind the women, white pillars of light flashing up from the ground into the air fifty to a hundred feet high, then down again to just the height of the women themselves.

Annie continued dancing, keeping hold of Tizbet's hand on one side and Lorette's on the other. The Bear Clan women

270

rocked back and forth, their eyes on the circle of dancing lights surrounding them. The face of her cousin on the other side of the fire showed sudden surprise, mouth half open in awe, as she looked behind Annie. "Nokomiss! Grandmother!" she said. The eyes of the woman next to her widened, and a sound escaped her lips "N'koh sheh! My mother!" No longer dancing lights without form, the spirits surrounding them took shape, moving with them, keeping the same rhythm.

Ancient ancestors and those who had more recently walked on enclosed them, clothed in fine regalia, faces kindly with expressions of deep love. Yet Annie could see through the forms to the woods beyond. The sacred fire flamed up, making bright reflections on the beads and shiny surfaces of the necklaces and earrings of Bear Clan and spirit women alike. Annie felt as though she were wrapped in a soft blanket of encompassing love, her own spirit woven into the multitude of spirits around her.

Behind the dancing figures, fog rose over the creek, lifting in swirling white streaks hundreds of feet in the air. Annie raised her head to see this new thing and her body froze in place. When she stopped moving, so did the others. As the fog brightened, the outer circle of spirit women began to fade, losing the clear delineation of their features. The beloved ancestors became wisps of translucent color, and then were gone.

Annie let go of Tizbet and Lorette's hands. The Bear Clan women turned toward the creek and saw whirling white fog separate into dozens of spinning columns taking human shapes.

The Water Spirits had heard the songs. Annie caught her breath sharply and reached out to them in welcome. The arms of the women around her were raised in the same gesture, held out at waist height, palms up. In response, the pillars of fog became the more solid shapes of mermen and merwomen, pale blue skin and darker turquoise hair that swirled around their heads. The scales over their bodies, arms and legs were in varying hues of blues and greens. Their eyes were deep purple in handsome and

271

lovely faces and their hands reached out to the women in gentle movements.

Voices of the water spirits came into Annie's mind, humming that echoed the chanting songs she and the women had sung. They were like vibrations in her head, but she could hear the words. Promises. Assurances. Soothing like the lullabies sung to crying babies. Gentle like the sounds of the waves coming in from the great lake behind them. Lilting like the sounds of children laughing.

As quickly as they came, they whirled back into white transparent shafts of light and melted down into the waters of the creek. The women stood by the dying fire and looked at each other. No one spoke. Each of them had heard the promises to help bring peace. Annie reached out to Lorette, a moment's embrace. Tizbet and her mother did the same as did others. Then they separated, each cherishing her own thoughts, warmed by the promises of the spirits to help bring about peace.

No one spoke as blankets were shaken out and folded, the fire extinguished with sand. The women walked single file back up the path beside the creek.

===========================

Nem-kee and Chip waited on the porch until the sun dropped behind the trees. The fire pit was ready. Chip lit the dried bark and twigs as the first car pulled into the driveway and Nem-kee waved it over onto the grass to make room for the others. In a short time, twenty-two other Thunder Clan men had arrived and made their way back to the field behind the house. Louie carried a hand drum and padded drumstick. Abalone shells with sacred plants were laid out and each man put some in the flames, as fragrance rose in curling white smoke.

Leading the ceremony, Nem-kee began singing. The sound of Louie's drum and their voices lifted skyward with the smoke. As one song ended, another began. Calling for the spirits. Honoring Nanabozho and asking his protection for the people and the precious earth around them. They stood a little apart from each other, looking into the fire or up into the darkening sky. The songs ended and Nem-kee spoke in the language. They responded at the end in a chorus of deep 'Ahau's.' He kept his body straight and an occasional eye on the grandfather stones around the fire just in case they decided to participate, but they lay still.

When their requests were completed and pleas given, Nem-kee leaned over and picked up a strange object fastened to a long thin rope that lay near the fire. It had a shape few of the other men had seen, a foot long thin oval slat of wood, pointed at both ends. The rope was fastened to a hole in its center.

"What's that?" asked Chip. The other men looked relieved that he had spoken their unasked question.

"Bull-roarer," said Nem-kee. "Got it from a Maori guy at the Indigenous Conference. Figured it might come in handy. Gonna call old Nanabozho with it."

"How does it work?" asked Chip. He saw suppressed amusement on the faces of a couple of the men.

"Whirl it around your head, just keep it going. You'll hear it." Nem-kee handed it to Chip, and showed how to wrap one end of the rope around his hand and held the thin rhomboid shaped slat on his other palm. "Takes some strength, needs somebody younger than me to do it."

"Over there," Nem-kee pointed to a place away from the group. As instructed, Chip tossed out the object and started whirling it out around his body, letting out the rope a little at a time until the full length was reached. The men stood by the fire, watching.

The sound began, higher at first as Chip rapidly spun it faster and then deepening as it slowed until it was a throbbing hum that filled the air with a deep growl. Chip kept it going, the pulsating sound changing with the angle and velocity of its spin. He spun it slower and its low voice was like that of thunder.

Nem-kee hoped Chip's arm would hold up long enough for them to get some kind of response.

Nem-kee felt the pulsing of the bull roarer throb within him, a low hum he felt inside his chest. Would the spirit being come, or send a message?

Overhead, the sky darkened with a large cloud that came in from the west. A real echo of thunder reverberated over the lake, and a strong wind flattened the grasses near the fire pit. Chip kept whirling the bull roarer, and its pulsing sound joined with the thunder. The dual sounds were so alike that Nem-kee couldn't tell them apart. Yes. Nanabozho heard and was responding.

One sharp flash of light, an ear-splitting crash, and a thin spear of lightning came down into the fire pit, blinding the men for a moment with its brilliance. They backed away, stumbling over the uneven ground, a few falling to their knees or sides. Chip's hand dropped to his side and the bull roarer on its long rope fell to the ground. Silence. Nem-kee stood erect, assured that when the time was right, the Sky Forces would help. Gradually, the men composed themselves.

Nem-kee's eyes focused again. He looked up. A sky full of stars, no cloud. A full moon rising. No wind. The men came back to the fire pit, murmuring among themselves.

"Powerful stuff, Nem-kee," said Louie.

"Yep. I think that did it."

Chip wrapped the rope around the bull roarer, brought it to Nem-kee and handed it over without comment. Louie picked up his drum and stuck the drumstick in his back pocket. A sharp sound from above made them look up, heads back, eyes probing the blackness.

Eagles flew in over the field from the direction of the lake, a dozen or more, shrieking a warning. They circled the men once, lifted up again, flew back out over the lake and were gone.

Nem-kee stood with his back to the dying fire and spoke of what he would soon ask the ones present. The men of the Thunder Clan listened and gave quiet assent. Each one came and shook his hand or embraced him and then went to their cars and trucks. Chip and Louie were the last.

"I need to get with you and Annie for a little bit, Chip," said Nem-kee. "Bring Tizbet." He got a small tobacco tie out of his pocket and gave it to Chip. Asking a favor. Proper way to ask.

"Sure. Where?"

"Gotta pay Annie back for cookin' for me; how about the restaurant? Are they serving?"

Chip thought for a minute. "I think so. They got some propane and a generator. You need a ride?"

"Nope, I'll ride with Annie." Nem-kee already had his cell phone out. He watched the light come on in the police car as Louie got in the driver's side. Once the tail lights were two red spots down the road, he called her.

"Annie? How's about gettin' somethin' to eat? My treat. You drive."

===============================

"I have no idea what he wants, Tiz." Chip backed out of the Mueller's driveway. Tizbet fastened her seatbelt and leaned back, trying to clear her head.

"Why us?" she asked.

"No clue. He and Annie will meet us at the restaurant. You hungry?"

"Sure. It's been a long day." She kept thinking about the whirling images of the water spirits and what she believed was the kindly face of her grandmother.

They talked about the warnings Nem-kee and Annie had made about some upcoming altercation between powerful spirits. Although Chip believed completely in what he had been

275

told and what he had seen, Tizbet was still somewhat skeptical that anything would actually happen. She didn't want to turn him off with her doubts, so she kept them to herself.

Nem-kee and Annie were already sitting in a booth. There were a few other people eating and talking. They appeared to be tourists stuck on the island until they could get away. One of the big ferry companies at Mackinaw had volunteered to send a boat without charge but it wouldn't arrive until tomorrow.

"Hey, did you hear? Some guys came over from the mainland and fixed the cell tower," said Chip. The electricity is supposed to be back on soon, too. One of the campers works for an electric company downstate, climbed up and repaired the transformer."

"They managed to put together some stew and dumplings here." said Annie.

Tizbet slid in next to Annie, and Chip sat down by Nem-kee.

"It ain't that bad, actually. Kinda worked up an appetite," said Nem-kee.

Tizbet and Chip ordered and the food came quickly. Big white fluffy dumplings sat on a thick stew with meat, potato, carrots and onions in a brown gravy. They all made small talk until they finished.

Nem-kee reached in his back pocket and pulled out a small address book. Annie opened her purse and removed one that was similar. "Phone numbers," he said. "Need to get them in this darned contraption. Don't know how." He held his cell phone out and laid it on the table next to the book.

"Neither do I," said Annie. She put her book and phone on the table next to the other. She handed Tizbet a tobacco tie. "Figured you kids would be able to do it faster. We don't have a lot of time to be fighting with phones."

For the next hour, Chip programmed the Thunder Clan men's phone numbers into Nem-kee's phone and Tizbet programmed the Bear Clan women's numbers into Annie's. Several cups of coffee and tea later, and they were done. Both of the elders now knew how to just push 'All' and they could round up the people they needed instantly.

Tizbet thought about the time she went to Annie's and found her with a blender on the kitchen counter filled with an herbal concoction. Annie had told her that the medicine was supposed to be stirred on the stove for the duration of the time it took to sing a particular healing song, but they had to be at a tribal meeting in a half hour.

She had a small tape recorder on the counter next to the blender, with a tape already in it. While Tizbet watched, Annie pushed a button on the blender with one hand and at the same time pushed a button on the recorder with her other hand. The whirring of the blender and the fast-forwarded chirping song on the recorder took about two minutes.

Tizbet would never forget the sound of their hooting belly laughs. Annie had said "For gosh sakes, Tiz, don't tell!" She never told. And now this. Technology and ancient wisdom. Incredible.

CHAPTER 31

Chip stood in the shower with water as hot as he could stand it, everything around him seen through white steam. It wasn't a sweat lodge, but it would do. He oriented himself to the four directions and softly sang the prayers, turning each time. East for renewal - springtime....South for planting - summer....West for the harvest - autumn....North for resting - winter... The song Nem-kee had taught him was part of his morning ritual with himself in the center. He breathed deeply, feeling himself go to that place of balance that came with the end of the song. This would be the day. He was ready. Nem-kee was waiting for him.

===================================

Tizbet drove the small ATV on the dirt road that ended at Annie's place. Her mother sat beside her, looking straight ahead. Over morning coffee they had shared their dreams. Foreboding. Today it would happen. A full picnic basket of food bounced on the back seat with every bump. Their hand drums were wrapped in a tan Pendleton blanket with broad red and black stripes that lay on the floor of the vehicle behind them. Annie had called everyone. They would come.

===================================

Shibizhee swam up out of the tunnel into Cathead Bay. Ganoosow-Makwa followed in his wake, huge white paws stroking out, then back toward the smaller white bears behind him. They emerged from the deep water of the lake and floated on the surface. Long pale rays of light from the rising sun reflected off the shining copper of Shibizhee's scales and the gleaming silver neck bands of the bears. Mishi-Ginebig's massive horned head lifted, his iridescent scales throwing tiny rainbows of color around him.

Shibizhee heard the call of a single loon that had seen them. It was echoed across the bay by others. He saw two cranes lift their long bodies from a shallow inlet and fly up over the trees where eagles nested. Shibizhee uttered a low growl and the heads of his army all disappeared under placid lake water.

The place for the battle had been chosen, and Shibizhee led the others underwater to the western end of Cathead Island. They emerged onto the deserted beach where the creek brought waters from inland springs into the lake. The fire from the women's ceremony was a gray pile of ashes.

Ganoosow-Makwa lumbered up the sand and onto the ledge of beach grass. He lay flat, covering a large area with his enormous body. His entourage of smaller white bears climbed up to surround him. Some rolled over onto their backs, writhing in pleasure, paws in the air. Shibizhee understood that after living for so long in the cold stone of their cavern, the small sounds he heard were comments on the wonder of sun and sand.

Mishi-Ginebig slid out of the water onto the beach, his iridescent scales and bejeweled head resplendent in sunlight. His long red tongue flicked out tasting pine-scented air. The end of his tail curled and unfurled as Shibizhee watched him find a warm place on the pale sand beneath the grassy rise where the bears reclined.

Shibizhee rested on the other side of the creek on a bed of wormwood, brushing the wispy leaves with the sides of his head, crushing them and releasing their intoxicating smell. He drew in a deep lungful and felt a sweet lightness as though he were floating. It was not time to rest, however. He rose to all fours and jumped down into the creek. He walked inland under an arch of trees. Striding up the creek, waters splashed as he entered deeper water away from his resting companions. The crayfish had been called and were waiting.

After a few moments he returned, looping in long strides down the flowing water with a mass of skittering gray crayfish behind him, legs and claws probing the pebbles on the creek bed as they shoved forward, climbing over each other in their haste. They clattered and clanked their way to the beach and surrounded Shibizhee on the sand.

Ganoosow-Makwa stood up and the mass of smaller white bears joined him. Mishi-Ginebig slid around and lifted his head toward Shibizhee, their massive copper scaled leader.

Shibizhee could see all of them watching and felt a tinge of excitement at what he was going to surprise them with next. He rose on his back legs and pawed the air in his rampant lion pose that was rather noble, if he thought so himself. He let out an appropriate roar and waved his paws over the dozens of small gray crayfish.

First their tiny gray claws broadened and thickened, and then their bodies and legs, growing larger and larger with each swipe of his paws. He dropped to his feet and shook his head back and forth, white horns glistening. The crayfish grew larger, swelling to ten times their original size, each one now six feet across. He roared again, and their dull color changed to a bright reddish orange. Their shiny black eye beads on short stalks turned back and forth as they looked at each other. They spread out across the sand, waving their claws above their bodies, digging their feet into the sand and circled Shibizhee in a parade of loud clattering dry chatter.

Ganoosow-Makwa and Mishi-Ginebig moved their heads slowly up and down in approval, and Shibizhee congratulated himself.

A low rumble of thunder sounded in the distance. The sky was clear, but when Shibizhee turned, he saw the beginning of dark clouds coming from the east. Not the usual direction for clouds. A light wind lifted the grasses and made new leaves tremble on the trees. The spikes on his back rose and his copper scaled tail whipped angrily. He roared back at the challenge, yellow-green eyes wide and sharp teeth and claws ready. It would be a final battle and he would destroy the hated one.

===

Nanabozho stood on the highest dune above the beach where just days before there was a forty-niner with young people singing and drumming. He held out his arms, his hands palms down, making the sand before him lift and fall in waves that rolled large pieces of driftwood about like dice. When he turned his hands over and raised them, the beach wood flew up into the air, and as he waved his hands in a sweeping gesture, the wood swung around. With one downward slash of one hand the spinning gray chunks of dry wood fell to the beach.

Nanabozho smiled to himself and brought his hands to his face, cupping them about his mouth. The sound he made was like the hollow trumpeting of the conch shell used by humans of the earth. He called the Sky spirits, the Thunderers, the Grandfathers, the Winds, and the Thunderbirds.

At his back, to the East, he felt the wind coming, lifting the bottom of his tunic up against his back, flattening out the leggings around his thighs and calves. He turned to greet the cool East Wind and his breath joined with it; as he exhaled, beams of golden light poured from his mouth. From the South, more wind came and raised the fringes on his sleeves and leggings. He faced that direction, breathed in its warmth and blew it out again in along green tendril that dropped to the ground sprouting tiny pale green leaves. A crisp wind from the west with the sharp smell of autumn leaf fires brushed his face and hands; he drew in its heat and exhaled a long plume of white smoke. From the North the sharp chill of wind-driven sleet encased him in a thin coating of ice that melted with the heat from his body; he sucked in the cold air and blew it out again in a cloud of snowflakes, each a unique bit of lace that floated down to melt into the sand.

Nanabozho called again, and the sound echoed across the bay to the opposite shore. From the West came a broad dark cloud. Beneath it, the sound of wings and cries of thousands of raptors, hawks and eagles preceded the mass of a second dark cloud of wings that rose and fell like a massive tsunami in the sky. The earth below them lay in shadow as they passed overhead, wings beating in synchrony, making even the tops of trees bend before them. They kept coming and the sky filled with the sounds of their voices, screeching a Valkyrie death cry to his enemies. His face broke into a wide smile and his amber eyes glistened with tears of joy. He ran down the dune to the beach below and raised his arms up in greeting to his beloved fellow warriors.

Behind him to the East, the low rumble of the Thunderers joined with the raptor's calls and small sharp shafts of lightning flickered in the fast approaching dark cloud. He turned to greet them. Under the larger birds, some of the younger Thunderbirds moved slowly and majestically as they came toward him. They tipped their wings slightly up and then slightly down in greeting. Their eyes flashed with sharp silver bursts of light. Nanabozho's heart lifted and he felt as though he were flying with them.

With his feet apart, standing firmly on the Earth he had helped to shape, on the place the humans called Turtle Island, Nanabozho gave thanks to those he had called to battle. They would conquer the hated one and all his minions.

===
=====

Chip and Nem-kee stood on the high dune overlooking Cathead Bay. They had heard the long hollow sound of Nanabozho's call coming from the South as they walked across the field behind them. Chip felt the hair on the back of his neck rise and tried to keep Nem-kee back in the shelter of the birches, but the old man insisted on going out in the open.

A wide dark rain cloud moved swiftly through the sky overhead, and threw a shadow over Cathead Island and the bay. Sky Forces responding to Nanabozho? Or to the people? Chip thought it looked like the thick dark cloud that carried thunderbirds when they attacked. Wind from the East pushed through the trees behind them and pressed their jackets and trousers against their bodies. Each time a short burst of thunder crashed, the sky brightened for an instant with the lightning that followed.

Chip pointed at the oncoming cloud from the West, thousands of birds flying under the higher cloud, over the mainland across the bay. "Are those eagles? They're huge!"

"Looks like it. I can make out some hawks. Nanabozho's called them," said Nem-kee. He sat down in the sand, cross-legged. Chip squatted, thinking he would make a smaller target in case the birds were interested in human prey. His knees started to give out and he eased himself down next to his great-uncle.

==

The raptors swerved to the South, a thick mass of wings that seemed to move in synchrony. Chip and Nem-kee leaned back, hands in the sand supporting them as they watched. The higher cloud hovered, not moving, casting its shadow over roiling waters in the bay. Chip felt a strange vibration beneath him and he jumped to his feet. The beach below rippled in waves that lifted the sand and dropped it again. Sand in the dune under them was moving. Nem-kee got to his feet. They ran back to the shelter of the trees and solid ground and saw the dune collapsing, sand sliding down to the beach.

"It's beginning! Gonna call the guys!" shouted Nem-kee over the rumbling of thunder and screeching of birds. Chip nodded and pulled his great-uncle back behind the birches. The cell phone was already in the old man's trembling hand.

"Here, let me do it," he said, gently taking the phone. He sent the texted message to 'All,' and handed it back to Nem-kee. Annie would get the message and call the women. Perhaps some of the women in the Thunder Clan and men of the Bear Clan would join them.

===

Shibizhee slipped into the lake waters and guided those behind him to an underwater sandbar just offshore from the beach where Nanabozho stood. The darkened sky above had turned the bay into a twilight scene of churning land. The sounds of thunder and cries of raptors were muted through the water.

Ganoosow-Makwa came to Shibizhee's side on the sandbar, conferring through gestures. The army of smaller bears came forward, waiting expectantly in a long row of bared teeth, silver claws kneading the sandbar. Shibizhee could see through the murk with his feline yellow-green eyes. The cave bears' sight had adjusted to dim light through eons under the earth.

Shibizhee motioned with one paw, and Mishi-Ginebig floated toward them, his scales dulled in the dim light, followed by a wriggling mass of poisonous Mississauga snakes twenty times their usual size. Their brown bodies with black markings settled onto the sandbar as Mishi-Ginebig came up to Shibizhee's other side. He tossed his head and Shibizhee nodded in a respectful response.

With one more gesture, Shibizhee brought the massive crayfish to array themselves behind him, their bright colors now in shadow. Their claws had changed, their edges now rimmed with sharpened metal. The time when they reconnoitered with the leader had been well spent in arming them for battle.

Shibizhee walked up and down the underwater sandbar, tossing his massive copper clad head in approval, reviewing his impressive followers. They were indeed a majestic army that would bring the final vengeance he had desired for millennia. He came to the end of the raised underwater ledge and stepped over onto a limestone rock.

A thousand eyes watched through the water as Shibizhee's copper-scaled body whirled and blurred, his long tail wrapped around, spinning in a small tornado of scales and water. He emerged in human form, clad in copper body armor. A copper helmet with arched white horns covered his head and face. The bright metal covered his arms, legs and feet. He was twice the size of any man. In one hand he carried a long steel sword with a brass handle and ornate brass inlay.

Shibizhee-now-warrior swung the sword. His rock and the sandbar lifted. He led his army forward toward the beach where Nanabozho stood, armed only with his war club, bow and arrows.

===========================

Chip and Nem-kee saw the dark rain cloud lift higher in the sky. It let some light into the bay, but still hovered overhead, not moving. The wind had died down, and the air was still. Chip felt as though everything was poised, waiting. Then from the center of the bay a long wave rose, then another, and an oval of concentric watery rings spread out, lifting and flowing toward the shore of Cathead Island and out into the lake. In the center, a long oval sandbar rose out of the water, covered with shapes that appeared small in the distance, but Chip knew they must be of some size in order to discern what they were from where he stood.

"What?" he breathed the question. Nem-kee just shook his head and uttered a low moan. The two men made their way carefully on a path through the woods that led to a place above the battle where they could watch. They saw a long line of white bears walking forward toward the shore of Cathead Island. The land under the animals spread out and moved with them

285

toward the beach. Behind the bears writhed large brown and black snakes, and on either side of them, a mass of reddish orange shapes with strange protrusions lifted up into the air clattered forward, looking like giant lobsters.

At one end of the progressing land mass, a warrior clad in copper-colored armor strode forward, swinging a long glinting sword. Chip saw the white horns on the man's helmet and sucked in his breath. Nem-kee grunted out one word, "Shibizhee."

The raptors circled lower and divided into smaller groups, circling Shibizhee and his minions.

Chip pointed at a man on the beach dressed in only a loin cloth and moccasins raise a bow and aim a long feathered arrow at the oncoming large white bears.

"Nanabozho!" said Nem-kee. The figure on the beach threw back his head and as the men watched, he grew in size to the same height as the warrior Shibizhee. He pulled hard on his bowstring and let fly a massive arrow.

A single enormous bear at the front of the line of smaller bears was the target, but he raised a paw and slapped it away. A second and third arrow met the same response. The bears kept moving forward and now were nearly at the beach.

"The Long-Tailed Bear. Ganoosow-Makwa is helping Shibizhee," said Nem-kee. Chip had only heard about that spirit being in stories as a child. His mind refused to accept what he was seeing. He turned away, trying to find something real to focus on. A birch tree. A patch of bracken. No. No. He felt as though he was watching everything on television, or in a dream. No. It could not be real.

Eagles descended, diving at the white animals, sharp claws and beaks ready. They landed on the smaller bears, tearing and slashing. The screeching of raptors and howling of bears joined with the sound of thunder rumbling out of the dark cloud.

Sharp bolts of lightning struck the sand water around the attackers, bathing the entire battleground with instant lights sharply extinguished.

Shibizhee-now-warrior strode onto the beach, sword held before him, directly toward Nanabozho. Clad only in a loin cloth, the tall handsome Nanabozho stood his ground. Thick ropes of muscles stood out on his chest, arms and legs. His lithe tan body needed no armor, and his movements were sure. He pulled a thick, knobbed war club from his belt and swung it back and forth before him as he advanced on Shibizhee.

Nanabozho blocked a slash from the sword with his war club. The long sword and war club came together again and again. He danced away from Shibizhee's long sword, laughing, his voice louder than the low rumbles of thunder.

Shibizhee threw back his head and responded with a lion roar. His voice drowned out his enemy's laughter and the thunder.

Nem-kee started to move through the trees to get a better view of the scene below, but Chip pulled him back.

The eagles kept diving. The grabbed some of the large snakes and rose in the air with long writhing bodies in their claws. Would they attack the humans? Chip felt his heart pounding in his chest as he placed firm hands on Nem-kee's shoulders. Could there ever be any peace between the two spirit beings below?

He heard the sound of massive wings, looked up, and saw thunderbirds dive out of the cloud above, large as the giant bear, joining the battle in a new onslaught.

Chip watched the melee of raptors make dive after dive, but some of the bears knocked the feathered assaulters out of the air into the water, where the snakes quickly put an end to them.

The bear that Nem-kee had called Ganoosow-Makwa stood on his hind legs, braced himself with his long tail, and used the crayfish like giant frisbees, slinging them at the attacking hawks. The sharp claws of the crayfish ripped through the soft feathers, slashing into flesh beneath. One after another, he flung out the flattened reddish crustaceans, bringing down dozens of the attackers to a watery death below.

So much destruction. Chip tried to suppress the anger he felt toward the crazed spirit beings, but failed. He wished he were some huge spirit being himself that could simply reach down and make them cease such mindless slaughter. On the beach, Nanabozho and Shibizhee battled on.

More raptors dove toward the bears that rose on their back legs clawing down smaller hawks. An enormous horned snake lifted its head out of the water and breathed yellowish fumes on the diving eagles. Several eagles fell into the waiting claws of red-orange crayfish.

"Mishi-Ginebig!" Nem-kee's voice was hoarse. "He is with Shibizhee!"

Chip remembered the story of the Great Serpent, and thought about his father's call about the disappearance of the Serpent Mound in Ohio. It had seemed impossible, a tale told to children, something from a time so long ago. No - he saw the serpent.

It was here, before him. A shaft of sunlight came through the cloud at that moment onto the massive spirit being, making his iridescent scales reflect a myriad of small rainbows. The serpent's jeweled head was resplendent, sending off faceted beams of colored light.

It tossed back its enormous horned head, shrugged and shuddered, and a huge net covered with iridescent scales whirled out into the air, snaring several thunderbirds, flinging them down under the water. His shed skin had become a weapon in the battle.

The raptors drew back, rose and compressed into a single group of beating wings and high pitched cries. Then the larger thunderbirds dove out of the cloud. Their eyes flashed bolts of lightning that penetrated the water, destroying snake after snake.

Their pale underbellies floated beside the risen sandbar, no longer moving.

On the water's surface floated the remains of what had been proud eagles and hawks. Near them, the razor sharp claws of the crayfish reached up in useless threats. Thunderbird eyes flashed severe bright shafts of lightning that caught the crustaceans on fire, turning several of their reddish-orange bodies into flames that slipped under the water, sending up small bursts of steam.

Yet the battle between Shibizhee and Nanabozho on the beach went on as each spirit being persevered, neither giving in to the other.

CHAPTER 32

Chip felt the others coming through the woods behind him before he heard them. Annie and Tizbet were the first, and he saw his father with other men and women standing in a long row along the edge of the high dune that overlooked the beach. Not only the Thunder and Bear Clan people, but those from other clans as well. Perhaps a hundred, perhaps more. They came out of the trees in a long row, holding hand drums.

Annie was holding Nem-kee's drum and her own. Tizbet had two drums in her hands, Chip's and hers. The men took their drums and drumsticks. Nem-kee shouted, a sharp high pitched cry, and then began the song for peace. The men and women picked up the beat, a steady heartbeat of sound. Their voices rose up into the air that was still filled with sounds of battle. Their song was insistent, demanding, humans planting their feet firmly on the land above the bay.

The two battling on the beach stopped and turned to look above them. Shibizhee's sword dropped to his side. Nanabozho's war club hung down in his hand. The opposing spirit beings backed away from each other.

Chip kept drumming and singing with the others, his eyes on the two still figures below. Nem-kee started a new song, one more demanding, more insistent on peace. No pleading or begging in his song, just firm determination in strong words like arrows shot from the mouths of humans at the top of the dunes. The battle must end. The fighting must cease. There must be no more display of vengeance and retribution. There must be no more threat by such powerful beings to the Earth and its people.

The drumming and firm demanding songs continued. Chip heard Tizbet's voice next to him, and her sharp intake of breath as he saw the figures on the beach gradually lose shape and substance. In seconds they turned into two glittering columns of mist. Then they were gone.

Nem-kee ended the song with sharp beats of his drum and all of the drumming and singing stopped. The sky lightened as the dark cloud above the bay lifted and thinned as though a wind were blowing it into greying wisps. Chip looked down and saw the bears walking into the water, following Ginoosow-Makwa. The large purple and white band of wampum on his neck glinted in the brightening sunlight before he went under the gentle waves. Radiant Mishi-Ginebig's head emerged once and faced the humans at the top of the dune. He flipped over and his new scales sent multicolored rainbows for an instant, and he was gone. The cloud of raptors circled the bay once, and flew out across the water over the mainland, flying farther and farther away until they were a small dark streak above the horizon.

Chip remained standing between Nem-kee and Tizbet, apprehensive. Was it over? Had they simply quit fighting and called the whole thing off? Would it begin again? He had a strong feeling that this was not the end - that something more was going to happen.

Under his feet, the earth vibrated. Another earthquake? He reached for Tizbet's hand, fearing the worst. Then it stopped. He turned and looked at Nem-kee, who simply shrugged and raised one eyebrow. What next?

The water in the bay below was moving in a long oval of waves as a long cylindrical white object began rising above the water, a pipe bowl on one end, a stem on the other, held up at each end by two huge hands. As the people watched, the hands inserted the pipe stem into the bowl.

==========================

Chip clutched Tizbet's hand even tighter as he saw Nanabozho rise from the bay, now over five hundred feet tall. He stood before the long line of Anishinabe dressed in only a loin cloth. The war club, bow and quiver were gone. The beloved spirit being of the Anishinabe held out toward them the Pipe that demanded peace. He had heard the people, and brought that which was most sacred.

==================================

In his true form, Shibizhee stood on the grassy ledge above the creek at the western end of the island, watching Nanabozho rise from the water holding the Pipe. It was over. The people demanded peace, and his old enemy responded. There could be no winner in the old battle. He would not avenge his mother's death at the hand of Nanabozho; nor would his own murder of Nanabozho's brother be avenged.

They had fought for centuries and it had finally come to an end. He felt the hard core of hatred that had lived so long in his belly lift up, coming up through his throat. He opened his mouth and saw a reddish-brown mist escape his lips, blood lust that dissipated into the spring air.

The cloud above was gone. Full sunlight felt warm on his back. Beneath the ledge, gentle waves washed up on the pale sand of the narrow beach. He jumped down and walked into the water, feeling small pebbles under his paws.

Shibizhee dove down into a deep cool channel, and swam slowly, considering what he should do. A thought flowed into his mind that filled him with a sensation like the narcotic of wormwood. The Megis. The shell that showed the way. The guide. He could bring the Megis and it would lead the way to a place where Earth, Sky and Underworld could once again find balance.

Spinning into a bright orb under water, Shibizhee became a ball of light that rose above the bay, up into the clear air.

=====================

Nem-kee left the others at the top of the dune; half slid down the sand to the beach and eased himself onto a large driftwood log at the base of the dune. His legs had about given out with standing so long, and his arms ached from the drumming.

Nanabozho had risen out of the lake with the Pipe and walked toward the people, becoming smaller with each step until he was the size of a man by the time he reached the edge of the water at the beach. He came toward Nem-kee holding the Pipe before him.

When he was still some distance away, a bright ball of light lifted out of the water behind Nanabozho, arched over his head and came to float just in front of Nem-kee. It broadened, blurred and spun into the human shape of John Mishipsea. He was dressed in a traditional deerskin tunic, leggings and moccasins, and held a large white cowrie shell. The Megis.

He looked at Nem-kee and turned to face Nanabozho who now stood still, the Pipe in both hands held out at waist height. As Nem-kee saw the two spirit beings face each other, he decided to speak.

"Looks like we can work this out now," Nem-kee said in what he hoped was a gentle manner. He drew in a breath and stood erect, ignoring his aching legs.

"I bring the Megis to help us find the way," said Mishipsea, still looking at Nanabozho.

Nanabozho said nothing, butt gave one nod of his head. Nem-kee cleared his throat. "There's a place back up there we sometimes call the Middle Ground." He gestured with one wrinkled hand up the dune to the clearing between his house and Annie's. It had remained a meadow since he was a boy, a good place for children to play and have picnics. As good a place as any. Mishipsea walked ahead with the Megis, holding it ahead of him like a beacon, followed by Nanabozho and Nem-kee. As they reached solid ground, the Megis lifted from Mishipsea's hands and began to glow, sending out a long golden beam of light that made a pathway through the trees.

The people at the top of the dune followed in a long line, carrying their hand drums, speaking softly among themselves.

293

As the sun slipped lower over Cathead Bay, the people gathered around the perimeter of the meadow called The Middle Ground.

The two spirit beings followed the glowing Megis to the center of the field and sat down cross-legged, facing each other, preparing to smoke the Pipe. The Megis floated above them and then descended, its light illuminating Nanabozho and Shibizhee in the gathering twilight.

Nem-kee and Chip stood next to Annie and Tizbet at the edge of the field closest to the cedars. Annie lifted her drum above her head and struck it once with her drumstick. She began the honor song, words of thanks to the two who were now passing the pipe between them, a thin white trail of smoke rising. Their mouths moved but the people could not hear their words. Other drums responded and picked up the strong beat as voices joined in and around the Middle Ground; the people sang their deepest approval and respect for the spirits of the Earth and Underworld.

A single eagle flew down over the cedars above Nem-kee's head, its wings spread wide as it circled the two spirit beings. Then it rose, riding the air back out over Cathead Bay, a spirit eagle sent by the Sky Forces. Nem-kee breathed a deep sigh of relief and resumed singing the honor song with his people. The battle had ended, making possible a new beginning.

EPILOGUE

Annie carried her old basket out to the weathered picnic table in her back yard where three men dressed in jeans and t-shirts were talking - Nem-kee, John Mishipsea and Nanabozho. The men were deep in conversation and she didn't want to interrupt. She set the basket down as quietly as possible, but all three looked up and went silent.

"Just thought you might want some lunch." She opened the top of the basket and took out plastic plates and eating utensils, cans of cold Vernor's ginger ale, and thick ham sandwiches. With a suppressed grin, she produced a box of Twinkies, giving Mishipsea a glance. He responded with a broad smile.

"I was just about ready to go, but thanks," said Nem-kee. He pushed himself up with his sinewy old arms and slowly eased his legs over the seat. "These guys have got some serious planning to do, and I'm ready for a nap."

Annie caught the hint. Not the right time for humans to get involved. So far, it looked as though the two spirit beings were more focused on the condition of the land and water than their personal concerns. Neither seemed to require much sleep for the past two days, and they had been discussing problems caused by pollution and invasive species in the Great Lakes and its environs.

Nem-kee was already walking across the field on the small path that led to his cabin. She turned to go back to her own house and overheard part of the discussion.

"It seems to me that weevils would solve the problem with loosestrife and Eurasian milfoil, but the only solution for frog-bit and curly leaf pondweed is just to pull them out, unless they are needed elsewhere." Mishipsea sounded like some of her professors.

"I could probably round up and enlarge enough muskrats to deal with the rusty crayfish. Softening up their shells would help, too." Nanabozho talked around his ham sandwich. Annie bent over to fasten the strap on her sandal, wanting to hear more.

"It wasn't that difficult to eliminate the sea lamprey. I checked first to see if they were running short somewhere – could have just resupplied the area. I ended up dropping them off at a cat food plant south of here. We could try the same thing with the Asian carp," said Mishipsea. It sounded like he was opening the box of Twinkies, but she didn't turn around.

"Humans could eat the carp, but it seems that they only eat them in Asia," said Nanabozho.

"Something ought to be done to stop ships from coming in and starting the problem."

Annie eavesdropped for a few minutes longer, checking out some rabbit droppings and a patch of wintergreen.

"If you could get enough Lake Erie water snakes, we could probably wipe out the round gobies. But it would take more salmon to eliminate the alewives. They evidently were a bigger problem earlier, but...."

Annie wondered when they would get around to figuring out the spiny and fishhook water fleas - and then there was the problem with zebra mussels. She forced herself to keep on going toward her house. Whatever those two came up with, it would be interesting. The Department of Natural Resources would have enough research questions to keep hundreds of doctoral students occupied into the next century.

Louie finished his third cup of coffee. "My treat," he said as he picked up the check. Chip and Tizbet sat across from him in the booth at the restaurant in Shipsea. Now that phones were working, electricity restored, and tourists gone on the ferry, they had spent the last couple of hours watching the Army Corps of Engineers building the pontoon bridge to the mainland.

Trucks were waiting on one side with gas for the fuel pumps on the island, and a line of campers and motorhomes waited on the other side to get back home. Life was back to what passed for normal on an island.

"You coming to the station?" Louie asked.

"We're going to stick around here for a while. Got some ideas for the pre-school program." Chip pushed their dishes aside and slapped a spiral binder on the table. Tizbet scootched over closer to him.

"Imagine having adults who only speak the Anishinabe language all day with them, Louie!" Her eyes sparkled with excitement. "We can get teachers from Canada, and the kids will be fluent in just months!"

Louie slid out of the seat and pulled out his wallet. "Never thought I'd see that happen. We've been losing that language with every elder that walks on." His phone vibrated and rang in his pants pocket.

"Yo, St. Sable here." It was his cousin at Sault Ste. Marie.

His face grew serious, and then his mouth opened but no sound came out. He shut his mouth and grunted. His eyes widened. "Uh huh…. What do you…? Uh huh…. Oh my God! Yup, never heard of such a thing…."

Louie closed his eyes and bit his lip. "Well, let me know how it goes."

He shut off the phone and turned to Chip and Tizbet. "The Locks up at the Soo - that let ships through into Lake Superior - are completely jammed up! Several freighters … from countries that brought in invasive species when they dumped their ballast … are totally covered with Zebra mussel shells - dead invasive plants - and stinking dead invasive fish!"

REFERENCES ABOUT MISHIBIZHEE

THE GREAT LYNX:

1995 Johnston, Basil. *The Manitous: The Spiritual World of the Ojibway.* Minnesota Historical Society Press.

1975 Johnston, Patronellla. *Tales of Nokomis.* The Nokomis Learning Center, Okemos, MI.

1982 Overholt, Thomas J. and J. Baird Callicott. *Clothed-in-Fur and Other Tales.* University Press of America, Inc., Lanham, Md. [Note: 'Now Great Lynx' is the title of Chapter 9, p.87; referencing Thompson's Motif Index.]

1956 and 1991. Schoolcraft, Henry Rowe. *Indian Legends.* Ed. Mentor L. Williams. Michigan State University Press, East Lansing, MI.

1995 Smith, Theresa S. *The Island of the Anishnaabeg,* 'Thunderers and Water Monsters in the Traditional Ojibwe Life-World.' University of Idaho Press, Moscow, Idaho.

Also see Wikipedia on line for references, and Norval Morriseau's depictions of Michipishu, The Underwater Panther.

www.ingramcontent.com/pod-product-compliance
Lightning Source LLC
Chambersburg PA
CBHW070738180626
46818CB00007B/2906